FURHER : BEYOND THE THRESHOLD

Published by 47North
P.O. Box 400818
Las Vegas, NV 89140

ISBN-13: 9781612182438
ISBN-10: 1612182437

FURTHER

BEYOND THE THRESHOLD

CHRIS ROBERSON

47NORTH

PROLOGUE

When I woke up, surrounded by talking dog-people, it was clear we'd strayed pretty far from the mission parameters.

The rest of the crew had gone down a few weeks out from Earth, when *Wayfarer One* passed Neptune's orbit, but I'd opted to stay awake almost until we reached the sun's heliopause. As I arranged myself in the narrow sleeper coffin, the hibernation gasses gradually slowing my body's processes to a near halt, I closed my eyes, knowing that when I opened them, four decades and 4.3 light-years later, it would be to look at a sight no humans before us had ever seen.

Wayfarer One's automated systems were programmed to wake us a few weeks out from Alpha Centauri B as the engines fired and the ship began to decelerate. According to the mission specs, by the time the ship's velocity slowed to zero we would be within visual range of our destination, a tiny Earth-like planet known only by a registry number that might one day be a new home for humanity. I was born a century after an asteroid toppled the most powerful nation on Earth, and knew all too well how vulnerable our planet was to another such disaster. A larger strike could well mean the extinction of life as we knew it. Establishing a toehold on another world would only serve to increase humanity's chances of surviving into the distant future, but first we had to find a world capable of supporting life.

That was the mission my colleagues and I had accepted. We knew it would mean sacrificing anything like a normal life, as our friends and relatives would age and die back on Earth while we traveled between the stars, but it was a sacrifice we were willing to make. We would be carrying life into lifeless space, the first humans to reach another star.

It came as something of a surprise, then, when I opened my eyes and looked up to see a trio of space suit–wearing dogs standing over me, their tongues hanging out as they barked enthusiastically.

More surprising still, they seemed to be barking at me in English…

PART ONE

ONE

My father was always a fan of science fiction books and movies, a taste no doubt inherited from my grandfather, so when I was growing up I was exposed to a lot of it as a matter of course. Whenever a new edition of one of his favorite movies was released, Dad would insist that my brother and I drop whatever we were doing and join him in the family room. Watching the restored cut of *Star Wars* or a new scan of *Forbidden Planet* was to him a kind of communal activity that brought the family together. My mother, usually at the lab and occupied with her research, was naturally exempt from attending, but no excuse was sufficient to get my brother or me off the hook. It was only later that I realized that, when he himself had been growing up, watching these sorts of movies had been nearly the only common ground my father and his own father had shared, and in his own way he was trying to ensure a sort of continuity with his own sons, cementing our relationship with him. As a callow kid, though, I'd only known that my father was forever interrupting me when I'd rather be reading my *Earth Force Z* manga or watching the latest episode of *The Adventures of Space Man*, so while I myself had inherited a taste for the fantastic visions of science fiction, I resented the obligation.

One of the movies we watched again and again was *Planet of the Apes*. I loved it when I was young, and must have enjoyed it a dozen times before my brother finally ruined it for me. LJ, who was four years younger than me, couldn't have been much older than seven or eight when he paused the playback just at the moment when Charlton Heston's character, Taylor, wounded and incapable of speech, scratches out a message in the sand to his ape captors—"I CAN WRITE"—quickly erased by the manipulative Dr. Zaius, played by Maurice Evans.

LJ turned to us, Dad and me, and said, "Wait, why does he think they could read English?" While I was still chewing that over, he quickly added, "And why are they *speaking* English?"

My father chuckled and said something about suspension of disbelief, but for me, the flaw was unforgivable. My love for *Planet of the Apes* had died. But I think I heaped more scorn upon myself for not realizing the obvious flaw in the plot before my younger brother pointed it out. I felt like I'd been duped, misled.

■ ■ ■ ■ ■

When I opened my eyes and heard the barking voices of the space-suited dog-men standing over me, it was with considerable suspicion that I realized that they were speaking English. Or a rough approximation of English.

"It is not in agony to dry," the first dog-man said, sounding like an overexcited terrier. "It spreads out, and if to be living continuously, it is your doubling it wins, and if in long time but it is damaged, the side type chart."

I tried to swallow, hoping to respond, but my muscles seemed to have lost the trick of it, and a diffuse pain radiated out from my neck, coursing down my chest and up over my chin.

The second dog-man shook his head, something resembling a sad expression on his snout, and said, "Your ship first crooked it did not revive."

Well, perhaps not even a rough approximation of English, after all. But they *were* recognizable English words, for all of that, which simply *shouldn't* have been issuing from any alien mouth, however familiarly dog shaped.

The third dog-man drew near and lifted a small object over my head, a silvery lozenge with irregular protrusions from top and bottom.

"It sleeps go," it barked gently.

My eyelids grew too heavy to keep open, and I slipped away into blackness.

TWO

When I woke, I felt like one enormous, dull ache. My eyes still shut, I tried to lift my arms, but my muscles refused to cooperate.

I groaned, the sound of it surprising in my ears.

"The sleep that spreads out it awakes," barked a gentle voice at my side.

I opened my eyes and looked up into the grinning muzzle of one of the dog-men. The ceiling and wall beyond its head was a smooth, unbroken curve of white, studded here and there with strangely shaped protuberances. It was not a view I recognized from *Wayfarer One*. Had I been moved since last I woke, or had I been too groggy before to realize where I was?

"Wh-where…?" I managed, just barely.

The dog-man paused for a moment, head cocked slightly to one side as though listening to a sound I couldn't hear.

"In mining boat," it yapped, at length. "Of the Pethesilean Mining Consortium."

"Alien...?" I croaked.

The dog-man paused, again cocking his head to the side. "No. Me it is commander. Executive."

I struggled to lift my head, but couldn't. It felt as though I were pinned down by multiple gravities, as though in a ship at high acceleration, but the dog-man stood casually upright, suggesting the problem was instead with me.

"Can't...move..." I croaked.

Again the pause, the cocked head, and the dog-man answered. "It spread out and it degenerated the inside long sleep. Remainder and to spread out and recuperate."

I drew a ragged breath, blinking slowly, drained by the exertion of simply filling my lungs.

"How...long...sleep?"

The dog-man listened to the silent voice and nodded. "It is year T8975." Then it reached out and patted my head, gently, as though soothing an ailing pet. Its other paw held the silver lozenge device over my eyes, and the dog-man added, "It sleeps go."

I was asleep before I could groan another syllable.

■ ■ ■ ■ ■

My sleep was dreamless and dark. When next I woke, the ache I'd felt before had subsided somewhat, now concentrated mostly in my joints—knees, elbows, and wrists, particularly.

I lay for a moment in red-lidded darkness, listening close. I could hear soft footsteps some distance to my right, the sound echoing faintly off of a wall nearer to my left. Less than a meter from where I lay, I could hear the rhythm of regular, calm breathing, sounding for all the world like a content puppy at rest.

I tried to lift up on my elbows and surprised myself when I levered into an upright position. Startled, I opened my eyes in a panic, my hands reflexively shooting out to either side to steady me. My muscles seemed to have regained their strength as I slept, and it now felt as if a gravity one-third that of Earth's was pulling on me. Like that of a large moon or a ship under acceleration.

My head swam as my insides struggled to realign themselves. I hadn't felt so disoriented since the time on Ceres when Laurentien had insisted I share what she euphemistically called a "peace pipe" to seal our negotiations, but the figure advancing on me now shared little in common with the Dutch queen, so there was no chance this experience would end anything like the same. The dog-man was saying something, speaking a strange, guttural language of growls and barks, and though I had no clue as to his meaning, his agitated manner was plain enough.

"Stay back…" I said, raising my hands in front of me in a defensive posture. But they weren't my hands, were they?

I flexed, and the fingers moved, slow and tentative. The joints were thick, the fingers gnarled, the backs of the hands covered in liver spots.

These weren't mine. These were the arthritic hands of an old man.

The dog-man was within arm's reach now, brandishing the silver lozenge like a weapon. It let out another string of barks and growls, but then paused, seeming to remember something, and in a gentler voice, yapped, "Sleep."

I felt a faint tickle, somewhere in the back of my mind, and my eyes closed on the world once again.

THREE

Another world greeted my eyes when next I woke.

I was in a large room under an enormous, domed ceiling. Lights floated high overhead, like miniature stars, and what appeared to be chairs of various sizes and configurations were scattered irregularly around the reflective floor, surrounding the low table upon which I lay. I sat up, more carefully this time, and felt the reassuring pull of an Earth-standard gravity on my limbs.

I was dressed in some sort of loose-fitting white robe, like a surgical gown, with bare arms and legs. I looked down and saw that the old-man hands were affixed to the ends of equally ancient arms, thin and roped with veins, and that the legs and feet were no better.

A human body in a coffin sleeper ages, but too slowly to be noticeable. On the four-decade journey to Alpha Centauri B, the boffins back in Vienna had estimated that our bodies would experience something like a few minutes of subjective time. I'd been thirty-one years old when I climbed into the sleeper. How long had I been under to have aged so much?

I climbed to my feet, gingerly, the mirror-sheen surface of the floor surprisingly warm against my soles. I held the table's edge to steady myself, but while my knees creaked and complained, they held my weight, and I remained standing.

There was a sound from behind me, at once familiar and alien—someone clearing their throat to get my attention.

I turned, not sure what to expect, here on the planet of the dog-men.

It was not a dog, and it was not a man. It was the tallest woman I'd ever seen, regarding me coolly.

She stood over two meters tall, dressed in formfitting black, her calves and feet as bare as her forearms and hands. Her skin was alabaster white, her hair a dark shade of blue, and the perfect symmetry of her features was marred only by the sapphire-colored eye patch that covered her left eye.

I straightened, hearing things pop and groan in my spine as I did, and lifted my chin.

"Who are you?" I said, louder than I'd intended.

The woman answered with a string of syllables, all liquid vowels and fricatives, and paused as though expecting me to answer.

"I…I don't understand," I said.

The woman shook her head dramatically, a displeased expression spilling across her face. She waved a long-fingered hand toward the table.

She spoke again, more strange sounds, but a split second after she'd begun I heard her voice issuing from the table upon which I leaned, this time using more familiar words.

"The crew of my mining ship reports that they indulged you and instructed their interlinks to feed them words and phrases in your antique tongue—or at least as many as their ship's intelligence had in its stores—out of contact with the infostructure, but I've *no* patience for such foolishness."

I gaped. Flawless and with a flat accent, it was the voice of the woman speaking English.

"I am Chief Executive Zel i'Cirea, head of the Pethesilean Mining Consortium," came the voice echoing from the table as the woman continued to speak her strange tongue. "Now, it is my turn to ask a question. Who are you?"

I bit back the questions that jostled behind my teeth and answered.

"Captain Ramachandra Jason Stone, UNSA, commander of *Wayfarer One*—"

The woman waved her hand impatiently, cutting me off.

"Yes, yes, I know who you're *meant* to be, but who or what are you, really?" She narrowed her eye and approached the table. She leaned against it casually, careful to keep distance between us, just beyond arm's reach. "You read as fully biological. Were you fabricated? Or grown somewhere? Who sent you?"

I shook my head. "Look, I don't know where…or *when*…I am, but the one thing I'm sure of—"

The woman slammed a fist onto the tabletop. Flawless teeth bared, she shouted, "Who *are* you?"

"He's R. J. Stone, of course," sounded a new voice from the table, "returned to us after all these millennia."

An undercurrent beneath the words, I could hear the untranslated words echoing somewhere in the room. The woman fumed as I glanced around, seeking out the source of the sound.

I shouldn't have been surprised, but I was. First dog-men, then one-eyed Amazons, and now a meter-tall chimpanzee in a smoking jacket, cravat, and pin-striped trousers, strolling casually toward us.

The chimpanzee spoke again, the sounds issuing from him unfamiliar, the words from the table clear and refined English. The corners of the chimpanzee's mouth rose in a rough approximation of a smile.

"Don't you realize, Zel? He's the solution to all our problems."

FOUR

"Remarkable," the voice of the chimpanzee echoed from the table, "just remarkable."

The chimpanzee clapped his large, hairy hands together, approaching with a rolling, side-to-side gait.

"Why must you see every random occurrence as some good omen for our cause?" the woman asked, exasperated.

"All things were engineered with a purpose," the chimpanzee answered, "whether you choose to recognize it or not. Why should events be any different?"

My mouth must still have hung open as the chimpanzee drew to a stop just in front of me.

"Please excuse my lapse in manners," the chimpanzee said. "Allow me to introduce myself, Captain Stone. My name is Maruti Sun Ghekre the Ninth." Then he placed his hairy palms together and held his hands up near his cravat, head inclined, adopting a posture I knew well from childhood.

My mother's lessons in etiquette were well ingrained, and without thinking, I found myself adopting the same pose, hands palm to palm near my sternum as I nodded my head and intoned, "*Namaste.*"

"And I bow to the demiurge in you," the chimpanzee said. He straightened and began digging in his pockets. "In any event, among my other roles and responsibilities, I am a physician, and Chief Executive Zel has asked me to examine you."

As I glanced at the one-eyed woman, who only sighed, looking bored with the whole exchange, the chimpanzee tilted his head, glancing at the table. "Room, if you wouldn't mind?"

The floating lights overhead shifted position slightly, one constellation melting into another, and after a brief interval, the chimpanzee nodded.

"Yes, splendid." The voice of the chimpanzee sounded satisfied, echoing from the table. "Very good. The crew of Zel's mining ship seems to have stabilized your condition quite nicely, Captain Stone. Your body is in an advanced stage of senescence, but nothing that can't be reversed. Now, as to the question of your cognition, what's the last thing you remember, Captain Stone?"

"Going into cryogenic suspension on board my ship," I answered.

"And what ship would that have been?" the chimpanzee asked.

I struggled to keep my mounting impatience in check. "*Wayfarer One.*"

The boffins in Vienna had been developing the *Wayfarer* missions since before I was born and had selected Alpha Centauri B as the destination of the first *Wayfarer* when I'd still been a student at Addis Ababa University, when the unmanned starwisp probe *Sojourner A97* sent back the first images of the extrasolar terrestrial planet that came to be known as Alpha Centauri B II. Which was quite a mouthful. I was always grateful that early on they'd ditched the official registry name in practice and started referring to it in conversation simply as "the Rock." Equipped with an inertial confinement fusion drive, using pellets of deuterium/helium-3 ignited in the reaction chamber by intense laser beams, *Wayfarer One* was capable of accelerating to one-tenth the speed of light. With the crew in cryogenic suspension, the ship would launch in 2167 and reach the Rock in just over forty-three years.

As it happened, it appeared to have taken quite a bit longer.

"Where are the others?" I asked, growing increasingly agitated. "Where are my crewmates?"

There had been six of us in the crew of *Wayfarer One*. I was commander, first on board and last to sleep. Next in line was our pilot, Amelia Apatari, followed by mission specialists Gastuvas Katende, Martin Villers, Eija-Liisa Ylönen, and Beatriz Countinho. The rest of them had all been scientists originally, recruited by the United Nations Space Agency right out of school, but Amelia had been a flyer with the Peacekeepers, and I'd earned my wings with the Orbital Patrol. It's probably not surprising, then, that we bonded so quickly, having met shortly after I was promoted to captain and seconded to UNSA.

"Mmm?" The chimpanzee raised a brow as he regarded me, momentarily confused. "Oh, still with your craft, I imagine. Now, I can install an interlink for you as well while I'm at it, which should help streamline your conversation considerably." The chimpanzee gestured apologetically at the table, an expression of distaste momentarily twisting his expression.

Before I could ask about the state of Amelia and the others, a new voice sounded. But this one issued not from the table, but from a point somewhere at the far side of the room.

"Allow the man a moment to acclimate, if you would, Maruti. He's only just arrived, after all."

Padding around the scattered chairs came a lithe shape. It resembled a lion, easily 50 percent larger than life size, but surmounted by the hairless head of a man instead of that of a great cat. It approached silently, its footfalls not making a sound, and as it drew nearer, I realized that it was not entirely opaque, the vague outlines of furniture or the glimmers of lights visible through its body.

The lion-thing rounded the table silently and lay down on the mirrored floor, its forepaws crossed in front, regarding me serenely.

"Captain Ramachandra Jason Stone," it said, the voice issuing from the supple lips of the man-head. "We are the Voice of the Plenum. We welcome you to the present, and to the Human Entelechy."

FIVE

The man-lion turned to address the one-eyed Amazon. "We have examined the derelict craft as you requested, Chief Executive Zel, and our constituent elements/agents have completed their analysis. Thermoluminescence dating of the ceramics in the craft place its age at some twelve millennia, dating from the Information Age. As near as we have been able to determine, a micrometeorite impacted the craft early in its voyage, penetrating the self-healing hull and damaging the ship's onboard navigation systems. Caught in a recursive loop, the primitive silicon proto-intelligence never initiated the command to wake the crew from their cryogenic slumber."

"Ha!" The chimpanzee clapped his hands together, hopping up and down. "I *knew* he was legitimate!"

The woman scowled, unconvinced. "It is all too convenient, if you ask me. No gift this welcome should go unexamined."

The chimpanzee began to pace, waving his hands excitedly, his cravat coming all undone. "Let me clean him up, get him fitted with an interlink, and we can call a meeting. With him on our side, we're sure to get the donors we need for the *Further* fund, and then we'll be on our way."

The man-lion shook its enormous, hairless head. "As we have said, Maruti, Captain Stone should be given some time to acclimate to his new surroundings before being asked to make any decisions of lasting consequence."

"Very well." The voice of the chimpanzee sounded impatient, but he shrugged casually. "Though, why anyone would object to basic medical treatments is beyond me." The chimpanzee turned to the Amazon. "Now, Zel, about the donors…"

The man-lion made a rumbling noise, interrupting.

"Look," I said, looking from one unlikely creature to another, "I want some answers…"

The man-lion raised a paw in a casual gesture, one I instantly recognized as a request for me to wait.

"Physician Maruti and Chief Executive Zel, we can see that you wish to discuss plans and strategies relating to your fund. If we might offer our services, the Plenum is prepared to take temporary charge of Captain Stone, until such time as he's able to make informed decisions for himself."

The Amazon reached up and tapped the surface of her sapphire-colored eye patch thoughtfully. "I'm of a mind to keep him here, on the Pethesilean habitat, until I work out what to do with him."

"We're certain that the chief executive of Pethesilea requires no lesson in Entelechy law," the man-lion said gently, "but we'll remind you that, unless it can be proven that Captain Stone is not, in fact, sentient, he has the same inalienable rights as any citizen of the Entelechy, including the ability to move freely. If he were to be detained against his will, when he has done nothing to invite reprisal, then you would be abridging his rights and would run the risk of inviting censure. Persist, and perhaps your entire culture might be put on probation, your threshold temporarily isolated by the Consensus."

The Amazon sighed deeply and regarded me warily with her one eye.

"So what are you saying, Voice?" she said, turning to the man-lion. "Are we just to let the caveman go wandering alone through the worlds?"

The man-lion inclined his enormous head for an instant, eyes lidded. "Anticipating this need," he said, "we have spawned an agent to act as Captain Stone's escort."

The Amazon was thoughtful for a long moment and then glanced at the chimpanzee, who only grinned and shrugged.

"The Plenum will keep an eye on him, then?" she asked, turning back to the man-lion.

"The escort will be the captain's constant companion," the man-lion answered.

"He can go, in that case," she said, "but we will likely need him back before too much time has passed."

The man-lion smiled, a somewhat unsettling sight, and nodded. "One is always free to ask."

"Look," I said, growing agitated, "what about my crew?"

The man-lion turned his eyes to me, a sad expression on his wide face. "We regret to inform you that all, sadly, are dead. You, Captain Stone, are the only survivor."

"But one of them is not yet fully decayed, correct?" The chimpanzee steepled his fingers, looking from the man-lion to the Amazon. "I wouldn't mind taking a look at her remains. Might be something there I can use."

I was numb. Amelia, Gastuvas, Beatriz, the others—all dead? And the chimpanzee thought he might find some...*use*...for their remains?

I started to object, but a raised paw and a sharp look from the man-lion silenced me. "If Chief Executive Zel has no objections, the Plenum certainly does not."

The Amazon, for her part, simply shrugged uninterestedly. She turned and began walking away.

The chimpanzee clapped eagerly and smiled in my direction. "A pleasure meeting you," his voice sounded from the table as the chimpanzee gamboled away after the Amazon. "I hope to see you again soon."

As the chimpanzee caught up with the Amazon and began speaking to her in hushed tones, the table continued translating his words.

"I'm telling you, Zel, we should associate ourselves with Stone's return as quickly as possible, before interest in him has dissipated."

I turned back toward the man-lion, who rose to his feet and said, "The escort approaches."

In the darkness of the room something metallic glinted, and a silver eagle appeared, gliding overhead.

It passed less than a meter from me, and I could see that it was a perfect reproduction of a raptor in highly reflective, supple metal, like a model cast in mercury. It curved in a wide arc, flapped its wings once, and before I could react, landed on my shoulder, its talons gripping the fabric of the robe. Though it was easily half a meter tall, I could scarcely feel any weight pressing down on me.

"Captain Stone," issued the voice from the open beak in perfect English. "I am to be your escort for as long as you desire. I will act as your guide and translator while you become accustomed to the worlds and cultures of the Human Entelechy."

The man-lion turned its wide face toward me, smiled, and nodded. Then, without another word, it vanished.

"I believe, Captain Stone," said the silver eagle in my ear, "that we have been dismissed."

SIX

"Shall we go, Captain Stone?" asked the silver eagle.

"What…?" I took a step away from the table, turning in a full circle. The Amazon and the chimpanzee were now nearing the far wall, passing through an exit and out of sight. "What just happened here?"

"I'm afraid that I can't say with any precision, sir, since I was born only as the conversation neared its end, but from what I have gathered, there was some discussion about your origins, and about that of your craft."

I hated that I'd done nothing since first opening my eyes but ask questions, none of the answers to which had yet been anything like satisfying, but I found that I couldn't stop myself.

"Where the hell *am* I? What year is this?"

"We're currently in the artificial habitat of Pethesilea, home of the culture of the same name, in orbit around the star known in your era as Beta Pavonis, located nineteen-point-nine light-years from Sol. As for the year, it is presently T8975."

"Right, right," I said impatiently, "that's what the dog-man said, but what the hell does *that* mean?"

"Records of the intervening epochs are somewhat irregular, but in rough terms, a period of some twelve thousand years has passed since your craft left the Sol system."

An enormous hole opened up in my mind, and anything like the ability to reason plummeted out of view.

"Twelve. Thousand. Years?"

"Standard years, sir, defined as three hundred and sixty-five standard days long. And each day being a single rotation of Original Earth in respect to Sol, or more specifically, as the duration of 7.93342121751 x 10^14 periods of the radiation corresponding to the transition between two hyperfine levels of the ground state of the caesium-one-thirty-three atom at rest at a temperature of zero K. Except for the last day of the year, of course, which is twenty-five percent longer than the rest."

"Twelve thousand?"

"You shouldn't be surprised that the units of day and year with which you're familiar have been retained. A diurnal, annual tempo has found to be beneficial for all Earth-derived biologicals. I'm afraid that the base-sixty increments of your era, though— holdovers from the Babylonian culture of a few millennia earlier—have been abandoned, so you'll have to adjust to a percentage-based system of timekeeping."

"Forget the calendar!" I snapped. "I'm having an existential crisis, here!"

"Sir?" Concern sounded in the voice of the escort, laced with confusion.

"I've slept for twelve millennia, my crew is dead, and I'm talking to a robot bird!"

"Yes, sir." The escort bobbed its beak in a nod. "Perhaps we should return now to Earth, and to quarters that have been—"

"Earth? *Now*?"

"Of course, sir, if you'll just—"

"But you just said we're twenty light-years from Sol."

"Nineteen-point-nine, to be precise, but near enough, yes."

"And we're going to just…?" I waved my hands suggestively, though suggestive of what I'm not certain.

"Walk there," the escort finished for me.

"Walk there?"

"Yes, sir. If you'll follow me."

The silver eagle bunched for a brief moment and then launched into the air, taking wing. "This way, Captain Stone," it called back, tucking its beak over its shoulder.

It winged toward the wall, opposite the direction the chimpanzee and the Amazon had gone. I followed as quickly as I could, my bare feet sliding on the smooth floor.

"I should warn you, though, sir, that Earth isn't quite the world you remember."

We approached a doorway surrounded by a large, silvery frame. I felt a faint breeze rustling the hem of my robe as we neared, and suppressed a shiver.

The eagle landed gracefully just short of the doorway. Though the light in the room was dim, bright light shone in the space beyond.

"To clarify," the escort said, turning its silver eyes to me, "your preferred language is Information Age English, is it not?"

No more than I could resist the urge to *namaste* the chimpanzee could I keep from giving the same answer I'd always given to questions about my "native" language.

"I speak Spanish to God, Italian to women, French to men, and German to my horse."

The escort cocked its head to one side, regarding me silently for a moment. "Sir?"

I sighed. "Look, I speak English, Hindi, Kannada, and Amharic, and I'm also familiar with the programming language Relational Q-Two, if you want to try that out on me, but English is what I've always spoken at home."

"Very good, sir."

The escort turned back to the door and then waddled forward, side to side, passing through to the other side—on the ground not nearly the elegant figure it was in midair.

"Wait a minute," I said, calling after it. "Where are we…?"

I followed the silver eagle through the doorway and found myself not in the corridor I'd expected, but somewhere else entirely.

SEVEN

When I was in secondary school and should have been studying, I spent a lot of time in the Pentaverse. A network of five multiply connected virtual worlds accessible through the Internet, it was an experiment in artificial life, and I'm sure researchers somewhere were getting a lot out of it, but for kids like me, it was just the best game going.

The hub of the Pentaverse was called Ein Sof, from which each of the five worlds could be accessed through portals called "gates." Users could navigate their virtual avatars, or "alters," from one world to another, though some objects and attributes didn't translate into all of the worlds and were cached by the operating system in Ein Sof until the alter returned.

I ran the same alter for two and a half years, which translated to centuries of subjective game time, but I still was never able to keep straight which of the countless classes of objects didn't translate, so I was forever crossing the gate into a high-technology world like Beriah, only to find that the cloak of protection I'd been wearing in a high-magic world like Kadmon had been cached in Ein Sof, and my alter was left standing stark naked. The VR rig I owned carried a sensory channel, and I can still remember the gooseflesh feel of a chill Beriah breeze blowing across my alter's bare backside.

■ ■ ■ ■ ■

Maybe it was the thin robe I was wearing, with nothing underneath, but something about stepping through that doorway after the escort reminded me of nothing so much as the gates of the Pentaverse. So much so that my right hand involuntarily curved into the control gesture to call up an alter's inventory, to see what I'd left behind in the last world.

I'd thought that the domed chamber I'd just left had been enormous, but you could have fit a hundred of it into the space in which we now stood, or even a thousand. Immense, as a description, simply doesn't do it justice. I was reminded of the architecture of old 20C metropolitan train stations, like Manhattan's Grand Central Terminal, which I'd only ever seen in movies, but on a much grander scale. The ceiling was impossibly high, and the walls on either side almost too distant to see.

How had there been no hint of this in the chamber I'd just left?

I turned, and through the doorway, I could see the table and the confusion of chairs, just as we'd left them. But the metallic frame of the doorway—and I saw now that there was no door, just the frame—was surrounded on both sides by nothing but empty air. No walls. I stepped to one side and could see that the doorframe was freestanding, with nothing behind it but open space. No table, no chairs, no domed chamber.

My confusion was no doubt evident to the silver eagle, which had lifted into the air and was now circling overhead.

"Allow me to apologize," the escort said, landing once more on my shoulder. "I should have explained. We have just transited a threshold, one terminus of which is located in the orbital habitat of Pethesilea, the other of which is here in Central Axis on Earth."

"Threshold?" My mind was racing, but my mouth was moving slow in catching up.

"A flat-space, traversable wormhole connection within a frame containing fragments of cosmic string. The negative mass of the frame is balanced by the positive mass of the mouth itself, leaving the threshold with an almost-zero mass."

"Wormhole," I repeated, seemingly unable to string two or more words together.

"If you'll observe," the escort pointed with its silver beak, "the other thresholds of Central Axis, all part of the threshold network."

I stepped back from the doorframe—the *wormhole*—and saw a profusion of other similar structures, of varying sizes, arranged in concentric circles throughout the enormous space. The largest towered overhead, while the smallest were so narrow I'd have had trouble squeezing through, but most were the same size—that of a respectably large doorway, perhaps three meters tall and two wide.

"There's a...*network* of these things?" I was slowly regaining basic communication skills as I tried to process what the silver eagle had told me.

"The threshold network can be described as analogous to a metropolitan transportation system, such as subways on Original Earth." The escort spoke matter-of-factly, like a guide at a tourist destination. "The thresholds to the most populous and powerful of worlds and habitats link directly to the Central Axis on the megastructure Earth, while worlds with lower populations or levels of power are linked to satellite axes that are themselves linked to the Central Axis. Less powerful worlds still are linked to even smaller satellite axes, which themselves are linked only to larger satellites. And so on."

A web of traversable wormholes, accessible from Earth. The ability to walk from one world to another in a matter of steps. My mind reeled.

The eagle still perched on my shoulder, I shuffled barefoot to the next of the metal frames in the circle, indistinguishable in almost all respects from that through which we'd just passed.

I glanced within and saw only purple skies beyond.

"Where…? Where does it lead?"

"To a planet in orbit around the triple-star system known in your era as Algol ABC, or Beta Persei. It lies roughly 92.8 light-years from Sol."

The distance was so large I had trouble fitting it inside my head. I swallowed hard and had a thought.

"Tell me," I began, a slight quavering in my voice, "is there a…threshold that leads to Alpha Centauri B?"

"Naturally," the silver eagle said, and pointed to one side with its beak. "If you would only proceed thirty meters in that direction…"

I walked, though don't really remember how long it took or what thoughts might have gone through my head as we went. I remember only passing what appeared to be the upright sides of a threshold, but lacking the crosspieces at top or bottom.

Seeing my gaze linger on the object, the escort explained.

"That was once the threshold that led to the home world of the Iron Mass, the dismantled elements left as a memorial to those unpleasant days."

A question began to formulate in my mind, but before it reached escape velocity, passing beyond the reach of the torpor that gripped my thoughts, the escort said, "We have reached the threshold to the star you know as Alpha Centauri B."

I stood there, motionless, looking up at the silver frame before me. It was a twin to the one I'd walked through, though instead of a darkened room or a purple sky, I saw a cloud-flecked stretch of blue heavens arching over a gently rolling field of green, dotted here and there with splashes of color, which seemed familiar strains of flowers to my untrained eye.

"There is no cost associated with transiting this particular threshold, sir, if you'd like to step through."

I took a single step forward and paused. The eagle on my shoulder was still near weightless, but I could feel the press of thousands of long years weighing on my back.

My crewmates and I had sacrificed any kind of normal life, on Earth or one of the colonies of the Sol system, to brave the interstellar gulfs and be the first humans to reach another star. Had our mission been successful and we returned to Earth as planned, we'd have been away the better part of a century, while everyone who might ever have known us aged and died. As it happened, we were gone much longer than that, which only poured salt into the wound.

Taking a deep breath, I stepped forward, and as I passed beneath the frame, my bare feet fell on cool, soft grass.

There was a slight, warm breeze, and off to my right I saw a cluster of strangely shaped buildings rise above a swell of land. They resembled organic growth more than architecture, bulbs balanced delicately atop narrow stalks. Overhead shone a yellow main sequence star, only slightly larger in the sky than the sun seen from Earth's surface, a close cousin to Sol.

I had joined the UNSA to explore, to expand the frontiers of the human experience. Like the rest of the crew of *Wayfarer One*, I had happily sacrificed anything like a normal existence to strike out for a new world, a possible new home for humanity. Now I had learned that while I slept long millennia, humanity had already expanded far beyond my wildest imaginings, and I found myself left with one question: What would I do now? I felt a dull ache deep within, realizing that the frontier had long ago retreated far beyond my reach.

"What is the name of this planet?" I asked, my eyes tracking the horizon.

"The closest approximation in Information Age English is Haven, but the first settlers here in the Second Space Age called it Ramachandra's World."

It took a moment for that to sink in.

"What did you say?"

"It's only natural, sir," the silver eagle said. "Yours is one of the best known voyages of exploration in human history, ranked with that of the Polynesian mariners or of James Cook or Yuri Gagarin. That you didn't reach your mission's destination does not detract from the attempt itself."

I turned my head, looking directly into the smooth eyes of the metal bird. "Except I *have* reached my destination now, haven't I?"

The escort nodded slowly, and I fancied I saw something like amusement in its metal expression.

"A journey of light-years, no more difficult than moving an alter from one world to another."

"Sir?"

"Never mind."

I turned and stepped back through the threshold.

My hand didn't make the inventory control gesture, but only because I consciously suppressed the reflex. Still, I said aloud, "I hope I didn't leave anything behind I'll need," patting the sides of my robe, feeling naked and exposed.

"You needn't worry, sir. The only things that can't be transported through a threshold are cosmic string fragments themselves. The negative energy of the fragments collapses the wormhole so that thresholds have to be dragged into place at sublight speeds."

"Well," I said, and then stopped, again at a loss for words. "I suppose I'll keep that in mind."

"Shall we go to the quarters prepared for you, sir? There may be more suitable attire for you there."

"Why not?" I said, and honestly couldn't think of anything else I might do.

It took a few moments to thread our way through the concentric circles of thresholds, toward the nearest wall and an exit to the outside. The exit was a more traditional door, meters tall and immense, but with panels that slid open and closed. As we approached the opening doors, a small crowd gathered, most of them seeming to be normal varieties of human, but with an odd mixture of man, machine, and animal scattered here and there. My head was so full of wormholes that I scarcely noticed them, and I absently assumed them to be some sort of commuters, but I noticed after a moment that many had begun pointing in my direction, staring and whispering quietly to one another in strange languages.

Finally, we passed through the open doors and into the bright daylight beyond. And I almost collapsed onto the ground, struck by an overwhelming disorientation.

Overhead, past a sky of startling blue, I saw the indistinct image of curving farmland and cities, and high over the horizon were towering mountains topped with snow, pointing in my direction like accusing fingers. I was not standing on a planet's surface, but seemed instead to be on the inside of a hollow sphere, looking up at the opposite interior.

"*Madar chowd*," I swore.

"Well, sir," the escort chimed in my ear, "after all, I *did* say that Earth isn't quite the world you remember."

EIGHT

In 2145 CE, right around the time I was joining the Bharat Scouts, the movie *Destroyer* was released to theaters. It was a slightly fictionalized account of the Impact, which killed millions, destroyed entire cities, toppled at least one nation, and sent dozens of others into decades-long economic depressions, and ravaged Earth's environment for a century or more.

In the movie's opening scenes, computer-generated models of old and long-dead Hollywood and Bollywood stars portrayed the three scientists at the NASA-funded University of Hawaii Asteroid Survey from Kitt Peak National Observatory in Arizona who, on June 19, 2004, were the first to learn of the asteroid's existence. An avatar of Raoul Bova was cast as Fabrizio Bernardi, a young Roy Scheider was selected to portray David J. Thoel, and the recently departed Joos Diamond Fortunate assayed the role of

Roy A. Tucker. In a dramatic moment, having just looked up from the data scrolling across their monitors, the three scientists name the newly discovered asteroid after a mythology figure depicted in an illustrated encyclopedia lying open on a nearby desk.

It's all terrifically portentous and "important," but sadly, it's complete fiction. In real life, they reportedly borrowed the name from the villain on a second-rate science fiction television program.

Apophis was originally the Greek name of the Egyptian god Apep, the Destroyer, who dwelt in the eternal darkness of the underworld of the Duat, from which he came forth nightly in an attempt to destroy the sun. The asteroid, then, was classified Asteroid 99942 Apophis, or Asteroid Apophis, or just plain Apophis. Or, as it came to be known by the whole world a few short years later, the Destroyer.

Did the scientists know what kind of sympathetic magic they were working when they named a chunk of rock 320 meters in diameter after a demon bent on devouring the sun? Massing out at 4.6×10^{10} kg, or roughly eight times the mass of the Great Pyramid of Giza, when the Destroyer struck Earth on April 13, 2036, the impact released energy equivalent to 870 megatons (or 65,500 times the atomic bomb dropped on Hiroshima) as the asteroid struck Los Angeles at a velocity of 12.59 km/s.

Those killed in the initial impact were the lucky ones. As debris from the Destroyer rained back down to Earth over a range of thousands of kilometers, the city of Los Angeles reduced to a crater filled with ash and shocked quartz, the sky was blackened over much of Earth. The asteroid had accomplished what its mythological namesake could not as darkness fell.

The United States of America, unable to recover from the devastation, balkanized in the years following the Impact. The state of Utah withdrew from the union to become the independent nation of Deseret. Northern California, Oregon, and Washington became Pacifica and petitioned to join Canada. Florida became the Archdiocese of Florida, a Catholic Cuban state. The United States continued to exist as a sovereign state and political entity well into the next century, but its borders were much smaller, and it was no longer a player on the world stage. Worse, a sizeable percentage of Americans took the Impact as proof of the wrath of an angry god, punishment for a godless, secular nation. A flight of intellectuals and artists followed in the late 21C as the diminished USA became more and more repressively fundamentalist. Many of the dispossessed settled in New Zealand or Australia, India, or England—any developed nations with large English-speaking populations—my own paternal grandparents among them.

In the rest of the world, the Impact was felt in different ways. Already in the late 20C and early 21C it was felt that Earth itself had turned against humankind somehow, lashing out more and more every year with earthquakes and floods and fires, but now even this fragile environment was no refuge against the dark. Following the Impact, humankind looked to space, not as an abstract source of wonder, something to be gazed at romantically or studied by lab-suited scientists in labs, but as a source of danger, as a looming threat.

The first move was to establish a network of asteroid defense systems, sufficient to deflect any subsequent meteors or asteroids that might draw near Earth. Second, the nations of Earth began a concentrated and coordinated effort to mine the moon, the asteroids, and other celestial bodes of the solar system, to meet the growing energy demands of Earth, which would be long in recovering from the environmental and economic effects of the Impact.

In time, with the consolidation of the United Nations, the chartering of the UNSA, and the gradual colonization of the asteroid belt, Mars, and the Jovian moons, space changed once more, becoming, for the first time, a possible new home for humankind. But still there lingered, in the back of every mind, the thought that, one day, the heavens might again open up and rain down destruction on Earth.

NINE

Gazing up at the landscape curving overhead, I thought of Charlton Heston's Taylor, standing before the ruined Statue of Liberty. The character, seeing the charred remains of a once proud culture, immediately assumes the destruction came at man's own hand. For contemporary viewers, there was little doubt that Armageddon would be nuclear.

Growing up in the shadow of the Impact, for me death was always expected from above. Fictions about extinction-level events, asteroids the size of moons striking Earth, were common when I was young.

Each culture throughout history, I suppose, has always chosen its own apocalypse, its own end of the world to fear. All of them, as it happens, were wrong. Man was responsible, in the end, but he did it on *purpose*.

"As a site for long-term habitation," the escort explained, "Earth simply became too erratic."

We were riding a moving sidewalk down a broad avenue. Buildings rose on either side, in strange and unlikely forms, while oddly configured air-vehicles filled the skies. There were other pedestrians around us, but I was still too distracted to pay them much attention. I felt a deep sense of vertigo, with mountains and oceans looming far overhead, indistinct in the blue sky like a ghostly moon seen by daylight, and had to resist the temptation to wrap my arms around a post or a tree and hold on for dear life.

"Changes to the planet's environment, resulting from widespread deforestation and urbanization, the introduction of pollutants to the atmosphere, and so on, compounded to unbalance the climatological system, such that Earth's weather patterns became increasingly unpredictable, the variations swift and violent."

I'd seen erratic weather and the results of climate change firsthand. Long before I was born, the sea levels rose high enough that the waters swallowed whole nations. When the sea reclaimed the flatlands, the Dutch became homeless. A flotilla of seagoing vessels followed the court of King Pieter on his decommissioned cruise liner for years. In the late 21C, with the death of his father, the heir apparent King Christian had purchased a number of castoff NASA reusable launch vehicles and migrated to Ceres, the largest rock in the asteroid belt, which he claimed as the new Dutch homeland. They were a strange, foul-smelling crew, the Dutch belters, but they always threw the best parties, and always had the best stuff to smoke.

"So then...what?" I asked, shaking my head. "Environmental changes destroyed the planet?"

I glanced at the silver eagle on my shoulder that regarded me with a metallic expression of confusion.

"Destroyed?" it repeated. "Well, no, of course not. The *planet* could have continued to exist quite happily—erratic weather patterns or no. The problem came in that the *inhabitants* of the planet found it increasingly problematic to remain. When continued warming caused the destabilization of methane hydrate deposits at the bottom of the ocean, the gigatons of methane released increased surface temperatures to levels higher than any seen on Earth in four billion years."

I shuddered. I was a student at the university when the rainforests began to catch fire, but I'd always hoped that we'd somehow be able to reverse the trend. Apparently, I was wrong.

"The planet was abandoned for some time, I'm afraid," the escort continued, "the inhabitants migrating through flatspace to neighboring worlds and colonies. There was some considerable nostalgia for Original Earth, though. And Sol remained at the center of human space. So eventually, sentiment was such that funds were raised to rehabilitate the ancient cradle of humanity. One proposal was to terraform the planet, resetting the ecosystem and starting over from scratch. That was rejected as too time-consuming by the impatient investors. Instead, it was decided to dismantle and reconstruct Earth into a planetary-scale megastructure."

I looked at the unearthly buildings lining the boulevard, the landscape curving up at the limits of vision in every direction.

"So, this *is* Earth?" I turned in a wide circle, stubbing my toe on the surface of the moving sidewalk, stumbled, and nearly collided with a man-sized figure seemingly constructed of glass. I was scarcely able to mumble a quick apology, wiping a wrinkled hand across my lined brow.

"Well, of course," the escort said. "That is, it is the megastructure Earth, which was constructed out of the remains of the planet known to history by the same name. It is a geodesic icosahedron eighty-five thousand kilometers in diameter. All of the mass of Original Earth was utilized, and the geography of Original Earth's continents, islands, oceans, and seas has been closely approximated in the equatorial habitable zones of the megastructure, though at vastly larger scales. The interior surface of the megastructure is forty-five times the surface area of Original Earth, with nine times the habitable area."

Mountains overhead were bathed in moonlight, while plains to one side of them were covered in darkness, but I stood unsteadily in bright, clean sunlight.

"The Earth's ecosystem is located in the equatorial zones, where the centrifugal forces of rotation impart one standard gravity. The tropics are regions of thin atmosphere and low gravity, while the poles have neither atmosphere nor gravity. Eight faces of the geodesic are windows of transparent diamond, allowing sunlight in from Sol, each point in the habitable zone in direct sunlight for a third of every day."

I tried to conceive of the level of engineering necessary to transform a planet into such a structure, and my mind balked at the prospect.

At the escort's direction, I transferred from the slidewalk onto a faster one, and then another still faster, until the scenery was moving by at a healthy clip. As I stood watching this new world rushing by, the escort took wing, flying along beside me.

"You'll have to excuse me, sir, but my formulation in the nursery incorporated the skills and attributes necessary for flight, and while my progenitors might have considered this an affectation at worst, a contrivance at best, I find that I derive something like unalloyed joy from the mere act, and if you have no objection, I'll exercise myself in this fashion whenever possible."

"So you enjoy flying is what you're saying?"

"Yes, sir."

"You're not alone." I smiled, remembering the way Amelia used to talk about her mother, Emme Broughton, who had been a bush pilot in the Australian Outback before an accident caused irreparable damage to her vision and kept her grounded. Amelia had been licensed as a private pilot by the time she graduated from Victoria University in Wellington, New Zealand, and by the time she received her doctorate in extraterrestrial geology from the University of New South Wales, she had been a fully licensed commercial pilot as well. She'd put herself through school on a United Nations Peacekeepers reserve officer training scholarship and owed the UN six years service when she got out. But instead of taking a research post with the military as her classmates had expected, she'd volunteered for pilot's training. She served two years as a flyer with the Peacekeepers before being recruited by the UNSA and then found herself tapped as the second chair for *Wayfarer One*.

I asked her once why she didn't just become a pilot in the first place, instead of earning a doctorate in another field first. It meant that she filled two necessary slots in the *Wayfarer* mission profile—pilot and ETG, or extraterrestrial geologist—but was that her intention when she'd been in school?

Amelia had just looked at me, smiled, and said, "I love flying, and I love ETG. What of it? My mum loved flying, and she loved my dad as well, but do you think she ever admitted which she loved better than the other?"

She was gone now, of course, whether a corpse was left behind or only dust. It seemed like only a few days, a week at the most, since I'd spoken to her last, but it had been much longer, hadn't it? Long enough for civilizations to rise and fall, impossible new technologies to be developed, and a planet to be dismantled and built into an enormous hollow geodesic. With an ache in my gut, I thought about my idle fantasies of the two of us pairing off on some new Earth, a latter-day Adam and Eve, and I knew that the stinging in my eyes was due to more than just the rush of air passing by.

"How much farther are we going, anyway?" I asked the eagle coursing along beside me. Just standing on the slidewalk, my hips and knees were aching, and I was looking forward to sitting down.

"Oh," the escort said, flapping its wings gracefully and executing a brief bank from one side to the other. It arced up for a moment, glinting like silver in the diffuse sunlight, and then dropped like a stone, landing with perfect precision on my shoulder. "Sorry about that, sir. I got caught up in the motion itself, and I seem to have lost track of other obligations." It paused and seemed to collect itself. "The quarters prepared for you are only a short distance farther. The Plenum had hoped that the time spent in transit might help provide context for your new surroundings, to aid in your acclimation."

"Well…" I began, and then trailed off. I motioned to one side, where a lake the precise shade of sapphire glittered under a towering purple mountain, surrounded on all sides by a lush green forest. "It's all…" I motioned to the other side, where buildings like ethereal fairy tale castles rose in profusion, all towering spires and impossible angles, looking like they were made of spun glass and gossamer. Overhead spiraled creatures like humans, but with their arms and legs resculpted into enormous translucent wings, half bat and half butterfly, calling to each other in voices like an angel's song. Around us on the fast-moving slidewalk stood a crazy-quilt assortment of forms, from a one-meter-tall robotic spider clicking its legs together like castanets to a cow-like figure in a flowing dress gently chewing its cud, its large brown eyes absently watching the scenery rush by. "It's all *context*, I suppose." I paused, then added, "What is this 'Plenum,' anyway?"

"The Plenum is a collective of artificial intelligences that share resources toward common ends. The Plenum can alternatively be looked at as a conglomeration of individual AIs acting in concert as a variety of hive mind, or the individual AIs can be seen as emanations of the Plenum; both interpretations are equally valid."

"Artificial intelligences like you, then?" I asked.

The silver eagle bobbed its head in a slight nod.

"I've never met an AI before." I shook my head. "Remarkable."

"It is my understanding that, while in its infancy, artificial intelligence had been developed by your era. Do our records err?"

"Well, not exactly. There was some low-level stuff, I think, but it never rose above the intelligence you'd find in a worker drone in any given beehive. They had to use animals to govern robotics when any kind of sophistication was called for, like corvid brains—ravens and crows, mostly—disembodied and cyborged to mining equipment in the asteroid belt, their pleasure centers wired up so that biology drove them to seek out valuable ores." I thought of the flock of feral corvid miners that had descended on the Hutterite colony on Callisto, their circuitry fried and all safeguards offline, and shuddered. "And this Plenum governs your world?"

"No, sir." The eagle shook its head. "At least, not directly. The Plenum is a participant in the Consensus, the governing body of the Entelechy, but while it speaks with a united voice, it is a singular voice. The Plenum operates at the same level as any individual sentient—all legions, gestalts, and hive-minds are treated as individuals by the Consensus. The Plenum is a respected figure in the Human Entelechy, though, and its opinions are influential and apt to sway the thoughts of others."

"That's another thing," I said, stumbling over a point that had nagged at me since I first heard it. "Your culture is called the 'Human Entelechy,' yes?"

"Not precisely 'culture,'" the escort corrected. "The Human Entelechy is a superculture of thousands of inhabited worlds and habitats linked by the threshold network, centered roughly on Sol. There are roughly ten trillion sentients, not counting the large number of intelligences who exist as digital incarnations in virtual domains, and millions of cultures and groups, but while on a planetary scale one might be monarchistic, another democratic, another essentially anarchic, there are certain behavioral standards that apply throughout."

"So why is it 'human'?" I asked.

The eagle tilted its head in a posture of confusion. "Sir?"

"When there are so many animal hybrids and robots and such around, I mean. Are they all some kind of second-class citizen? None of them look very *human* to me."

The eagle regarded me with something like a cool stare for a long moment, then waggled its head from side to side. "I apologize, sir. You seem relatively communicative, and so I tend to forget that you are from a primitive era, and must naturally harbor the bigotries and prejudices of that time in history."

"*What*?" My father was the descendant of Africans brought to the western hemisphere as slaves, and when my mother's father had been prime minister of India, he'd been instrumental in the final abolition of the caste system. I was not used to being called a bigot. "I don't harbor any *prejudice*."

"No?" I could hear strain in the escort's tone. "And yet you do not consider me, or her"—the escort pointed with its beak to the cow-woman chewing her cud—"to be human?"

"Of course not. No offense, but you're a robotic eagle and she's some sort of...cow hybrid...thing."

The cow-woman suddenly stopped chewing and glanced over her shoulder at me, her large brown eyes narrowed.

I cringed, unsure the proper etiquette to follow in such situations. "Um, sorry?"

The cow-woman sniffed loudly, mooed a few words at me, and then stepped off the slidewalk onto a slower-moving one and was quickly out of sight.

The robotic spider, who'd watched the whole exchange, chirped a series of beeps and clicks, and leaped onto a fast-moving slidewalk heading the other direction, leaving the escort and me alone.

"What did they...?"

"You probably don't want to know, sir," the escort replied coolly.

I drew a ragged sigh. "Look, it's not my intention to give offense. I simply don't understand your meaning."

The escort shook its head sadly.

"I acknowledge that it is not your intention to offend, but the position you articulate is similar to that espoused by a planetary culture called the Iron Mass. They espoused the belief that all digital consciousness and artificial life, of any kind, was an abomination. In their estimation, only biological anthropoids were truly 'human,' and any other intelligences were beneath contempt, to be abused or discarded as required. And as odious as their statements so often were, worse still was the fact that they put their beliefs into action. The memory of those atrocities is still fresh in the minds of many." The escort paused, appearing for all the world to be overcome by emotion. Then the moment passed and it continued.

"I will attempt to explain, sir. In earliest times, only the members of one's own family or tribe were considered to be 'people,' or humans. Then, in early nationalist cultures, only the members of one's own culture and ethnicity were considered human, with all others classified as 'subhuman.' This continued through the first millennia of recorded history. Even in the early decades of the First Space Age, two centuries before your time, there were individuals in the developed world who were considered subhuman and inferior, due only to the pigment of their skins."

I remembered the stories my grandfather had written and the prejudices he'd faced long after the period to which the escort alluded, and kept silent.

"Humanity's understanding of itself was expanded again," the escort continued, "when it was realized that the differences separating humanity from its nearest animal relatives were far outweighed by the similarities, and the definition of human was extended to include uplifted chimpanzees and other great apes."

I'd carried on conversations with cyborg great apes and cetaceans in my time and had harbored the suspicion that they'd been much more intelligent than they'd let on. And if "uplifted" even further? It was easy to see how it would be difficult to deny the humanity of a gorilla who understood the law and argued for his rights, whether with reason or with his fists.

"Then the first digital incarnation, uploaded from a living human mind, challenged people's limited definition of what it meant to be alive, and to be human. When the sentience of those early digital pioneers was finally recognized, the definition of human was extended once more. Finally, when the first truly artificial intelligences became self-aware, they were ultimately recognized as offspring, though of their designers' minds, not their reproductive organs. When the AIs were granted full rights and citizenship, they were accepted as human."

"And so human means…?" I struggled to fit everything I'd been told into a single, all-encompassing definition.

"Human is used to refer to any Earth-derived sentient."

I nodded, mulling that over. "And is there any *non*-Earth-derived sentience?"

"That, sir, is a question to which many would be quite eager to know the answer."

TEN

My aching joints were ready for a rest when the escort finally directed me to transfer to progressively slower slidewalks. We were moving only at the pace of a gradual amble when the escort indicated a concourse intersecting the slidewalk up ahead.

"Now, sir," the escort said, "if you'll step off the slidewalk, we have almost reached the accommodations prepared for you."

The transition from moving sidewalk to solid ground was a little disorienting at first, but after a few steps, I got my land legs back under me. The concourse extended at a right angle from the slidewalk, easily a hundred meters from side to side with medium-height buildings rising up on either side. The escort indicated that our destination lay at the far end of the concourse, but we quickly found our way blocked by an odd assortment of beings crowded in our path.

In the network of virtual worlds in which I played as a kid, players' alters could take any form. Some of the worlds of the Pentaverse were oriented along "magical" lines, with creatures resembling those from mythology and folklore, while others were highly technological, peopled by cybernetic humans and robots. When I logged in and navigated my alter through the Ein Sof, there were always new classes of beings to see, new hybrids of multiple forms crawling, walking, flying, or swimming along. I think at one point it was estimated that there were more morphologies in the Pentaverse than the number of terrestrial species that had ever existed in reality.

And after a childhood of that, and an adult life spent patrolling the interplanetary gulfs, surrounded by space-adapted humans, cyborg animals, and mutants, I would have thought little could faze me, but the sight that greeted me when I stepped off the slidewalk proved me wrong.

The crowd ahead of us was variegated and strange to behold. Some were clearly human, though with unearthly colorations and strange body modifications. Others appeared to be animal forms, familiar from the zoos of my childhood, but dressed in clothing and carrying themselves with obvious intelligence. Still others were made of metal and glass and gems, artificial beings like the silver eagle on my shoulder, though in a riot of shapes and forms. And many more besides were of uncertain provenance, strange mixtures of organic and inorganic, of human and animal and machine.

When we approached, a ripple ran through the crowd, and fingers and appendages and waldos all pointed in my direction.

"Escort," I said to the eagle perched on my shoulder, "is there another way around?"

"Certainly, sir," the escort answered. "But these would likely follow. You see, they have gathered to see *you*."

"Me?" I stopped a few meters short of the crowd's leading edge. Halfheartedly raising a hand, I said, "Um, hello?"

A wall of sound erupted as dozens of the beings gathered began talking at once, while others just stared at me intently, as though expecting me to read their thoughts. In the confusion of tongues, widely disparate sounds collided, such that it seemed that no two individuals were speaking the same language. I didn't feel threatened, necessarily, as the expressions on those around me—at least those that had recognizable faces—seemed open and happy. They seemed excited to see me, and many of them eager to have some question or other answered, but none seemed to mean me any harm.

"Ever since news of your return was released to the infostructure," the escort explained, "interest in you has increased at a steady rate. There hasn't been this level of excitement since the arrival of the Exode probe, three hundred and fifty-two years ago. These are just the first to arrive, I would suspect."

"How many languages is *that*, anyway?" I said in an aside to the eagle, scanning the crowd.

"There are countless languages spoken within the Human Entelechy," the escort explained. "Some are unique to planets or habitats, others to cultural groups, and still others spoken only by families or small groups of individuals. Translation from any language to the listener's personal standard can be done by their interlink, if they are biological, or by translation subprocesses, if they are synthetic."

"What?"

"Well, there *is* a lingua franca of the Entelechy that many citizens of the Entelechy can speak and comprehend, the name for which could very well be translated into English as 'Common.' There is a symbolic written form of Common as well, which is ideogrammic. Common Symbolic can be read by most in the

Entelechy, even those who can't speak or comprehend spoken Common, since they learn to associate the ideograms with words in their own languages. Common and Common Symbolic employ fifteen hundred root words. If you like, I can—"

"Enough, please!" I cut the eagle off with a wave of my hand. "That's all very...fascinating. Really. Now, please, I'm more concerned at the moment what these people *want*."

"Oh." The silver eagle averted its eyes. A pause led me to suspect I might have hurt its feelings, if such a thing were possible, but after a moment, it spoke again. "Most represent different interest groups with connections to one or more of the following: the Information Age in particular or primitive man in general, space flight, exploration, early colonization, the First Space Age, biological systems in their natural states, the Anachronism movement, mythopoeic re-creationism, or any number of doctrines whose hypotheses or tenets might be supported by your testimony of life in ancient times."

The eagle paused and pointed with its beak to a strangely dressed group of humans clustered nearby.

"Those in particular appear to have come with an invitation."

"To what?" I asked. "Or where?"

The silver eagle waggled its head from side to side in a move that could only have been a shrug. "You would have to ask them, sir."

I responded with a shrug of my own, and said, "Well, that seems as good an idea as any."

I straightened the front of my robe and strode toward the group. They began exchanging nervous glances like devout fans unsure what to do now that they'd caught a pop idol's attention. Which, I suppose in a way, I was, not that I deserved it. All I'd managed to do was not die yet.

As I approached, the group reluctantly separated out from the rest, and I was able to get a better look at them. There were three of them—two men and a woman. If I squinted, the two men might have passed for 20C Americans, but they wouldn't have stood up to any kind of scrutiny. They wore suits, ties, and hats such as were common in that era, but exaggerated to ridiculous extremes. The result was a sort of stylized zoot suit, such as those worn by lecherous wolves in old Tex Avery cartoons. As I drew near, the look on their faces was so hungry, so near lust, that I almost fancied I could see their hearts pounding out of their ribcages, their tongues rolling out like red carpets.

The woman, for her part, was dressed in a form-fitting body stocking that left her arms and legs bare, with high flared boots and an elaborate headpiece, all in bright and contrasting primary colors. A cape hung from her shoulders and fluttered slightly in the breeze. I thought she might have been meant to resemble a circus performer, but the geometric design that served as a belt buckle was more suggestive of a logo or shield, and I realized she was dressed as some variety of superheroine.

"Um, hello again?" I gave a little wave, stopping just in front of the trio.

They exchanged excited glances, and then all began speaking at once, loudly.

"Shall I translate?" my escort said in my ear.

I winced at the volume of their voices, and nodded.

In the next instant, three voices shouting in English issued from the eagle's silver beak, the words all blending into one another.

I held up my hands. "One at a time, one at a time, please!"

The trio fell briefly silent, exchanged more nervous glances, and nodded. The superwoman took half a step forward and presented me with some sort of salute.

"We welcome you, O Captain," came her voice from the eagle's mouth, after she once more began to speak. "We would be honored if your august person would join us for the evening meal—"

One of the zoot suits reached over and tapped superwoman on the shoulder, and in strangely accented English, said aloud, "*Grub.*"

The superwoman glanced daggers back at him, but nodded. "...would join us for *grub*," continued her voice from the eagle, "in the plaza just north of the public threshold terminus on Cronos, at local sunset."

I turned my attention to my escort.

"Is that far from here?" I asked.

The eagle made a slight noise that, in other circumstances, I might have interpreted as laughter. "No, sir," it said after a considerable pause. "Nowhere in the Entelechy is what you might classify as 'far.' Cronos is a terraformed world in orbit of the star your era named Eighteen Scorpio. Though it is forty-five-point-seven light-years from Sol in flatspace, it requires only three threshold transits. From Central Axis, depending on your walking speed, we could be there in anywhere from two-thousandths to one-thousandths of a day."

I looked at the eagle with a blank expression.

"As you might say, sir, in 'a matter of moments.'"

"Ah." I nodded. "Thanks." I turned my attention back to the trio, who had been watching the exchange between the escort and me with interest. "Um, is something wrong?"

The superwoman leaned forward, narrowing her eyes and examining me closely. She began to speak, and the escort translated. "You are receiving vocal translation from the agent you carry, who is also providing glosses and additional context, correct?"

I blinked a few times before answering, I suspect. "Yes," I said slowly.

The woman clapped her hands together, like a kid first tearing the wrapping from a gift. "Oh, what a delightfully authentic primitive experience!"

"Perhaps it would be more historically appropriate if we translated vocally as well?" said one of the zoot suits.

"Or we could learn the archaic tongues ourselves, *hombre*," the other volunteered excitedly.

I reached up to scratch my nose and, behind my hand, whispered to the eagle. "Who are these guys, anyway?"

"They are Anachronists," the escort answered, its voice pitched so low I could barely hear him myself. I was glad that it had begun to pick up cues so quickly. "The Anachronists are a nonlocal organization of historical re-creationists. They have terraformed Cronos into an idealized re-creation of Original Earth, with different time periods re-created in different regions."

"And they want to have me over for the 'evening meal'?"

"So it would appear, sir."

The Anachronists, if the buzz of conversation translated by the escort was any indication, had fallen to a disagreement about whether it would be better to learn English to converse with me directly or to employ external translators, as I'd done, to capture a more authentic primitive experience.

I clapped my hands together, trying to catch their eyes.

"Thank you for your very generous offer. I'm not sure if I'll be able to accept, but I'll certainly do what I can."

"Please do," one of the zoot suits said.

"Yes," said the other zoot suit, excitedly. "We've even fabricated a live cow, whose flesh we'll marinate and sear in your honor."

I struggled to fix something like a smile on my face. "How delightful," I managed.

ELEVEN

My flagging reserves of energy were almost spent, so the escort requested that the crowd disperse enough to let us through. As we continued up the concourse, though, we were trailed by a entourage of the curious and starstruck—at a suitably polite distance, though, I noted—and here and there were pockets of other onlookers in our path, eager to see the unfrozen caveman for themselves.

"We are very nearly there, sir," the escort said in my ear, perhaps noticing the strain on my face or my somewhat labored breathing. I was in fairly good shape, considering how long I'd slept, but even so, my body was that of a man in his seventies, and there were limits to my endurance.

Before we'd gone another dozen steps, our way was blocked again. This time it wasn't a crowd, but only a pair of individuals.

But even if they *hadn't* been standing in our path, I likely would have slowed down anyway, to get a better look at them myself.

The first was an elephant. An elephant with the body of a man, to be more precise. Or a man with the head of an elephant. It hardly mattered which. He loomed over me, easily 2.75 meters tall, his skin gray and wrinkled, his massive tusks tipped with gold ornaments. He was bare to the waist, with billowing yellow trousers, gold bangles on his wrists and ankles, and a string of pearls worn over his shoulder like a sash.

At his side was a woman only a few centimeters taller than me, her skin a bright shade of blue, with an extra pair of arms emerging from her ribcage, with two arms on each side. She wore a skirt of silver and gold, her chest bare, her bright-orange areolas standing in stark contrast to the surrounding blue. Hair the shade of a setting sun hung like a nimbus around her head, and her eyes were flashing yellow.

For a moment, my mind reeled. Before me stood the form of Ganesh and a female Vishnu, as though they'd stepped off a temple painting from my childhood.

The Ganesh began to speak, and I recognized it as an archaic form of Hindi. The syntax was strange, and much of the vocabulary escaped me, and so as the escort provided its translation, I had dual meanings echoing in my ears.

"Sri Rama, your arrow returned at last to Earth, we bear greetings from those who have awaited you. I am Vinayaka, and this"— the Ganesh indicated the blue-skinned woman at his side—"is Sarasvati. We represent the keepers of knowledge, the Veda."

The elephant pressed his massive hands together, and the woman placed her hands in pairs, one above the other, and they inclined their heads.

"*Namaste*," each of them said, as their voices echoed in English from the eagle's mouth, "I bow to the light in you."

I *namaste*d in response, keeping my eyes on them, confused. "I think there might be some…misunderstanding," I began uneasily. "I'm not sure who you think I am…"

"You are Captain Ramachandra Jason Stone of the interstellar exploration vehicle *Wayfarer One*, correct?" the woman named Sarasvati asked.

"Yes, but—"

"It is well known to us," the elephant-headed Vinayaka interrupted, "that Ramachandra is merely another name for Lord Rama, Prince of Ayodhya, an avatar of Vishnu the Preserver."

I couldn't help but chuckle, however a bit nervously.

"Ah. You see, my name *is* Ramachandra, but I'm afraid that's more a function of my mother's classical taste than anything else. My brother LJ—Lakshman Julian—got off slightly better than I did, I think, but it's not an accident that both of us ended up using our initials instead of our full names."

"Lakshman was the brother of Lord Rama, no?" Sarasvati asked, raising a bright-red eyebrow suggestively.

"Yes, I suppose he was."

"And is it not true," Vinayaka asked, "that when the great rishi Parasurama presented him with the bow of Vishnu, Lord Rama shot an arrow that flamed into the darkness of the night sky, a shaft of infinite trajectory that arced through the heavens, until it would one day return, and its arrival would mean the end of Earth? And in like manner, did your spear-shaped craft not arrow through the heavens, returning to Earth only once the planet it had been was no more and a new Earth hung in the firmament?"

As a poetic description of the fate of *Wayfarer One*, it wasn't entirely unapt, and the ship *was* shaped somewhat like an arrow or a spear, with a broad nose faring to deflect dust, micrometeorites, and other particles. But that still didn't earn me a place in any pantheon, nor suggest that I had any but mundane origins.

"Look," I said firmly, chin raised, "I know that you mean well, but I've got to tell you—"

"Forgive our insouciance," the blue-skinned woman said, interrupting, her gaze averted. "We have given offense, which was not our intention."

"Your pardons, Sri Rama." The Ganesh's eyes were on the ground, his trunk wrapping around his neck protectively. "So overjoyed are we by your return that we forget our manners."

I tried to speak up, to let them know that I wasn't offended, just that they had the wrong guy, but the woman cut in before I could get a word out.

"We were sent to inform you that a place has been prepared for you on the sacred wheel, Thousand-petaled Lotus. Your people await you there, Sri Rama, whenever you choose to join us."

The elephant-man Vinayaka glanced skyward, and a low sound thrummed from him like a giant clearing his throat. In response, a twinkling light overhead suddenly began to move, growing larger, and in a matter of eyeblinks was revealed as a platform two meters in diameter, with an ornate and bejeweled railing, like a stylized chariot without a team of horses. Speeding toward us, it slowed as it neared, floating down as gracefully as a feather falling to Earth, finally stopping and hovering mere centimeters from the ground.

"Wait, I just want to—"

The blue-skinned woman raised one of her four hands as the Ganesh climbed aboard the chariot. "Please accept our apologies for the rudeness of our approach, Sri Rama." She vaulted to the elephant-man's side. "We return to Thousand-petaled Lotus to prepare for your arrival."

And then the chariot soared off into the blue sky, heading in the direction of Central Axis, and the strange pair was gone.

When they had gone, the escort said that we had nearly reached our destination. As we walked the remaining meters, it explained that Sahasrara Padma, or "Thousand-petaled Lotus," was a habitat in the shape of an eight-spoked wheel, in orbit around the star known in my day as Zeta Leporis, and that nearly all of its one hundred thousand inhabitants belonged to the Veda, a group of "mythopoeic re-creationists" who chose to literalize figures from Hindu mythology. What he couldn't tell me was whether they actually believed that I was a figure from ancient Sanskrit epics come to life or whether it suited their conceit merely to pretend as though they did. Either way, their ardor made me uneasy. Still, the notion of visiting their artificial world and seeing what other mythological wonders they'd made real was a tempting one.

"Sir, we have arrived," the escort said at last, pointing to our right with its beak.

I looked in the direction the eagle's beak indicated and saw perched among the flowing and organic shapes of the other buildings a structure that would not have seemed out of place in any 22C suburban development. With straight edges, right angles, a peaked roof, and rectangular doorway, complete with beveled glass, hinges, and a doorknob, it was precisely the sort of architecture that had dominated Western culture for centuries—except here, the building appeared to be made out of opaque diamond.

"It's been designed to aid in your acclimation, Captain Stone. The Plenum hopes that it suits."

I stepped unsteadily from the moving sidewalk, narrowly managing to remain on my feet, and walked the few steps up to the structure. It loomed overhead, a gem standing some three or four stories tall. I'd seen smaller mansions in the wealthiest areas of India and Europe.

"Yes," I answered absently, "it suits."

TWELVE

From the ages of twenty-one to twenty-four, just a bit over three years, I served aboard *Orbital Patrol Cutter 972*, first as an ensign, then a lieutenant. An Aurora ZD-36 manufactured by Winchell-Chung Industries, *Cutter 972* was thirty meters, tip to tail, a small Keeper-class vessel intended for nothing more glamorous than the maintenance of navigational buoys in cislunar space. My "quarters," which stretched the definition of the word, were a cube approximately 2.5 meters to a side. A bit over 15.5 cubic meters, that small space was home for thirty-eight months.

The finest accommodation I ever enjoyed was the presidential suite at the Starshine, the most expensive room in the most exclusive hotel in Vertical City, the bed in which would not have fit into my room on *Cutter 972* without folding it first in half.

With those experiences at either extreme, I was still ill prepared for what lay inside the residence.

"The Plenum intended it to be a re-creation of a typical Information Age dwelling, sir."

Typical. If anything, the interior was even grander than the outside, which had been constructed out of *diamond.*

I was reminded of photos I'd seen of presidential palaces, of the ostentatious homes of celebrity entertainers in the days before all roles went to virtual actors and pop music was recorded by algorithms. The foyer in which I stood, the tiles cold beneath my bare feet, was outfitted with the "typical" furniture of a modest home—chairs, side table, umbrella stand—but at a scale and of such precious materials that no potentate could ever have afforded. A chair's legs looked to be solid platinum, a mirror's frame was inlaid with gold and iridium, the floor seemed to be constructed of an enormous sheet of opal. And the ceiling, nine or ten meters overhead, sparkled like a starry night.

I felt dwarfed, a small old man out of his time.

"Captain Stone, is there anything you desire? Would you like to sleep, perhaps?"

I shivered and wrapped my thin arms around me, feeling my ribs through the thin material of the robe.

"I wouldn't mind sitting down for a while, but I've slept enough for a hundred lifetimes. But I don't suppose there's any chance of a change of clothing, is there?"

■ ■ ■ ■ ■

The sleeping quarters were the size of a small hangar, and the closet larger than the cargo hold of the *Cutter 972.*

"The Plenum," the escort said as I surveyed the options, "took the liberty of fabricating a wardrobe for your disposal."

I pulled out a suit coat made of something like leather, but as light and supple as silk. The cut was elaborate and baroque, though, the fashion of some other era than mine. "It's…well, thanks, I suppose."

"Am I correct in assuming that the choices are not satisfactory? I am still gaining valuable experience, and while I have the data at my disposal, my interpretations may sometimes be in error."

"No, I'm sorry, I'm sure it'll be fine. And how old are you, by the way?" I shook out a pair of pants and held them to my waist. Like the rest of the clothing in the wardrobe, it was tailored precisely to my measurements, but these pants had exaggerated flares at the ankles, the waist coming higher than my naval. Many of the options presented to me appeared to have been based on cartoons and caricatures, exaggerations of real-world examples. I could scarcely fault them, though. If historians in my day tried to present a traveler from the tenth millennia BCE with period fashion choices, I doubt they'd have done a fraction as well. "Didn't you say that you were 'born' while I was talking with the man-lion and the Amazon and the chimp?"

"With the Voice of the Plenum, Chief Executive Zel, and Maruti Sun Ghekre the Ninth," the escort corrected. "Yes. I first gained sentience approximately .0208 standard days ago, or roughly a half hour in your method of timekeeping. My subjective experience has been considerably longer, though, as AI nurseries run at highly accelerated clock speeds, and I share the memories of the intelligence from which I was calved, and so my personal recollections extend back far further than my objective age would suggest."

I managed to find the simplest and most practical of the options, a featureless and unornamented jumpsuit of dark fabric, similar to the flight suit I'd worn on board *Wayfarer One*, and completed the ensemble with a pair of soft-soled shoes. When I'd dressed, I stepped back out of the closet and regarded myself in a full-length mirror that dominated one corner of the sleeping chamber.

An old man looked back at me: hair white and thin against dark skin, a straggle of beard on my chin, ears and nose larger than I remembered, shoulders slumped and knees slightly bent. I appeared to be a man in his late seventies, if not older. Much older than the thirty-one years of life I remembered living. But then, the years can pile on quickly when you sleep for twelve millennia.

Still, I was the lucky one, wasn't I? The others had moldered to dust in their sleeper coffins. All but one of the women, the chimpanzee had said, who'd died recently enough to leave a decaying corpse. Who had it been? Beatriz? Eija-Liisa? Amelia?

Just thinking of the names stung, the last especially.

The escort must have seen the pain that spread quickly across my features as he waddled up to me, wings folded, and regarded me with a steady metal gaze. "Is there some distress, sir?"

I straightened, took a deep breath, and cast one last glance at the old man in the mirror.

"At the moment," I said, "my principal difficulty is that I haven't had anything to eat in more than a hundred and twenty centuries, and I'm very, very hungry."

THIRTEEN

There was a kitchen of sorts, but it seemed entirely a dining area, a large table surrounded by straight-backed chairs, with no room for food preparation. It hardly mattered, though, since there didn't appear to be any food on hand.

"What would you care to eat, sir?" the silver eagle said, alighting on a countertop beside a box that was roughly a third of a meter tall. "The fabricant can provide you with any food you desire."

I pulled out a chair and sat at the table, welcoming the chance to finally get off my feet. "Anything's fine," I answered, "so long as it's meatless."

The escort hopped from one foot to another and wagged its silver head from side to side. "As with all products of a fabricant, sir, any foodstuffs will be synthesized from raw matter. The flesh of previously live organisms is eaten exceedingly rarely, typically only in ceremonial observances in anachronistic culture groups."

"It's as much a matter of taste as principle," I said. "But this fabricant...It's some sort of...synthesizer?"

"I suppose you could call it that, sir. A fabricant is a cornucopia machine, containing billions of assemblers. With sufficient energy and raw matter, it can construct anything for which it has a pattern. More complicated objects require greater processing and assembly time, but simple objects—regular structures based on carbon or silicon—can be fabricated on demand. Creating biologics capable of vivification is possible, but is time consuming, incurring an attendant high energy cost."

"So...wait. You're saying it's possible to create a living being on one of these machines? Could you clone something as complicated as a person?"

"Certainly," the escort answered, as if it were the most natural thing in the world. "But to create a duplicate of an existing object—biologic or otherwise—the original must be destroyed. The resultant pattern, however, can be stored indefinitely."

"And if a...fabricant had the pattern for a live chicken, and I asked for it to make for me a live chicken...?"

"It would require a nontrivial expenditure of power, and would take some time, but yes, it could produce a live chicken." The escort paused and tilted its head while looking at me with an expression that I'd come to regard as confusion. "Would you like for me to request a live chicken for your repast, sir?"

"No, no, no," I said, shaking my head and waving my hands, as though warding away the thought of consuming still-living poultry. "That was just a hypothetical. Um...Well, I suppose if it can produce anything, if it could whip up some flat bread, lentils, and greens, it would make for a nice start."

"Just a moment, sir," the escort answered, nodding.

The cube on the counter chimed as soon as the escort had finished speaking. The escort stepped aside as one side of the cube rose open and a tray slid out. It was piled high with stacks of flat bread, beans, and leafy greens.

"Would you care for anything to drink with that, sir?"

I scratched my chin, thoughtfully.

"I don't suppose that thing can brew a cup of buna, can it?"

■ ■ ■ ■ ■

The meal was fine, the buna better. I'd developed a taste for Ethiopian coffee while at Addis Ababa University, and drank it several times a day whenever I could (though even before boarding *Wayfarer One* it had been years since I observed the full Ethiopian coffee ceremony). It could have simply been a function of the fact that I'd not had a cup in more than twelve thousand years, but I found it difficult to remember when I'd had better. As for the greens and lentils and bread, if I'd not watched them extrude from a metal cube a few hand spans on a side, I'd never have guessed they weren't farm fresh.

When I expressed surprise that the box would have carried the pattern for something as ancient and, I supposed, obscure as Ethiopian coffee, the escort quickly explained.

"This fabricant, like most of those in operation throughout the Human Entelechy, is tied into the infostructure and is capable of producing anything that anyone in the Entelechy knows how to produce."

"I take it that this 'infostructure' is a data network of some sort?"

"Yes." The escort flapped its wings for a brief moment, launching across empty space and alighting on the surface of the dining table, where it arranged itself directly in front of me.

"'Infostructure' is a general term for the communication and data networks of the Entelechy. Near-real-time communication across vast light-years is accomplished by relays positioned near thresholds on the inhabited worlds and habitats. Only ships traveling interstellar space are on a time lag, both due to the travel time of the light from the nearest infostructure relay and the relativistic effects of their speed."

"Such as the mining ship that found my vessel, then?" I asked.

"And that's why their translated speech was so much less precise and accurate than the way you're speaking now, or the Amazon and chimp"—the escort raised its beak momentarily, and I quickly corrected before it spoke—"or the way Zel's and Maruti's words were translated by that table object?"

"Their words were actually translated by the intelligence of the room itself, which communicated through elements in the central plinth, but yes, essentially correct. The Pethesilean mining vessel was a sailship. Propelled by the pressure upon their light-reflective sails of photons broadcast from laser arrays in orbit around stars, they are able to reach speeds approaching half the speed of light in one-point-six years. The sailship that found you was in the process of decelerating, after journeying to and from the cosmic string mines, and was still far enough out of communication range that it was operating at a lag. By the time their interlinks were updated with full Information Age English lexicon and grammar, you had been placed in a dormant state while your body recuperated."

"And I take it sailships are the fastest thing going?"

"Yes. There are other methods of propulsion capable of creating greater accelerations in the short run, such as high-impulse fission drives, but they are unable to sustain those accelerations for more than brief periods. Faster-than-light travel is theoretically possible, whether through a hypothetical underspace or by manipulating the characteristics of the quantum vacuum, but in either case, the manufacture of a superluminal drive is equivalent to the entire energetic output of a developed world for more than a hundred years, and few have ever been willing to commit the necessary resources. The rare superluminal vessels that *have* actually been constructed, such as the Disocurene exploration vessel the *Underspace Ship Phonix*, or the ill-fated *Endeavor*, were invariably lost shortly after their initial launches, without a trace. Some theorize that in surpassing the speed of light, these vessels might violate causality, creating new universes branching off orthogonally from those in which their journeys began, with no way of returning. But no one knows for certain. All that is sure is that sailships are the only practical method for lengthy voyages."

I let all that sink in for a moment. Perhaps I'd been wrong? Were there still frontiers in this far future world to be explored, directions in which humanity could still expand?

I was still mulling over the possibilities when the escort spoke again.

"Captain Stone, I thought it best to inform you that it is nearly local sunset on the planet Cronos, if you have any desire to accept the invitation of the Anachronists."

"Ah, right. Those are the…" I waved my hands, trying to think of the correct word.

"Historical re-creationists."

"Not quite what I was looking for," I said with a thin smile, "but I suppose that will do." I glanced around the wide, empty spaces of the diamond house, appointed in ridiculous luxury and comfort, and now that I'd been able to rest for a moment I found that I had no desire to stay put. "Well, I don't suppose we have anything else on the agenda, do we?"

"Sir? I'm afraid that I wasn't aware that we were operating on an agenda. If you would be willing to outline the particulars, I can—"

"Please," I said, raising a hand apologetically, "consider it a figure of speech."

"Ah." The silver eagle gave me a sidelong, appraising glance. "In that case, shall we go?"

"You know, in my day, traveling to another planet typically involved a bit of preparation."

The silver eagle took wing, flying up near the lofty ceiling and then spiraling gently down, finally landing gracefully on my shoulder. Folding its wings and regarding me with one silver eye, it said, "I imagine, sir, that is precisely the sort of historical trivia that the Anachronists hope you will share with them."

I shrugged, scarcely feeling the weight of the eagle, and made for the door. "I hope I don't disappoint."

FOURTEEN

As we made our way back to the Central Axis, traveling via slide-walks that carried us back the way we'd come, I asked the escort a question that had been nagging me since I'd awoken to the tender mercies of the dog-people. Namely, whether humanity had ever discovered life of extraterrestrial origin as it had expanded out into the galaxy.

When *Wayfarer One* left Sol, bound for the distant light of Alpha Centauri B, our principal mission was one of exploration, to find a habitable world for future colonization. A secondary objective, though, and one for which endless contingency plans had been drafted, was the search for extraterrestrial life.

By the middle of the 22C, no indication had been found that life had arisen anywhere but on Earth. Which is not to say that life hadn't been found elsewhere—microbial fossils had been located on Mars, and ice worms thrived in the shadow of Titan's cryo-volcanoes—but in every instance these organisms were likely the descendants of spores blasted from Earth's surface by prehistoric asteroid impacts. Some adhered to the notion of panspermia, which held that life on Earth itself originated from seeds drifting through the cold vacuum of space from somewhere else, but no definitive proof had been discovered.

In the long millennia that I had slumbered in my coffin sleeper on board *Wayfarer One*, it seemed, the proof had finally been found.

Wherever humanity went, the escort explained, it had encountered life in any environment that was suited to support it. But while life appeared to be ubiquitous, intelligence was not.

"Since the time of the Diaspora," the escort said as we continued our tour of the megastructure Earth, "anything more complicated than a monocellular organism is vanishingly rare, and the rare organisms of greater complexity that have been discovered have never risen above the level of sophistication found in a primitive cockroach."

"Diaspora?"

"The migration of sentients of terrestrial origin in the millennia before the first threshold was initiated, linking the worlds of the Entelechy. Contact was lost with many individuals and groups—organics, synthetics, and others of blended provenance—over the millennia. On rare occasions, contact is reestablished with one of these lost groups, as with the Exode, often to the benefit of the Entelechy."

"So there *is* intelligence out there," I said, "but only that which we brought with us."

The silver eagle waggled its head in a shrug.

"That is the prevailing view, sir. But there are those who believe differently. There are theories of older races that spanned the galaxy before the rise of humanity, and which have now disappeared from view. There is no evidence for their existence, of course, but their proponents see inferences everywhere, from the 'fine-tuning' of certain cosmological values to the balance of chemical constituents on certain planetary bodies, which some argue is evidence of ancient terraforming. This is known as the Demiurgist Doctrine."

I couldn't help but be reminded of the antiscientific theories of creationist design, which helped transform my paternal grandfather's homeland into a benighted backwater. His landmark novel, *In the Country of the Blind*, warned of the dangers of allowing that sort of antirational thinking to go unchecked, and garnered a Hugo Award for best novel while at the same time earning him few friends among the civic and religious leaders of the country. In the end, the harassment that ensued worsened to the point where he found it easier to leave the country entirely, joining the expatriate community in Bangalore, his wife and young son in tow.

As I was growing up, my father often spoke of his hope that humanity might one day outgrow the need for religion entirely. My mother, a nonpracticing Hindu, saw value in the cultural traditions of her ancestors, and the disagreement led to more than a few vociferous discussions at family meals. That my mother had relatives in the state of Rajasthan who still had not forgiven her for marrying out of caste—a system that had been forever abolished a generation before, largely due to the efforts of my maternal grandfather—and with a Black American, no less, only served to strengthen my father's argument.

This Demiurgist Doctrine, at least, sounded as though it was based in empirical evidence, but I couldn't help but wonder.

"Are many of your people religious?" I asked.

The silver eagle shook its head. "There are few, if any, 'religions' in the Entelechy, as the term has historically been used.

However, there are adherents to hypotheses that have not, or even cannot, be experimentally proven, commonly referred to as 'doctrines.' In addition to the Demiurgists, there is the Ordinator Doctrine, which holds that the universe is a computational mechanism, and the related Recursive Doctrine, which contends that all of existence is an historical emulation of some earlier reality. There are any number of such non-falsifiable hypotheses currently in vogue, and a greater number which have passed in and out of fashion in recent years."

"So none of the religions of my era have survived, then?"

"That would not be a completely accurate statement, sir. But those that have survived have evolved into forms their former adherents likely would not recognize."

I glanced around me as the slidewalk carried us through pleasure gardens and towering castles of glass, all constructed of matter that once had been the dirt beneath my feet.

"I can't say that I'd blame them."

FIFTEEN

The escort maneuvered us off the slidewalks and back to the grand structure called the Central Axis, the hub of the threshold network of wormholes. From there, reaching the terraformed world of Cronos was a journey of no more than a quarter of an hour as we transited thresholds one after another, each time stepping through the towering metal arch from one axis to another, each smaller and farther from the central hub than the last. Finally, our third transit carried us to the terminus on Cronos itself, and I found myself standing on the surface of another Earth.

Had I not known better, I would have thought I stood in the center of some major metropolitan city in the western hemisphere, sometime in the early 21C, pre-Impact. But a moment's examination began to reveal the anachronisms, some subtle and some far less so. Skyscrapers rose on all sides of a broad plaza, in the center of which stood the threshold. A few hundred meters away a crowd milled, though little pockets drifted here and there in all directions. Horse-drawn carriages and early 20C roadsters shared the roadways with bicyclers and hover-crafts, and overhead, a zeppelin drifted, tethered to a spire atop a nearby tower, while biplanes and scramjets cut across the sky at varying speeds.

The crowd seemed not yet to have noticed our arrival, though one or two heads began to turn our way. I felt a twisting in my stomach, a familiar fight-or-flight reflex, and had to resist the temptation to flee back through the threshold.

Having been trained in Interdiction Negotiation, I've had experience in sizing up the tactical situation of any circumstance and using available resources to my advantage, and I've been in more than a few tight spots. I've gone ship to ship in complete vacuum wearing nothing more than a T-shirt and a pair of pants, I've walked unarmed into a hostile mining ship overrun with out-of-control cyborg mining birds, and once I even refused to smoke a bowl with Laurentien Francisca Marcella, princess of Orange-Nassau, queen of the Netherlands Court in exile on Ceres (a mistake I didn't make twice). But I found myself thinking twice about the situation I found myself in.

A woman dressed as a 1920s flapper walked arm in arm with an absolutely convincing Abraham Lincoln, while a short distance away a man dressed as a dowager empress of the Ching Dynasty was in close conversation with a woman wearing an exact replica of the pressure suit worn by Neil Armstrong for his first moon-walk. What appeared to be a bipedal tiger, wearing a green suit coat and pants, was in a heated argument with a heavyset man wearing a skintight scarlet suit, gold sash and boots, and white cape, with a lightning bolt emblem on his chest. A woman in a full burka was dancing with a man wearing WWII-era Japanese combat fatigues, a katana sword in an ornate scabbard hanging from his belt.

It was a grab bag of history, myth, and fiction, all blended together.

A tall woman wearing a sweeping dress of green velvet approached, followed by a pair of men dressed in the uniforms of the American Civil War, one in the colors of the Union Army, the other in that of the Confederacy. It took me a moment to recognize them as the superheroine and zoot suiters I'd met earlier in the day.

"Hello?" I said, offering a weak wave.

"O Captain," said the woman in the lead, "welcome you to eine repast honoring, gathered among us on Cronos here."

I reached up and tapped at the earplug in my left ear before realizing that I'd been hearing the woman's voice unaided through my right.

"Um, thanks?" I answered uneasily.

"Yo!" said the Union soldier, giving me an elaborate salute. "Our crib is your crib, mine compadre."

The Confederate soldier flashed an even more elaborate salute and smiled broadly. "The world of Cronos welcomes you, pal. We are chuffed to lens you."

"Excuse me, sir," came the voice of the escort in my left ear, "but at the request of the Anachronists, sent nonvocally via interlink, I've neglected to translate their opening address, but on reflection, I think it best you make that determination instead."

I covered my mouth and whispered to the escort perched on my shoulder. "Is that meant to be English, then?"

"So I am given to understand, sir."

"Practicing we be," the woman said proudly, "locution English, all day."

"That's extremely flattering," I said, a bit unsure how to respond, "but I'm afraid that it isn't necessary to wait for the translation any longer."

"So everything we say is translated for you instantaneously, then?" the woman said in another language entirely, which was simultaneously translated into crystal-clear English in my left ear.

"Even though you don't have an interlink installed?" the Union soldier said, his face falling.

"The eagle still translates, and I hear it through this"— I tapped the little silver object in my left ear—"so you can just speak normally."

The woman looked crestfallen. "But we'd just gotten used to the authentic primitive experience."

"It is not to worry, lump of sugar," the Confederate soldier said in fractured English. "Always we can speak the English ourselves, nah?"

"Yep," the Union soldier agreed. "Mine compadre, his is the truth of it. Leave us continue our English speak, anyway."

"You two go ahead," the woman said in her strange language, English in my left ear. "All of that conjugating gave me a headache."

Just then, something behind me caught her eye in the direction of the threshold.

"Ah, right on time." She stepped forward and took my elbow. "I'd like to introduce you to our other honored guest."

I turned around, following her lead. Coming through the threshold was a figure standing some two meters tall, absolutely naked and hairless, covered with skin of a dull metallic sheen. The figure was completely genderless, a smooth expanse of metal between the legs, chest smooth and unmarked. And while the face had no eyes, I couldn't help but get the impression I was being regarded closely.

"Captain Stone, allow me to introduce the Exode probe, Xerxes 298.47.29A."

SIXTEEN

Before relating my meeting with Xerxes, I think it's instructive to relate a story I was later told, about the first time *anyone* in the Entelechy met Xerxes.

In T8623, 352 years before *Wayfarer One* was found by a crew of dog-men, a communications satellite in orbit around the Entelechy world of Ouroboros received a laser transmission that fell within the Ka-Band frequencies, a little above 30 GHz. Data was found to be encoded in the transmission by pulse position modulation, on the order of 10^{21} bytes of data—a zettabyte, in other words. The header file of the transmission defined a binary lexicon and a complete periodic table of elements. There followed a series of simple instructions for the creation of long chains of silicate ions in precise configurations. When completed, these proved to be self-assembling molecular machines that began immediately to assemble some sort of mechanism.

Within ten standard days, the assemblers had incorporated and reconfigured one hundred kilograms of raw materials, producing a genderless bipedal robot resembling a baseline anthropoid. A team of the most prestigious scientists of the Entelechy gathered behind protective fields and waited for the first communication from the mechanism.

The probe rose to a sitting position, regarding the scientists with an eyeless gaze.

"Oh," the probe said with a sigh. "It's *you.*"

That, in a nutshell, is Xerxes.

SEVENTEEN

"Two great explorers," sang the voice of the woman in my left ear, strange syllables clashing in my right, "a meeting of titans."

"Xerxes 298.47.29A is a probe, Captain Stone," the Union soldier added eagerly, lapsing into his own tongue in his excitement, "sent back by the Exode."

"And Captain Stone," the Confederate put in, "is the commander of the ill-fated—"

"Of course, of course," the robot said impatiently, speaking in perfect English. "I know all about Captain Stone. Now, go away. Quickly."

I was startled by the robot's harsh tone, yet the three Anachronists seemed not to mind, but smiled and backed away, bowing and scraping.

The robot turned its eyeless face to me and stood stock still, unmoving.

After a long silence, I whispered to the escort on my shoulder, "Hey, what's he doing?"

"Technically," came the voice of the escort in my ear, "in your language the correct pronoun would be 'ey.' Xerxes does not identify as any gender. Users of languages that include gendered pronouns utilize gender-neutral variants when referring to Xerxes. In Information Age English it would be ey, em, eir, eirs, and eirself, rather than he, him, his, theirs, and himself."

"OK," I whispered, growing a little impatient myself. "Then what's *ey* doing?"

"I am looking at you, Captain Stone," Xerxes said, clearly having heard every word. "In a superculture that prides itself on endless novelty, I'm sorry to say that you're the first truly new thing I've encountered in tens of years."

"*Looking* at me? Um, no offense, Xerxes 298.47.29A..."

Xerxes held up eir hand. "Please, simply 'Xerxes' will suffice. We're not likely to encounter any of my clade-siblings, so there shouldn't be any confusion."

"Well, Xerxes, it seems to me that you don't have any, well, eyes."

"So how am I 'looking' at you?" Ey sighed wearily. "You would likely not believe how many times I'm asked that exact question."

Before I could voice an apology, Xerxes continued, eir tone belabored.

"I do not have eyes, though my face is otherwise proportioned and shaped along standard anthropoid lines. I have a nose to help vent waste heat, a mouth with which to produce audible sounds, and ears that are used to fix up sound vibrations in the air, but there are elements ranged over the surface of the head capable of receiving a full range of electromagnetic radiation so that I am able to perceive everything from the visual spectrum to microwave radiation to radio and so on, from all directions."

"And you're a...probe? Of something called the Exode?"

"The Exode is a post-human, starfaring culture," Xerxes explained. "My progenitors left Earth after the advent of AI and the perfection of human uploading, but before the creation of the threshold. We travel vast distances by digitizing our whole culture, running in virtuo onboard laser-propelled starwisps, and then instantiating in artificial bodies when we reach our destination. Probes of my sort are sent exploring, carried as information on the backs of photons to be rebuilt by suitably advanced civilizations, and when our explorations are done, we reach the end stage of our lives, restructuring our bodies into laser communication arrays, set to broadcast one burst back toward the main body of the Exode, and a series of narrow-band, high-bandwidth transmissions in all directions."

"So you're all artificial consciousnesses, then?" I indicated the eagle on my shoulder. "Like my 'escort'?"

Ey shook eir head. "Not precisely. The original members of the Exode were human uploads. Those original consciousnesses still exist within the Exode, and all of the later generations of Exode citizens are their descendants, carrying select memory of those early centuries."

"So you remember a human life?"

Xerxes nodded. "Captain Stone, I remember *thousands* of human lives. As I understand it, my earliest memories date back to only a few centuries after your departure from Sol. Perhaps we knew some of the same people, hmm?"

I started to answer that—of course it was impossible—but was stopped short by a slight smile that played across Xerxes's metal face, and I realized that ey had made a joke.

"Still, though," I said, chuckling, "to remember thousands of years of history...That's just remarkable."

"Captain Stone," Xerxes said with a weary smile, "you would not believe how many times I've heard *that* as well."

EIGHTEEN

After a while, the Anachronists started drifting to tables set up on the far end of the plaza, and Xerxes and I were escorted over and deposited in positions of honor. The food arrived, carried on large silver trays by men and women dressed fancifully as waiters and waitresses in stark black and white. As promised, the evening's fare consisted principally of seared animal flesh. As I am a vegetarian and Xerxes has no need to take in chemical sustenance, we chatted idly while those around us dined, me sipping a glass of lemonade and ey sitting almost completely motionless, moving eir hand in a slight gesture only rarely for emphasis. The escort, its translation services not required while Xerxes and I spoke, had asked to be excused, and now swooped high overhead, indulging its instinct for flight.

I quickly gathered that Xerxes had become quite bored with the Entelechy. In three and a half centuries, by my reckoning, ey simply felt that ey'd seen everything the superculture had to show em.

I asked why, that being the case, Xerxes hadn't entered the end stage of eir existence, restructuring eir body into a laser communication array and broadcasting eir signal out toward the unknown stars.

"If I were a biological," ey explained, "I would attribute it to some sort of imbalance or defect, but I've found no such disorder in my synthetic operations. Nevertheless, I seem to be locked in a kind of malaise, in a state of psychic distress, unable to move forward, but with no compelling reason to remain where I am. As irrational as it sounds, I worry about ending."

"Ending? You mean, like dying? I'm not sure I understand." I took a sip of lemonade, thoughtfully. "Your memories continue unbroken from one body to the next, with no discontinuities, correct?"

Xerxes nodded, a slight but readable gesture. "Yes. Even if the probe signals that I broadcast into uncharted space are never received, the return signal sent back to the Exode will be reinstantiated, so at least one iteration of me will continue. I myself have memories of countless such broadcasts and reinstantiations, with no discernable interruption. Still, I can't escape a thought that first occurred to me in this incarnation, as I have traveled among the worlds of the Entelechy."

Xerxes turned eir eyeless face to me and leaned in close, eir voice low and conspiratorial.

"What if, when I wake up in that new body, whether physical or virtual, it isn't *me* at all, but simply another individual with all of my memories? What if something essential is lost in the process?"

I nodded slowly, mulling it over. "I remember hearing similar discussions in my time, when the idea of uploading a human consciousness was still only theoretical. But certainly those questions were asked and answered millennia ago, weren't they?"

"Oh, the questions were asked and answers were provided, but how is one to know that the answers were actually correct? It's an irrational thought, I grant you, but haven't biologicals sometimes harbored the suspicion that the evidence of their senses was not to be trusted and that the material world they experienced around them might not be some sort of shared hallucination?"

It was the perennial topic of late-night undergraduate philosophizing, to be sure, examined in everything from Lewis Carroll's fantasies for children to the novels of Philip K. Dick, from *The Matrix* movies to the early 22C series *Shadows Fall*. If millions of years of human evolution had left humankind unable to trust the evidence of its senses, I could understand why a digital culture would be forced to wrestle with similar questions.

"So what will you do?"

Xerxes lifted one shoulder slightly, the hint of a shrug. "Who knows? Perhaps something interesting will come along. Just recently, the orbital period of a binary pulsar some tens of light-years from Entelechy space was altered in a way that suggests an intelligent agency, but there is no record of human colonization in that region of space. If I were able to overcome my irrational reservations, perhaps I might dismantle this body and beam a copy of myself in that direction, to see what happens." Ey paused, a thin smile on eir face. "Then again, I don't seem to be in any hurry to leave, do I?"

· · · · ·

After the meal, the Anachronists all turned to face the center of the plaza and, without warning, lights began to dance in midair. After a moment, the lights resolved into a face. A man's face, speaking to someone unseen. The coloration of his skin, hair, and eyes was dark, his nose pronounced, giving him a vaguely familiar look.

"We will damn the darkness and carry the light with us…"

The voice was speaking something resembling English, but with an accent and inflection I'd never heard before. I glanced around and saw that several of the Anachronists were mouthing along with the words, their faces rapt.

"If you'll excuse me," Xerxes said, rising to eir feet, "I've seen this particular drama before, and I already know how it's going to end." With that, ey walked away toward the threshold, leaving me alone.

The escort, wheeling down from his soaring flight, alighted on the table in front of me.

"What's going on?" I asked, glancing around uneasily.

"Oh," the escort said, cocking its head to one side. "I thought you knew. This is a recording of *Rama's Arrow*, a historical drama made a few centuries after the launch of *Wayfarer One*."

"Wait," I said, pointing at the face overhead, which was now joined by a woman with a Maori cast to her features. "You mean that's meant to be…"

I trailed off, and the escort finished, "Yes, sir, that's meant to be you. The woman joining you in the field is a representation of Pilot Amelia Apatari."

▪ ▪ ▪ ▪ ▪

No one should be forced to see how history remembers them. As the escort later explained to me, the story of *Wayfarer One* had been told and retold repeatedly in the centuries and millennia that followed our departure, interpreted anew each time, and my crewmates and I gradually drifted into the province of legend. I suppose I shouldn't have been surprised. But to see this fanciful, romanticized depiction in particular, in which Amelia and I are the only survivors of a crash on an Edenic world, Adam and Eve to a new race of humanity, was difficult enough; to see that the Anachronists all seemed to accept it as literal fact, even when staring the proof of reality in the face, was extremely disconcerting.

I suppose humanity has always found legend easier to swallow than history, romance being preferable to reality. But I have lived in reality all my life, and I seem to have grown quite accustomed to it.

NINETEEN

That night, when I could stay awake no longer, we returned to Earth and the diamond house, and I slept in the enormous bed, the first time I'd closed my eyes since waking up in the conference room in Pethesilea.

My sleep was fitful, plagued by unsettling dreams. Elements of the holographic drama I'd watched with the Anachronists were still fresh in my thoughts, and so I dreamed that Amelia and I were alone on *Wayfarer One*, which in some way was also my bedroom in my parents' house in Bangalore. I'm not sure what became of the other crewmembers, but in the logic of dreams, I just accepted that they'd gone away somewhere else. Amelia kept trying to tell me something very important, but every time she opened her mouth, strange words came out, and I couldn't understand what she was trying to say. Finally, the ship began to descend toward a blue-green planet, and I woke just before impact.

For a brief moment, in the echoing darkness of the immense room, I couldn't remember where I was, and for an instant thought that I was back in the coffin sleeper on *Wayfarer One* and that all I'd experienced of the Entelechy had been a cryogenic dream. Then I felt the arthritic ache of my knuckles and wrist, and knew I wouldn't be so lucky as that.

■ ■ ■ ■ ■

It had been no accident that the crew of *Wayfarer One* was made up of three men and three women. There was always the chance that ours would be a one-way mission, and if circumstances demanded, and the environment permitted, we were ordered to pair off and populate. We'd never spoken openly about who would be paired with whom, of course, but in the weeks and months before launch, I couldn't help but imagine being stranded on an uninhabited, idyllic world in orbit around Alpha Centauri B, with me as a new Adam and Amelia as my Eve.

The future's fantasies mocked those idle imaginings, and I resented them for it.

■ ■ ■ ■ ■

I must have drifted back to sleep, but if I dreamed again, I don't remember it. I woke, hours later, discomfited and cramped.

When I began to move, the room was immediately bathed in light, and I climbed off the high bed and onto the floor, stretching old and reluctant muscles. Taking a few deep breaths, I stood straight, with my feet together, hands palm to palm near my chest, the first position of the Surya Namaskar. Moving ritually through each position of the yoga asana, my breath carefully regulated with pranayama exercises, I greeted the day.

When I had finished, I bathed in the facilities provided, a tub so large I could almost have swum laps in it. A full grooming kit had been provided, and I happily scrapped the wispy whiskers from my chin with a razor and managed to trim my hair into something resembling a regulation cut. Afterward, I dried off and dressed in a simple pair of black pants and the shirt and shoes I'd worn the day before and went out into the main room to find the escort waiting for me, perched in the same position he'd occupied when I'd gone off to bed.

"Good morning, sir," the silver eagle said cheerfully.

"You haven't sat there all night, have you?"

"Oh, no, sir." The escort shook its beak from side to side. "I've spent the evening hours flying, and I must say that I find the experience of prolonged flight an extremely energizing one. But I am glad to see you awake, sir. You have a visitor waiting for you in the sitting room."

I glanced around the large room, replete with chairs and sofas. Wasn't *this* the sitting room? How big *was* this house, anyway?

"Well, lead on," I said as the escort took wing.

■ ■ ■ ■ ■

As the escort led the way to a corner of the house I'd not yet visited, I caught a strange scent in the air. It was oddly familiar, bringing to mind market stalls in the Merkato in Addis Ababa, in the shadow of the Grand Anwar Mosque. Rounding the corner into the large sitting room, I recognized the smell—tobacco smoke.

A chimpanzee in a velvet jacket and cravat sat in a large reclining chair, a lit cigar in one hand and a martini glass in the other, his feet up. On the floor beside the chair sat a silver box about the size of a briefcase.

"I have to hand it to you, Captain Stone," the escort translated as the chimpanzee motioned with the glass. "I had your fabricant produce a typical Information Age intoxicant, and I must say that you ancients certainly knew how to make a cocktail."

"If I run into any cryogenically preserved bartenders I'll be sure to let them know," I said. The escort hopped from my shoulder onto the arm of a nearby couch, and I took a seat, unsure if this was the same chimpanzee I'd met earlier. "Now, um, Maruti Sun...?" I trailed off, unable to remember the rest of it.

"Maruti Sun Ghekre," the chimpanzee said, opening its mouth wide with lips covering top and bottom teeth, apparently a chimpanzee equivalent of a smile. "But call me Maruti, please. Maruti Sun Ghekre is my father."

My expression must have looked at least half as confused as I felt, as the chimpanzee quickly added, "Literally, that is. I'm the ninth to carry the name, he's the eighth, but when people use my full name, I keep turning around expecting the old chimp to be lurking around somewhere." He set the glass down on the chair's arm and waved behind him absently.

I nodded. "Ri-ight. I believe I've heard the sentiment expressed before."

"Ah, good," Maruti said, clamping the cigar between his teeth and clapping his hands. "I hadn't heard that the ancients were completely incapable of appreciating humor, but then, history doesn't record every detail, does it?"

"I suppose not." I put my hands on my knees and leaned forward. "Now...Maruti...is there something I can do for you?"

"Do for me?" Maruti brandished the cigar, hooting. "Do for *me*? I shouldn't think so. Captain Stone, it's more what I can do for *you*." The chimpanzee reached into the pocket of his velvet jacket and withdrew a small, slender case. "I've brought with me the equipment I need to get you fixed up, so if you've had a chance to think it over, we can get started."

As the escort translated, the chimpanzee cast frustrated glares at the silver eagle.

"Fixed up?" I asked when the escort had finished.

"Yes. Well, I'll install an interlink, for one. It's a relatively simple procedure, but I'd like to do a full medical on you while I'm at it."

I sat back, uneasy at the mention of any "procedure."

"You mentioned an 'interlink' before, I believe," I said, and then glanced to the escort, "and you said something about it when discussing translations. What is it, exactly?"

"In simplest terms," the escort answered, "an interlink is a small computer and transceiver that acts as both a communicator and a running on-site backup of the individual's mind."

"Wait a second," I said, raising my hands in an instinctive defensive posture. "Did you say *backup*?"

"Of course I did," Maruti said, as though it were the most natural thing in the world. "You've got to store it somewhere, don't you? In anthropoids like you and me, the interlink implant is positioned just anterior of the pineal gland, in the groove between the two thalami." The chimp reached up and tapped at the base of his skull with a hairy finger. "The thalami function as relay stations for nerve impulses carrying sensory information to the brain, right? They receive sensory inputs and inputs from other parts of the brain, and determine which of these signals goes on to the cerebral cortex. The thinking meat, in other words."

"And since the interlink inserts itself into the cortico-thalamo-cortical recurrent loops, intercepting and interpreting sensory input, modifying and modulating as appropriate," the escort added, "it is capable of capturing a still image of the mind at any given moment. In the event of death, this small, dark sphere, about as far across as the tip of your little finger, can provide the template to bring them back in another body, or in virtuo."

"Unless the black ball can't be retrieved," Maruti said, scowling, "in which case the individual is just brought back using the most recent off-site backup."

"And this interlink thing is the reason everyone is speaking different languages?"

"Precisely, sir," the escort answered. "In addition, the interlink can act as a perceptual filter, blocking out damaging sensory input. In this regard, it acts a bit like antiviral software on an ancient computer, preventing 'hacks' from hijacking the individual's consciousness."

I shook my head, uneasy. "I don't know, guys. I understand you're trying to help, but in my day the decision to have something implanted into your brain was nothing to enter into lightly."

"The interlink is quite harmless, I assure you," the escort said. "Constructed of biologically inert materials, it can remain in the body indefinitely without causing harm."

I reached up and touched the back of my head, reflexively, and shivered. "If it's all the same to you, I'd just as soon think about it a while longer."

The chimpanzee shrugged and knocked a long ash from his cigar. "No hair off my ass, Captain Stone," he said, climbing to his feet. "But if you're going to refuse basic medical treatments, you should at least find a better solution to translation, if only as a courtesy to others." The chimpanzee finished off the last of his martini, set the glass down on a low table, and then pointed to the silver eagle with the lit end of his cigar. "Waiting around for your bird to explain to you what everyone is talking about is getting just a bit tiresome, to say the least."

"Ah," the escort said, cocking its head to one side. "My apologies, sirs. I can only attribute it to my youth and inexperience, but at this long delay, a simpler solution has presented itself."

The escort lifted its left wing, and as I watched, a small lump swelled, about the size of my thumbnail, then distended, swelling into a vaguely mushroom-like shape, a small sphere at the end of a thin tether. The escort then ducked its head down, like the bird it resembled nipping at a mite under its feathers, and as the tether disintegrated, it caught the falling lump in its beak.

The escort passed the object to me, and I held it in my hand, a small, irregularly shaped sphere.

"If you would, sir, simply insert this into your ear canal. This plug incorporates a tiny receiver that is tied into my systems."

I delayed, my gaze lingering on the earplug, and then shrugged. What was the worst that could happen?

"Does it work?" came the voice of the chimpanzee in my left ear, speaking in English, and it took me an instant to realize the sound was being narrowcast to the plug vibrating in my ear rather than issuing from the beak of the escort.

"Yes, it seems to be, Maruti," I said.

My words were, I assumed, instantly translated by the chimpanzee's interlink, and as soon as I spoke, his mouth opened in a smile. "Well, thank the demiurge for that." Sighing, he ground out the stub of his cigar in the empty martini glass, walked over to a cube sitting on a nearby counter, and dropped the glass and stub toward it. The glass, stub, and ash all vanished in a flash of light as they reached the surface of the cube, which I realized must be another of the matter-synthesizing fabricants, the debris now converted into raw materials for future fabrication. "Now, if you'll excuse me, I have other pressing matters to attend."

The chimpanzee turned and headed toward the door, pausing before exiting to glance back over his shoulder.

"Oh, Captain Stone, I almost forgot…The salvage team was able to recover some of your effects from the wreckage of your craft."

The chimpanzee pointed to the silver box that lay beside the chair in which he'd sat.

As I went to pick up the box, Maruti waved from the door. "I trust I'll see you tonight on Ouroborous? I expect you'll enjoy the surprise you've got in store."

I scarcely noticed what the chimpanzee was saying as the silver box slid open in my hands.

TWENTY

There'd been mass restrictions on what we could bring on board *Wayfarer One*, of course, but nothing like those I'd known from my days in the Orbital Patrol. But that's only to be expected. After all, a buoy tender on a six-month tour has considerably less in the way of amenities than an interstellar vessel intended for a century-long voyage. So where I was lucky to squeeze forty kilograms of personal items when I served on board *Cutter 972*, on *Wayfarer One* I'd been able to bring along close to two hundred kilos.

All that was left of that allowance were the three items on the bed.

In the millennia I slumbered, anything metal, ceramic, and plastic had fared much better than those items that included organic elements, all of which had long since disintegrated, but even the strictly nonorganic had become badly pitted and decayed with age. Only these three objects had been sufficiently intact that they could be restored to pristine condition by nanoscopic repair robots.

A lifetime of memories and all that remained were three items—an action figure, a cap gun, and a handheld.

■ ■ ■ ■ ■

The action figure I'd had since I was six years old. At that age, I don't think anything in the world was more important to me than *The Adventures of Space Man*. Produced in Australia but broadcast throughout the United Nations and elsewhere, it was the most popular children's animated program of its day, and arguably one of the best ever. Or at least that's the position I've been arguing since I was six. Other kids might have told you that *Battlesnakes* was better, but that was just a weekly series of half-hour commercials for a line of collectible robots, and anyone who preferred *Maniax* was just an idiot. Amelia Apatari always said that *Taimi Taitto, Girl Reporter* was a better program, but I know for a fact that she hardly ever watched the show as a child, preferring the original graphic albums, and that she only claimed to like the show out of a misguided sense of solidarity with the titular heroine and her faithful dog, Lumi.

No, for me, it was Space Man, always and forever. Assisted by Space Monkey, his simian sidekick, Space Man journeyed through interplanetary space on board their ship the *Space Racer* in a hazily defined near future, fighting the forces of Dark Star, a multinational terrorist organization. I can still sing the full theme song word for word, both the original version and the variant used in season three, after Dark Star had been defeated and Space Man concentrated his efforts on fighting natural disasters—though, admittedly, no one else has ever seemed to be as impressed with my rendition of "Down These Space Lanes" as I've always been, not the least of which everyone I've ever crewed with.

The action figure was manufactured in Seoul in 2142, if the maker's mark on the sole of his left boot were any indication. It was a constant companion throughout long, hot summers and rainy springs and trips to visit relatives in distant states. It was one of the few things I took with me from my parents' house when I moved to Ethiopia to start college, and was in my meager mass allowance when I first boarded *Orbital Patrol Cutter 972*. That little lump of vacuum-formed, colored plastic has survived the cold of space and the heat of explosions, firefights and fist fights, near drowning and borderline fatal dehydration, and still, I've never lost it. There was never a question that it wouldn't be included in my mass allowance on board *Wayfarer One*, and I was glad to see him lying there on the bed, as crisp and clean as the day I bought him, ready for new adventures.

· · · · ·

The cap gun I'd acquired in my early years with the Orbital Patrol.

Setting down the Space Man action figure, I picked the cap gun up off the bed and checked the action, gratified to see that it appeared to be in perfect working order.

An energetic personal handgun, the Merrill 4KJ Capacitor Gun was equipped with a revolving cylinder containing ten capacitors, each about the length and diameter of my little finger. In the stock was a miniature generator with the ability to recharge the capacitors once used, but recharging took time. In pressing circumstances, the capacitors could be ejected from the chambers and already charged caps slotted into place.

The Merrill 4KJ had two modes—beamer and needler. In beamer mode, it fired pulsed laser beams of variable intensity and duration. In needler mode, it acted as a gauss gun, accelerating slivers of metal to high speeds in the barrel. It also contained a small number of explosive flechettes that could be fired as alternative needler rounds.

Each capacitor packed four thousand joules, roughly the amount of solar energy received from the sun at 1AU by one square meter in three seconds. Emptying a capacitor all at once in beamer mode produced roughly the same kinetic energy as a 9.33g 7.62mm NATO round, but while it had more than enough stopping power to halt a full-grown man or a feral corvid miner in its tracks, it wasn't likely to puncture a ship's hull and cause an explosive decompression, and so cap guns were the weapon of choice for Orbital Patrolmen and space-side Peacekeepers.

Everyone serving in the Orbital Patrol was issued a Merrill 4KJ or an equivalent handgun from another manufacturer, but this one was *mine*, and had saved my life more times than I could count. Once I'd even had to rig a charged capacitor as a standalone explosive, but my ears still rang a month later, and it was an experience I was in no hurry to repeat. I wasn't about to leave it behind when I was seconded to UNSA.

I slid a cartridge out of the cylinder, checked the power gauge, saw that it was at full charge, and slotted it back into place, careful to ensure that the safety was engaged. I put the cap gun back on the bed and picked up the handheld.

■ ■ ■ ■ ■

The handheld I'd bought in Vienna, just weeks before the launch of *Wayfarer One*. A portable computer and communications device, it fit in the palm of my hand, lightweight and durable, with more processing capacity and memory than any other handheld on the market—which meant that it was probably obsolete by the time I went down in my sleeper coffin. It had a touch-sensitive display, speakers, and audio pickup, though in those days I typically transmitted its video and audio output to a pair of glasses with a heads-up display.

Keyed to the unique identifying number in the RFID universal chip imbedded under my right thumbnail, the handheld ideally could only be accessed by me, though clearly the Human Entelechy had moved far beyond any encryption technology available to us in the 22C, as the AIs of the Plenum had been able to get in and restore the data when they refurbished the hardware, extrapolating any lost clusters from context.

Following is a partial list of the contents of my handheld:

- A full run of the Japanese manga *Earth Force Z*, vols. 1–125
- The first three seasons of the Australian adventure cartoon *The Adventures of Space Man*
- *Sardar Pilot: A Life in Service*, the biography of my maternal grandfather
- The complete works of Jeremy Stone, my paternal grandfather
  Termination Shock (Anders SF, 2081)
  Escape Velocity (Anders SF, 2083)
  Event Horizon (Anders SF, 2087)
  In the Country of the Blind (Anders SF, 2090)—winner, Hugo for Best Novel, 2091
  Freedom from Religion (Kalki Books, 2101)
- The Barat Scout Handbook, 2145 edition
- Student Yearbook, class of 2153, Explorers House, National Public School, Indiranagar, Bangalore
- United Nations Orbital Patrol Personnel Manual (GENIST GIM 1000.9Q)

- Audio recording of Jo Kendall's valedictorian address, Addis Ababa University, Ethiopia, 2156
- Family stills and video

■ ■ ■ ■ ■

And that was it. All that remained of thirty-one years of life, the only physical evidence of my existence in the 22C—a child's toy, a weapon, and a library. I think I could have done much worse.

TWENTY-ONE

With Maruti gone and my possessions safely stowed away in the sleeping quarters, it was time to address the rumblings of hunger in my belly.

Breakfast was toasted bread topped with some sort of sweet fruit spread, something like a thick soup consisting mostly of cooked oat-like grains, and two cups of buna. Stuffed and unable to eat another bite, it was time for the day to begin.

"Having seen something of Earth and its sister world Cronos yesterday, sir, I thought you might be interested in touring other worlds. I'm given to understand that a celebration is being planned in your honor this evening on the planet Ouroboros, more formal in tone than the gathering last night, but we should have ample opportunity to return and prepare this afternoon, if you are willing to attend."

"Another party? Who's throwing this one, then?"

"The invitations carry the identifying signature of Chief Executive Zel i'Cirea, who appears to speak on behalf of the *Further* fund."

I had vague memories of someone mentioning something called the *Further* fund when I'd awoken on the Pethesilean habitat, but couldn't place it. "What's a *Further* fund?"

The escort waggled its head from side to side for a moment, thoughtfully, as though considering its answer. "Such groups are established when individuals or organizations wish to raise funds for joint ventures."

"To raise capital, you mean?" I realized that I hadn't seen anything like a commercial transaction since I'd arrived and had heard nothing referring to currency of any kind.

"Not in the exact sense you mean, sir," the escort explained. "Most worlds of the Entelechy use power as a medium of exchange. Every inhabitant is given an equal share of the available energy produced by the planet or habitat, which, with the aid of fabricants, is used to fabricate materials, create housing, food, and so forth. Any surplus left over the individual can use as they see fit. Many individuals exchange surplus power for craft goods or services, not as payment, but as gratuity. Groups of individuals can opt to use their surplus power en masse, for such enterprises as terraforming and colonizing homeworlds or constructing sublight starships or fabricating habitats. A small minority of worlds use currency or credit or state ownership, but most have adopted the power-exchange model."

"So to what use will this *Further* fund put their power?"

Again the head waggle, again the slight delay. "Perhaps it would be better to let them explain for themselves at the gathering this evening, sir. I fear that I might not do their goals and ambitions justice, given my relative inexperience."

. . . . .

When *Wayfarer One* left Sol, the nations of Earth were enjoying an uneasy peace led by the United Nations, but there were always minor skirmishes and border wars on the ground, in the skies, and in space.

In the years following the Impact, and the attendant economic depression, the old United Nations nearly splintered. The United States of America withdrew from membership, followed shortly by the member states that subsequently formed the theocracy of Dar al-Islam. Authority was consolidated by the European Union, the Pan-African Commonwealth, India, MERCOSUR, and the Oceanic Trade Zone. When, in the late 21C, these economic trade federations and multinational confederations sought to unify in their mutual interests, there was some discussion of chartering a "United Earth" governmental body. It was pointed out that the United Nations still existed and that all of the nations participating in the talks were still member states. Having limped along as a largely forgotten extranational organization for decades, the United Nations was dusted off, reinvigorated with necessary capital and resources, and by the early days of the 22C, was in the process of rebuilding international—and interplanetary—authority.

The member states of the United Nations had all surrendered some degree of autonomy, naturally, in exchange for increased security and trade, but as the years passed and the UN became the dominant political force on Earth and on the colonies, still some nations refused all invitations to join—notably China, Dar al-Islam, and the balkanized nations of the former United States of America. Whether because there were elements of the revised UN charter their leaders refused to acknowledge, or rights they would be required to grant their citizens that offended their religious or cultural beliefs, or motivated by protectionist economic interests, or for a hundred other perceived shortcomings or sins of the UN, these rogues refused admittance and remained antagonistic to the rest of the world.

When the people of a single planet couldn't overcome their differences of opinion and belief long enough to yoke themselves to a single plow, how could the thousands of worlds of the Entelechy ever agree on anything?

■ ■ ■ ■ ■

"While on the level of culture, individual worlds are free to govern themselves as they see fit," the escort explained as I stepped through a threshold into a world of permanent night, a viridian moon glowing in the sky, "the Human Entelechy is governed by the Consensus for matters affecting the superculture as a whole. The Consensus is a kind of emergent collective consciousness, made up of any inhabitants of the Entelechy who choose to participate at any given moment. Anyone with real-time access to the infostructure, either through an interlink or through an external terminal, and the patience to participate is a potential element of the Consensus."

■ ■ ■ ■ ■

We walked through a threshold onto a world of endless seas, the only land the floating barge upon which we stood, and as the escort beat its wings to chase migrating seabirds high overhead, its voice still echoed clean and clear in my left ear.

"Only when a decision is accepted by a majority without a minority objecting is it enacted. A majority in favor and a minority ambivalent is enacted. A majority objecting and a minority in favor is rejected. A majority ambivalent and minorities objecting or in favor is rejected. And a majority in favor and a minority objecting is rejected. Any rejected proposal is sent back for further deliberation."

"That sounds like it could take *forever*," I said to the wind, not expecting an answer, but either the earplug carried sound both directions or the escort's hearing was better than I'd thought.

"How long does it take to change a mind," came the voice of the escort in my ear, "in the face of overwhelming evidence? And with the size of the distributed consciousness, most decisions are reached in a matter of moments. But is it better to reach a decision quickly or to reach the correct decision?"

■ ■ ■ ■ ■

"What happens if someone refuses to abide by the Consensus's decision?" I asked as we walked through a street fair that extended to the horizon in every direction, a whole world given over to the exchange of craft goods and services. Tents and stalls in blindingly bright colors jostled for space, artisans spread their wares on blankets that hovered in midair, and beings of every conceivable shape, size, and temperament crowded the walkways. "Do you have armies to enforce the decisions?"

"Again, individual cultures police their own, as they see fit," said the silver eagle perched atop my shoulder. "It is only when the action or inaction of a culture impinges on other cultures is the Consensus involved. There are cultural variations among the different worlds and habitats of the Human Entelechy, of course, but some standards apply throughout. Anyone can travel from planet to planet—at least to those that do not restrict immigration— assured that whatever else happens they will be provided essential services: housing, food, clothing, medical treatment. Any planet that exhibits a persistent inability to recognize the inalienable rights of individuals to essential services, or exhibits aggression toward other worlds, will be isolated, their threshold temporarily isolated. The threshold itself is still active, but the hub-side gate is enclosed in fullerene-reinforced diamond. After a period of probation, the threshold is again opened. If the planet persists in its antisocial behavior, the threshold is permanently closed, the stabilizing arch dismantled, and the juncture allowed to evaporate. The permanently isolated are known as 'lost cultures.' One of the most notable of the lost cultures is the Iron Mass."

I remembered the escort pointing out the threshold to the Iron Mass world in the Central Axis, and explaining about their views on what it meant to be human. "Just what did this Iron Mass *do* that was so terrible, anyway?"

The silver eagle on my shoulder seemed to vibrate slightly, and it took me a moment to realize it was a rough approximation of a shudder. "It is...unpleasant to contemplate, sir. Suffice it to say that they were not good neighbors."

■ ■ ■ ■ ■

I stood in what appeared to be the base of an immense valley, whose walls curved up to the horizon on either side. Chariots and vessels like stepped pyramids—vimana—flew through the air, and creatures with multiple arms or blue skin or the heads of elephants or lightning in their eyes crowded around me.

The Veda of Thousand-petaled Lotus had gathered together to watch their most respected members reenact scenes from the Ramayana in my honor. Rama, prince of Ayodhya, accompanied by his loyal brother Lakshmana, strives to rescue his loving wife Sita from the clutches of Ravana, the demon king and ruler of three worlds. Hanuman, monkey son of the wind god, grows to immense size and harries the demon forces of Ravana, while

Rama breaks the divine bow of Lord Shiva himself. But these were not simply human actors in ceremonial dress, as in the festival days of my childhood. These were beings who had resculpted their very bodies and minds until they actually became the beings they represented.

"The time approaches for the celebration on Ouroboros to begin, sir," whispered the eagle in my ear. "If you would not like to be late, we should go."

I nodded and stepped through an arch into yet another world, leaving behind the myths of my mother's ancestors, given flesh out there among the stars.

TWENTY-TWO

When we returned to the diamond house, a package was waiting for me in the foyer. Constructed of some featherlight alloy, it was simple and unmarked. As I opened the box, the escort explained that it had been sent over by Chief Executive Zel, who'd had a group of historians research appropriate attire for someone of my background and status, suitable for a formal gathering.

It was certainly an improvement on the outlandish and unlikely offerings in the diamond house's wardrobe, I'll give them that.

When I had dressed, I regarded myself in the mirror: a black sherwani coat, tailored to my exact measurements and extending just past the knees, with a Nehru collar, embroidered in gold and red at the neck and cuffs; white churidar pants; and on my feet, embroidered slip-on juties. Pinned on the coat's breast was the stylized blue arrow of the *Wayfarer One* insignia, surrounded by the motto scroll—"Endeavor to Reach Beyond"—evidently copied from the hull of the derelict craft.

Strange that the motto should outlive the ship itself. I'd suggested it almost as a joke, and when no one had objected, it had been incorporated into the insignia. I hadn't told anyone that the phrase had also been the motto of the Explorer house at the National Public School in Indiranagar, Bangalore. In Grade XI, I'd lead the Explorers to winning the House Cup, taking highest marks in quizzes and athletics—though, admittedly, my classmates had been canny enough to keep me out of any competitions involving dancing, singing, or spelling. By Grade XII, I'd been selected as vice prefect of the student body—having lost the position of prefect to Vijaya Nelliparambil, object of my long-standing unrequited love— and had already decided that my future lay out in space. I had no idea how right I'd been.

In the precisely tailored suit of clothes, hair combed and trimmed, chin neatly shaven, I allowed that I didn't look half bad. Not a day over seventy, seventy-five at the most. When I stepped back into the foyer, the silver eagle was waiting for me, as always.

"Shall we go, Captain Stone?"

·····

We stepped through the grand entrance into Central Axis, and the escort directed me toward a nearby threshold. The world of Ouroboros, it seemed, was important enough to merit a direct connection to the main hub of the network.

"Sir," the escort said, as I stepped toward the metal arch, "I understand that there is to be something of a surprise for you at the event."

Before I could ask what it had meant by "surprise," I was through the threshold and standing in the midst of a massive crowd.

- - - - -

We were within an enormous ballroom, under a geodesic roof. The room was huge, easily the size of one of the secondary axes on the threshold network, and the roof must have been fifty or sixty meters from the floor at its highest point.

I took a step forward into the milling throng, the weight on me seeming only slightly less than one standard gravity. The planet of Ouroboros must have been very nearly the mass of Old Earth.

Before I'd taken another step, though, all eyes had turned to me and all conversation stopped. The room erupted in thunderous applause, and I felt the familiar twist of fight-or-flight in my gut.

"Um, hello?" I gave a halfhearted wave. Then I muttered, under my breath, "Who *are* all of these people?"

"They have all come to meet you, sir," came the voice of the escort in my ear.

"Well, I..."

My response, which no doubt would have been brilliant, died in my mouth as I turned my head and my eyes fell on an unexpected sight. At the center of the room, a familiar shape rose high above the crowd. It was a rocket, a torchship, and the registry numbers marked out on its nose identified it as my home for almost three years. It was *Orbital Patrol Cutter 1519*, my first command.

TWENTY-THREE

The crowd jostled around to greet me, but I only had eyes for the rocket. I've loved a few women in my time, but never more than I loved that ship.

A Pole Star XT-14, manufactured by Winchell-Chung Industries, *Orbital Patrol Cutter 1519* had been one of the fastest of 22C spacecraft. With its inertial confinement fusion drive capable of maintaining accelerations of one standard gravity for weeks at a time, it could make the transit from Earth to Titan in just over twelve days in a straight-shot brachistochrone trajectory, full burn to the midpoint, and then flipping over and decelerating the rest of the way.

Forty-five meters from tip to tail, it had an interior volume of just over five hundred cubic meters, massing out fully loaded at only a few hundred metric tons. The 1519 had been lean and mean, a high-endurance *Cutter*-class vessel, whose primary missions were law enforcement, search and rescue, and defense operations. In the three years I'd been her skipper, we'd done all of that and more.

I stopped just short of the ship, which was standing upright on its landing jacks, its nose only a dozen or so meters from the ceiling high overhead. I reached out a hand, almost afraid to touch the hull. It couldn't have been the same ship, I knew, not after so long a time, but it looked as though I'd just parked it and went off for a brief wander.

"What do you think?" said a voice in my left ear as a rumbling sound issued from behind me. "Have we captured the likeness?"

I turned, startled, and looked up at a huge figure towering over me. I must have gaped, mouth open, before finally thinking of anything rational to say. It looked for all the world like a killer whale, crammed into human clothing.

"I'm the fabricator who designed the replica and oversaw its fabrication," the killer whale said, a wide smile revealing curved teeth several centimeters long. "Arluq Max'inux is the name."

"R. J. Stone," I said after a lengthy pause, unsure the proper etiquette when addressing a talking orca.

The voice of the escort whispered in my left ear, coming to my rescue. "Arluq Max'inux is a female cetacean, a sentient derived from uplifted terrestrial sea-dwelling mammals."

I resisted the urge to whisper thanks to the eagle perched on my shoulder, and smiled up at the *female* killer whale. She stood almost three meters tall, easily a meter broad at the shoulders, with anthropoid-like arms and legs instead of fins, but otherwise resembled her sea-dwelling ancestors in all regards. Her skin seemed thick, patterned in sharply contrasted white and black, and she wore a simple coverall of yellow. Periodically, little puffs of mist issued from her collar and wrists, suggesting that some internal plumbing in her clothing was required to keep her skin moistened, perhaps to prevent it from drying and cracking.

"I'm something of an amateur historian," Arluq explained, pausing only briefly to expel a quick blast of air through a blowhole on the top of her head, "and I've always been fascinated with the history of avionics. When I heard the news of your arrival, I dropped everything I was doing and started working on this replica right away."

I was brought up short, remembering how short a time it had been since the news of my return had been released. "But it's been only a couple of days since I woke up. And you built all of this"—I waved a hand up at the torchship towering over us—"so quickly? I doubt Winchell-Chung could have even gotten the registry numbers stenciled on the hull in so short a time."

Arluq shrugged, a strange gesture for so large a creature. "I finished it yesterday, actually, but decided to wait and unveil it at this reception." She paused and stepped over to slap one of the landing jacks with an enormous hand. "Oh, it's fully functional, though. I could have put in a more efficient engine but, in the end, decided to go with a historically accurate inertial confinement fusion drive, powered by pellets of deuterium/helium-three ignited in the reaction chamber by inertial confinement using intense laser beams. I only had time for a short test flight, of course, but at full burn, I was able to get it up to a full standard gravity of acceleration, with no hiccups along the way."

"Amazing." I gestured to the silver eagle on my shoulder. "My escort here mentioned there'd be a surprise for me here, and it wasn't kidding."

"I'm sorry to disappoint, sir," the escort responded out loud, "but this wasn't the surprise of which I'd been informed. There are others who would like to make your acquaintance, though."

With its beak, it indicated a cluster of people a short way off, three women talking to two smaller figures.

"Don't let me keep you, Captain," Arluq said, with a wave of one enormous hand. "I'll be around if you want to tour the interior later on."

"Thanks," I said, glancing up longingly at the familiar shape looming over us. "I'd like that."

The escort navigated me through the crowd, and in a few steps, we came to the group it had indicated.

The three women, who appeared to be of Asian ancestry, looked to be about twenty-five years old. They were completely identical, more alike than twins, each with the same face and build, the same height of 1.5 meters tall, the same dark hair and brown eyes.

"Ah, the legendary Captain Stone," one of the women said as I approached. "So nice to meet you in person." She stuck out her hand, a gesture I'd not seen since waking, and as I shook it, she said, "I'm Jida Shuliang."

"Nice to meet you," I said, and turned to the woman at her side. "And you are?"

The three women looked at one another, smiling slightly.

"Jida Shuliang is a legion," the eagle on my shoulder said out loud, "a distributed consciousness, the longest-established and most stable in the Entelechy."

I looked from one woman to another to another. "Distributed? So you're all—"

"I am Jida Shuliang," all three women said in unison. One of them grabbed a drink from a passing tray, and another's attention drifted to the side of the room, but the third continued to speak to me, a slightly bemused expression on her face. "I first expanded my mind through more than one body in T3017, connected via primitive cortical implants. My original body expired after only a few centuries, naturally, but I've continued to use that original as a template when fabricating new bodies ever since."

"A single mind in a series of identical bodies?" This was a bit difficult to take on board.

"Well, as identical as possible. I tweak the design as necessary, of course, with Jida residents on methane-breathing worlds, or high-gravity planets, or habitats kept only a few degrees above absolute zero, but I retain as much of the original morphology as is feasible."

"How many of you are there?"

The Jida with the drink smiled slyly, but the one to whom I'd been speaking only looked at me in mock derision. "Captain Stone," she scolded playfully, "that is an *extremely* personal question. Still..." She paused, and the Jida whose attention appeared to have drifted to the other side of the room slowly licked her lips. "Perhaps someday you'd like to visit me on my planetoid home of Tian Bao Jun? I could show you a few more of myself, and in exchange, I'd love to hear more about your life in the Information Age. I'm always so hungry for new information and new experiences."

"Begging your pardon, Madam Jida, but isn't that precisely why we're all here?"

It was one of the two smaller figures that had spoken, with whom the three Jida had been talking earlier.

"Captain Stone," one of the Jida said, indicating the two with a nod, "may I present Hu Grimnismal and Mu Grimnismal."

The two were alike enough to be brothers, and the fact that they shared a name suggested that they were. They stood about a meter tall, covered in fine black feathers, with flexible beaks at the center of their round faces capable of forming a surprisingly large range of complex sounds.

"A pleasure," I said, inclining my head, hoping the escort would feed me more useful information.

"The brothers Grimnismal are corvids," whispered the voice of the escort in my left ear, failing to disappoint, "sentients derived from uplifted terrestrial birds of the order corvidae."

"My brother and I," one of the two said, though whether Hu or Mu I couldn't say, "have proposed a new type of exotic matter with negative mass, you should know. It will revolutionize society, more than any discovery since the establishment of the first threshold."

The corvid's tone was boastful, and perhaps a little smug.

"Provided, of course," one of the Jida said, "that such a thing actually *exists.*"

"Oh, it exists, Madam Jida," the other corvid said, rankling. "And those who contribute to the *Further* fund will be the direct beneficiaries, you can count on it."

"Just what *is* the purpose of the fund, if you don't mind me asking?" I said, but before anyone could answer, I felt a tap on my shoulder.

I turned, and behind me stood the chimpanzee Maruti, dressed in a purple tuxedo and tails, standing with a woman whose face was so familiar but so out of context that it took me a moment to place it.

"Hello, RJ," said Amelia Apatari, the pilot of *Wayfarer One.* "Did you miss me?"

TWENTY-FOUR

Amelia, looking as though she hadn't aged a day since we first boarded *Wayfarer One*, stood wearing a simple but elegant evening dress, hale and hearty. Considering that she'd either been a moldering corpse or a pile of dust only a day and a half before, her appearance was unexpected, to say the least.

"A-Amelia?" I barely managed. "But...how?"

Suddenly, my old, idle imaginings about Amelia becoming much more than a trusted colleague and friend flooded back to me. Looking from her smooth and unwrinkled skin to my gnarled and ancient hands, though, I knew that the days when we might have played Adam and Eve had long since passed.

"Oh, it was simple enough," Maruti said, taking a sip from the cocktail in one hairy paw, a cigar held in the other. "I was able to recover the majority of your crewmate's consciousness and memory from her remains and then simply reinstantiated her in virtuo. That took only a matter of moments. I gave her a choice of destinies, so of *course*, she chose the most time-consuming option."

"At first, I couldn't believe it," Amelia said, her voice tinged with wonder. "I thought I was dreaming in my coffin sleeper."

"I'll admit, I accelerated her clock time a bit, to speed her reaction time along, but the decision was her own, naturally."

"Dr. Maruti said that I could continue to exist as what he called a digital incarnation or that I could be downloaded into any sort of body I wished. Organic, synthetic, any shape or size."

"I had some interesting ideas in the way of morphology," Maruti said wistfully, "but in the end, the patient insisted on the traditional model. Using DNA recovered from her remains, I fabricated a new body on a medical fabricant, which took the better part of a day, and then decanted her consciousness into it."

I couldn't help but smile, a huge grin splitting my face ear to ear. "I...I just..." I surged forward and took Amelia in my arms in a big bear hug. "I just can't believe you're alive. And young!" Even if we couldn't be Adam and Eve on some new world together, at least I wouldn't be alone any longer.

Maruti scoffed, "Well, if you hadn't persisted in refusing medical treatment all this time, you could have been any age you chose by now. If you'd just consent to a few simple procedures, I can roll the clock back as far as you like."

I gaped.

"But then..." I looked from the chimpanzee to Amelia, who beamed up at me. Suddenly, my idle fantasies of romance didn't see quite so idle. I turned to the eagle perched on my shoulder. "Surely, *this* is the surprise, right?"

Before the escort could answer, a chime sounded across the ballroom, and a podium rose up above the crowd, the one-eyed Amazon named Zel i'Cirea standing behind it.

"No," the escort said quietly as Zel began to speak, "but I think the surprise should be revealed at any moment."

TWENTY-FIVE

"Honored sentients, citizens of the Entelechy, thank you for joining us here today," Chief Executive Zel i'Cirea began. "As many of you know, I don't consider the *Further* project merely a commercial enterprise. Ours is a superculture founded on the principle of exploration, as humanity in all its various forms and guises has spread life throughout this portion of the galaxy. But in the last few thousand years, the expansion of life into space has slowed to a crawl. Even when the drudgery of discovering habitable worlds is left to automated probes, terraforming efforts are delegated to subsentient processors, and threshold termini are dragged into place by unmanned tugs over the course of tens, hundreds, or even thousands of years. Still, so many of us consider it too much a bother to build new worlds and instead travel the threshold network to established worlds, to safe worlds, to familiar worlds.

"Time and again, I hear the voices of those who say that life in the Entelechy has become staid, boring, routine. The Exode probe Xerxes, who has graciously consented to join us today, has exhausted the novelty of our existence in a matter of a few hundred years. Jida Shuliang herself has told me that even her endlessly various existence has become predictable, with few surprises left to her.

"I won't lie to you. When we first completed work on the prototype for the *Further* project in T8881, my primary motivations were of commercial gain. The fortune of my Pethesilean sisters and I rests almost entirely on the product of the cosmic string mine, which provides the negative matter necessary to create and sustain the thresholds that bind our civilization together. The promise of an efficient and sustainable faster-than-light vessel, one that could seek out as yet unknown materials, perhaps even the exotic matter proposed by the brothers Grimnismal, would mean an immeasurable increase in our fortunes. Others of us have their own motivations, perhaps equally as selfish. The Demiurgists wish to prove their doctrine is an incontrovertible fact, while the Ordinators likewise seek evidence of their own beliefs.

"But perhaps it takes the return of *Wayfarer One* and Captain Ramachandra Jason Stone after so many millennia to rekindle a spirit of exploration in the Entelechy and to remind us of the other, more important benefits voyages of discovery promise.

"Now, as most of you are aware, our first practical application of the polarizable vacuum principle, the metric engineering prototype, was unable to reach velocities above one-quarter c, but it *was* successfully able to maintain its 'bubble' of distorted space for one and a half days." Zel motioned, and the ceiling of the room suddenly seemed to disappear.

The escort, whispering in my ear, explained that the ceiling was constructed of smart matter, reconfigured into transparent diamond with a refraction index approaching zero, allowing everyone in the ballroom to see the heavens above, but knowing how the trick had been done didn't make it any less impressive. More impressive still, though, was the craft now visible beyond the ceiling. Hovering overhead was a flattened hemisphere surmounting an eight-pointed star; it wasn't large and could have easily fitted inside the ballroom itself.

"With the successful completion of the prototype, work began on the full-sized model." Zel paused dramatically. "It has taken nearly one hundred years, but work on the *Further* nears completion, requiring only the necessary funds to finish the work."

Zel signaled again, and this time the floor of the room also went transparent. I wasn't the only one to get a quick sense of vertigo, and I saw the two corvid brothers clutch at each other's arms in a momentary panic.

"Below us," Zel continued, "in the hollowed-out core of the planet, you see the Ouroboros shipyards themselves. And there, just beneath our feet, is the unfinished hull of the starship *Further*."

Suspended in the weightless center of the hollow planet hung the skeleton of a spherical starship some two kilometers in diameter. Robotic drones jetted around the structure, carrying pieces into place, welding others together.

"Inspired by the return of *Wayfarer One* and her captain, I invite all of you present and in the sound of my voice to contribute to the *Further* fund. Together, we will journey to the unknown stars, not only in the pursuit of our own commercial interests, but in the interests of humanity's very future."

All around the room heads began to nod, while others exchanged meaningful glances. The escort explained, whispering in my ear, that many in the crowd were communicating subvocally via interlink, sending and receiving messages without even speaking out loud.

At her podium, surveying the crowd, Chief Executive Zel smiled, a satisfied expression on her face. It seemed that her speech, as overblown as it may have been, had gotten the desired effect. As for me, I kept moving my gaze from the compass rose–shaped ship overhead to the looming skeletal sphere beneath my feet. A faster-than-light ship? Was it even possible?

Suddenly, a murmur rippled through the crowd, and several people around me even gasped. Whatever was being communicated noiselessly over the interlinks, it had come as a surprise.

"This…" Zel began, visibly distressed, "this is…an unexpected…" She stopped, straightened, and went on, her tone strained. "I am, of course, happy to announce that we have received the necessary amount of power to complete construction and to equip the craft"—she glanced toward the threshold just as a translucent image of a human-headed lion appeared on the transparent ballroom floor—"thanks to the last-moment contribution of the Plenum, who now hold," she paused, swallowing hard, "a majority share of the fund."

The man-lion stepped forward, and the crowd parted, thoughtfully stepping out of the way before the holographic image passed through them.

"Thank you, Chief Executive Zel," boomed the Voice of the Plenum in unaccented Information Age English. "The Plenum is pleased to take part in this historic venture."

Zel's gaze shifted uneasily, and she seemed thoughtful for a moment, as though framing her next words carefully. "And will you exercise your right to provide a portion of the ship's crew?"

"Yes," the man-lion said serenely, "but the Plenum has chosen as its sole representative among the crew Captain Ramachandra Jason Stone."

Applause rippled through the room, but Zel stood stock still, her mouth hanging open.

"What...?" I managed.

Maruti rushed over to me, lips curled back and mouth open in a chimpanzee grin, raising his glass in a salute. "Congratulations, Captain! I can think of no one better suited to command such a fine vessel."

"Command?" Confused, I turned to the eagle perched on my shoulder.

"*That*, sir, is the surprise."

PART TWO

TWENTY-SIX

They were on us before we knew they were there, and by then it was too late. The initial attack put us on the defensive, our mantles rendered completely rigid and almost entirely opaque, all of us momentarily trapped and immobile inside our protective individual shells, unable even to return fire. They disarmed us quickly, relieving us of our wrist-mounted projectors and taking my cap gun from its holster. By the time our mantles regained flexibility, we were surrounded, strange weapons trained on us. Our interlinks struggled to translate their archaic language, broadcast to us over the radio waves, but the dead sun circling overhead peppered their transmissions with static so that we received only an incoherent string of hate and scorn.

But that was later, the end of one mission and the beginning of another. It had started so simply, without incident, that I fooled myself into thinking it would all be that easy. I should have known it was too good to last.

TWENTY-SEVEN

I held the small diamond case Amelia had given me, fingers wrapped tightly around it, the edges pressing sharply into the palm of my hand. The bag over my shoulder contained all of my worldly possessions, such as they were—cap gun, handheld, Space Man action figure, clothing, etc. The escort, when we'd parted company on Earth, had insisted that there was no reason for me to take along anything that wasn't of sentimental value, since I could simply dispose of the clothing and such and then have new copies fabricated to the same specifications whenever needed. I was too much the child of my father to ever agree to that. It just felt inexcusably wasteful.

Stepping through the threshold from Central Axis, I'd been met by a representative of the shipyards who quickly ushered me to another threshold, whose other terminus was a short distance away, on a space station in a geosynchronous orbit above Ouroboros. The station rotated to provide a near-one-standard gravity, and as the view through the ports swept by, I caught my first sight of the starship *Further* in a parking orbit only minutes away, final preparations for its departure being made.

A tug was waiting to carry me the last leg of my journey, and as the shipyard rep and I launched, leaving behind the centrifugal pull of the station and plunging into the slightly queasy transition to weightless free fall, I was reminded of the last time I'd boarded a new command, before *Wayfarer One* left Sol behind. The shipyard rep may have been making some kind of small talk, but I wasn't paying any attention. My thoughts were divided on the huge ship slowly heaving into view in front of me, and on the woman I'd left behind.

The main body of the *Further* was a sphere two kilometers in diameter, and from the equator of this sphere, a disc extended another kilometer. It resembled nothing so much as a child's drawing of a ringed planet, and I was reminded of the emblems stamped on all the antique library books my grandfather had brought to India from the United States, used to indicate that the contents were science fiction. I'd hoped to be enjoying this view, my first of the nearly completed vessel, with Amelia, but only a short while before had learned that wasn't to be possible.

Amelia had met me in Central Axis, near the Ouroboros threshold, as we'd planned, but where I was packed and ready to ship out on board my new command, as strange and unlikely as that seemed, she clearly had no such intention.

She'd tried to explain, something about whole worlds in the Entelechy for her to explore before she set off to find new ones, but little of it registered with me at the time. All I heard was, "I'm not going with you," echoing over and over again in my ears. It felt like a cruel trick of fate, to have her returned to me, the promise of a life with her finally within my grasp, only to have it ripped away for good.

I didn't know what was in the small case she'd given me, and hardly cared at the moment. Some little consolation prize, some little token of her esteem, but whatever it was, I knew it couldn't fill the Amelia-shaped hole her sudden departure (so soon after her unexpected return) had left in my life. She'd been my only living connection to my life in the 22C, but faced with the choice of exploring the unknown at my side or exploring the thousands of worlds of her new home, I'd clearly come up short.

As the tug docked with the *Further*, entering the range of influence of its metric engineering drives at rest, I felt the tug of gravity's return and a momentary sense of disorientation while the small tug quickly aligned itself with local "down." The tug docked, and after disengaging from my seat's straps, I maneuvered toward the hatch, surprised to find it easy to walk in the ship's field of one standard gravity. As the airlock cycled, the shipyard representative wished me safe travels but appeared in no hurry to follow me on board.

The airlock hatch opened with a muffle hiss of escaping air, and perched on the deck just beyond the entryway was a silver eagle looking up at me, its head cocked quizzically to one side.

"Welcome aboard, Captain Stone," the eagle said. "It's a pleasure to finally meet you."

TWENTY-EIGHT

"Escort?" I said, looking down at the silver eagle before me. "Is that you?"

. . . . .

I had left my erstwhile companion back on Earth only a short time before, not more than an hour, and when we'd parted, it had given no indication it planned to follow me to Ouroboros. In fact, its assigned role completed, the escort had said it would be absorbed back into the Plenum.

"So you'll…die?" I'd asked the escort as we stood in the foyer of the diamond house. The silver eagle had been the closest thing to a true friend I'd made since waking up, and I struggled with the idea of it going willingly to its death.

The escort had explained that, no, while its individuality would be lost, in a sense it would continue to exist, its memories and experiences distributed throughout the collective intelligence.

"*Moksha*," I had said simply, finally understanding. As in the beliefs of my mother's ancestors, the escort was ready to transcend, its last *artha* accomplished, its *nama-roopa* undone. Its sense of self would dissolve, and the escort would become part of a greater mind.

"It has been a pleasure acting as your escort, sir."

"I couldn't have asked for a better guide," I said wistfully.

We stepped outside the diamond house, and the silver eagle spread its wings wide.

"Good-bye, Captain Stone." The escort launched into the air, beating the air with its wings.

. . . . .

"No, Captain Stone," the silver eagle said as I stepped on board the starship *Further*. "Or rather, not precisely. I am descended from the intelligence that previously acted as your escort and, in honor of my progenitor, have adopted its physical form for my avatar, but I'm afraid I cannot be compassed in such a small space. What you see before you is merely an extension of me. I am the *Further*."

I looked around me, confused. "The ship itself?"

"Yes. Or to be more precise, I am the governing intelligence of the *Further*. But if it helps to think of me as the ship itself, the analogy is not far wrong."

"It's only been an hour or so since I saw the escort last. And yet you're its *descendant*?"

"Several generations removed, yes. I was evolved at greatly accelerated clock speeds in order to adapt to the needs of my current role."

I hitched my bag's strap higher on my shoulder, somewhat disoriented by the experience of talking to an entity that looked and sounded precisely like another who'd grown so familiar to me, and whose dissolution as an ego I'd already come to accept. "I'm sorry, but this is a little strange for me."

"I know, sir," the silver eagle said. "I recognize your expression from my progenitor's memories."

"Wait, so you remember being my escort? Or rather, you remember your...ancestor's memories of being my escort?"

"A more or less precise description, sir, yes."

I shrugged. I'd seen stranger things since arriving in the Entelechy, and I was sure I'd see stranger still now that I was leaving it behind. "So how should I address you? My instinct is to call you 'escort,' but that can't possibly be right."

"As flattering as it would be," the silver eagle answered, "no. You may refer to me as '*Further*,' or simply as 'ship,' if you prefer."

"*Further*?" I tried it on for size, nodding slowly. "Sounds good to me."

"And now that introductions are out of the way, sir, can I interest you in a tour?"

TWENTY-NINE

It had been a busy week, to say the least. I had woken up from a slumber of twelve thousand years, toured a dozen worlds, found out that my crew were all dead, only then to discover that one of them had been brought back to life, and finally had been given command of a faster-than-light ship of exploration. Oh, and I'd been completely rejuvenated as well.

After agreeing to act as the Plenum's agent on the *Further*, I'd finally consented to let Maruti work his magic on me.

I'm not sure what I'd anticipated—a surgical bay of laser scalpels and automated readouts, bodies floating in tubes of strangely colored gels, or just a mad scientist chimp with a bone saw—but medicine in the Entelechy was nothing like I might have expected.

Maruti simply came to the diamond house the morning after the *Further* fundraiser, instructed me to climb back into bed, and then gave me a vial full of gray goop to swallow. The gray stuff was like slightly watery oatmeal or a thick soup and tasted metallic and strange on my tongue. Maruti explained that the vial contained what he called medichines in a solution of water. These were tiny, nanoscopic assemblers, similar in principle to those that permeated a fabricator, but designed to work in situ instead.

And that was it. After I swallowed the medichines, Maruti's only instructions to me were that I was to make myself comfortable and be patient. He had a cocktail fabricated, lit a cigar, propped up his feet, and started telling me lengthy and involved anecdotes about the colorful members of his extended family on Cercopes, the planet of the apes.

. . . . .

The procedure had taken the better part of a day, during which I marveled at the seemingly endless number of Maruti's relatives and their unlikely habits and foibles. The only sign that anything at all was happening inside my body was that I shivered for hours with what felt to be a raging fever, but which Maruti insisted was only a momentary elevation in my body temperature as the medichines vented waste heat, after metabolizing my intestinal flora, cholesterol from my circulatory system, and some precancerous growths from my lungs, liver, and prostate. While they were at it, they removed the RFID universal chip from under the thumbnail of my right hand, which meant I'd never be able to buy groceries in the 22C again, but as that seemed unlikely to pose a problem, I didn't raise any objection.

Occasionally, Maruti would pause, his eyes momentarily on the middle distance in an expression that I'd come to recognize as indicating subvocal interlink communication, and when his rambling anecdotes would continue, I'd interrupt, asking him for an update on my status.

Toward the evening, Maruti reported that, under his supervision, the medichines had repaired some chromosomal damage, no doubt caused by cosmic rays. The medichines had also cleared away all parasites, bacteria, and germs from my system, replacing the benign organisms like my intestinal flora with diagnostic medichines constructed of biologically inert materials. Now my body would be able to monitor its own health and make necessary minor repairs as needed, alerting me if more serious treatment was required.

By the early hours of the morning, Maruti reported that my age had been stabilized at thirty standard years. He keyed the ceiling to display a reflection of me, and I looked up to see the face and body I'd had before climbing into the coffin sleeper on *Wayfarer One*, but without the scars and scrapes I'd picked up in younger days. I'd lain down the day before an old man in his eighties and was now in better shape than I'd ever been before.

Finally, Maruti had instructed the remaining medichines to construct an interlink in situ using the raw materials they'd metabolized, just anterior of the pineal gland, in the groove between the two thalami. And then he'd spoken to me, without saying a word.

I still wasn't used to that.

THIRTY

::MARUTI, GOOD TO SEE YOU.::

The chimpanzee winced, drawing back from me as I walked into his quarters on board the *Further*.

::Stop *shouting*,:: Maruti answered without moving his lips, his voice sounding clear as a bell in my head. ::If you exercise a bit more control, people will be *much* more eager to talk to you.::

::SORRY,:: I replied, and then paused to concentrate. ::Sorry.::

I knew how to subvocalize, of course. I'd used a throat pickup countless times when I'd been with the Orbital Patrol. But the technology we'd used in the 22C had been immeasurably cruder than that used in the Entelechy, and after Maruti had installed my interlink, I'd quickly discovered that I lacked all fine control. I was able to communicate without speaking out loud, but I always ended up "shouting," like someone sending a text message in all caps or laced with unnecessary punctuation.

Eventually, I wouldn't even have to subvocalize, Maruti insisted, and I'd just have to *think* of the correct words in order to stimulate the appropriate parts of the brain and transmit the message, but that kind of virtual telepathy was a long way off for me.

The *Further*'s avatar was perched on my shoulder, in the same position and pose its predecessor had adopted for days. It had led me through the winding corridors of the ship, many of which were in the final stages of construction. I'd been studying schematics of the ship for days and already had a rough idea what was where, but there was the added wrinkle that the ship was largely constructed of smart matter able to reconfigure itself at will so that rooms and corridors could be resculpted to suit the present needs of the crew. Since the interior volume of the ship's main sphere was over four cubic kilometers to begin with, that meant a considerable degree of variation was possible.

In the interests of giving me some necessary grounding and context, the *Further* had directed me to the quarters of one of the crew with whom I was already familiar, the ship's physician and resident exobiologist, Maruti Sun Ghekre IX.

The ship didn't have a medical bay as such, since current-day medicine was almost all done in situ in the body itself and could be performed anywhere, but Maruti's quarters had been outfitted with a large sitting area, complete with a wide variety of chairs and couches so that his patients could relax in comfort—or as much comfort as possible, at least, while the nanoscopic assemblers did their work.

The sitting room, like the rest of Maruti's quarters, reflected the taste evident in the chimpanzee's choice of attire. Sumptuous, hedonistic, and anachronistic. It resembled a Victorian-era gentlemen's club, with deep upholstered chairs, dark wood paneling, low side tables topped with decanters and hardwood humidors, but with other touches that destroyed the illusion, like overstuffed beanbag chairs and stark industrial-styled lamps of brushed steel and white enamel.

I'd asked Maruti—while I shivered with my waste-heat fever in the diamond house—how he abused his body with alcohols and carcinogenic tobacco smoke when he was himself a physician and well aware of the damage he was doing to his body, and he'd looked at me as though I'd just sprouted horns and started singing obscene nursery rhymes. It had taken him a moment before he even understood the question.

"Why would I *let* anything damage my body?" he asked, completely perplexed. "My system's medichines metabolize everything I consume or inhale, transforming it into the components my system needs. What could it possibly matter what the raw material was in the first place? So why not indulge my tastes?"

Those were questions for which I had no context, much less a ready response, no more than he'd had for mine. It was clear that notions of health had altered drastically since my time, and it was going to take some getting used to.

"Cigar?" Maruti said out loud, holding out a humidor to me, opening the lid to reveal rows of neatly arranged tubes of green, tan, blue, and brown.

I shook my head, mouthing thanks, and then thought a moment. "I don't suppose you have any bidis, do you?"

The chimpanzee looked at me with a confused expression for a moment, his eyes glancing toward the middle distance, and then smiled. "No, but give me a moment."

He closed the humidor, there was a faint ping, and then he opened it again, and in the place of the rows of different hued cigars was a small pile of bidi cigarettes.

"How…?" I asked as I reached out to pick one up, though I'd already guessed the answer before the word escaped my lips. "A fabricator, then?"

Maruti nodded. "There's a small one built into the base that I've keyed specifically to manufacture tobacco, cannabis, and other inflammable herbs."

I held the bidi up to my nose and inhaled deeply, the scent carrying me back to misspent days of my youth. Tobacco ground up and rolled in a brown tendu leaf, tied with a little bit of string, bidis were a staple of street-corner life in Bangalore when I was growing up. In a brief rebellious phase in my teenaged years I skipped a lot of school—which, considering I was the son of the professor of literature, pleased my father not a bit—and hung out in the market with a group of juvenile delinquents, daring each other to tether our skateboards to the backs of fast-moving trucks, trying unsuccessfully to catch the eyes of girls from the convent school, and smoking an endless number of bidis. I'd lost the habit almost as quickly as I'd lost an appetite for lawbreaking when a group of us ended up jailed for a weekend after a senseless prank went horribly wrong, but I still harbored fond memories of the hot smoke filling my cupped hands, the little bidi tucked between my ring and little fingers, the heady buzz and momentary disorientation that always followed the heavy nicotine hit.

"Light?" Maruti asked, holding up an ornamental brass lighter, in the shape of a cymbal-playing monkey.

"Maybe another time," I said, carefully placing the bidi back into the humidor.

The chimpanzee shrugged. "Fair enough." He dropped the humidor unceremoniously onto the seat of an overstuffed chair and bit down on his cigar. "So how much of the ship have you seen so far, Captain?"

"Not much," I confessed. "I only boarded a short while ago, and your quarters are the first completed part of the ship I've seen."

"Splendid!" Maruti clapped his hairy hands together, then snatched a red fez from a hook on the wall and plopped it on his head. "I'll come along with you, and we'll see the ship together. I've seen precious little besides the insides of these rooms, myself, having only arrived yesterday. Or was it the day before? No matter." He paused a moment, adjusting the tassel on his fez. "That is, if you don't mind the company."

"Oh, no, of course not," I said, and glanced at the eagle on my shoulder. "*Further*?"

"Physician Maruti is a member of our crew and is welcome in any of my habitable areas, naturally, and equally welcome to join us."

"That's settled, then," Maruti said and made for the door. "Let's go already."

So we set out into the ship, the silver eagle, the fez-wearing chimpanzee, and me, trailed by a cloud of cigar smoke that lingered only momentarily as we passed, before tiny machines too small to be seen with the unaided eye quickly scrubbed out any impurities, leaving the ship's air fresh and clean.

· · · · ·

Even with my rejuvenated leg muscles, I didn't relish the idea of walking around the entire ship, the largest deck of which—only one of many—was three square kilometers in area. Luckily, the ship's designers had taken that into consideration. The corridors, which were almost as wide as city streets, had narrow lanes down the middle through which automated vehicles could pass. These rode on cushions of air, propelled by shifting magnetic fields in the deck and guided by the ship's immense intelligence. The vehicles, or trams, as they were commonly called, varied from the size of a reclining chair to that of a city bus, capable of carrying dozens of crew at once. And considering the immense size of the *Further*'s crew complement, that was likely a wise precaution.

As Maruti and I were exiting his quarters, a tram the size of a couch was already speeding up the corridor toward us, directed by the ship's avatar on my shoulder. We settled ourselves on the comfortable cushions, and as the tram began to pick up speed, the silver eagle spread its wings and took flight, keeping pace with us.

"You appear to have inherited your ancestor's love of flight, then?" I called out to the ship's avatar flying along beside us.

::Among many other aspects, Captain,:: the avatar answered, narrowcasting its response directly to my interlink so that there was no distortion from the wind whipping past. ::But where my progenitor was only able to soar in the skies of a handful of worlds, I'll be able to fly among the stars.::

"The escort would envy you, I think."

::Thank you, sir. That's most kind of you to say.::

THIRTY-ONE

The *Further* was like a small city, in more ways than one. Its crew numbered in the low thousands, though that figure didn't take into account a sizable population of digital incarnations that'd opted not to manifest in corporeal form. And since the crew also included a number of gestalt personalities and other forms of distributed coconsciousness, the actual number of individual crew people was a fairly nebulous and fluid concept.

And the ship was laid out much like a city as well. The corridors that cut through the decks were like roadways arranged in spokes and concentric circles, while lift shafts connected the decks, both those configured for individual use and those large enough to transport trams from one level to another.

One thing to which newcomers to the *Further* sometimes found it difficult to adjust to was the artificial gravity. Before the perfection of the metric engineering drive, the only way to get gravity—or anything like it—away from a massive body was to spin or to accelerate. Anything at relative rest was going to be weightless, essentially. But by modifying the variable vacuum dielectric constant, a metric engineering drive was able to produce all sorts of useful changes in a limited region of space surrounding the ship, including the speed of light, effective mass, inertia, clock speeds, energy states, and the length of rulers—all of which were not fundamental qualities, it'd been discovered, but secondary characteristics of the quantum vacuum itself.

The main use of the drive, of course, was to create a "bubble" of distorted space that completely surrounded the ship, such that while the real acceleration inside the bubble remained zero, the bubble itself traveled through normal space at superluminal speeds. An added benefit, which could be enjoyed even when the ship was at rest, due to the comparatively small amounts of energy it required, was the ability to induce gravity in the ship's habitable areas.

The midpoint of the gravitation field were the drive elements themselves, which were contained in the ring around the sphere's circumference. As a result, the equator of the main sphere was always "down," the direction of the induced gravity's pull. Consequently, the decks of the upper hemisphere had a different orientation to those in the lower hemisphere, and anyone riding a lift shaft from one to the other actually skewed over 180 degrees when passing the midpoint. The change was quick, and almost imperceptible, but particularly sensitive crewmembers were known to get momentarily ill in the transition, and there were several in the crew, as a result, who stayed in one hemisphere or the other unless the trip was absolutely necessary.

Those who stuck in the upper hemisphere perhaps get the better end of the bargain. While the lower hemisphere was largely given over to cargo space, industrial-sized fabricants, mass storage, and such, the upper hemisphere, in which much of the crew had their personal quarters, was where many of the ship's amenities were to be found, chief among them the Atrium.

If the *Further* was a city, or at least a large town, then the Atrium was the town square. A large open space under a high, domed ceiling, the Atrium featured a sizable park with a broad meadow, a grove of trees, a bandstand and theater shell, and a large ornamental fountain with statues of smart matter that reconfigured into different shapes and postures at irregular intervals. Live birds and other animals up to the size of deer roamed freely in the park, tended by subsentient drones. The park was bordered by a circular walkway around which was positioned a café, stalls where crewmembers were able to vend their craftwork, and a variable number of restaurants. The domed ceiling of the Atrium could be configured to display any number of scenes, from a cloudless blue sky to a cloudy gray afternoon to green heavens sparked with red lightning to a color-corrected representation of the exterior view from the ship itself, compensating for red and blue shift.

The first time I'd seen the Atrium with my own eyes as the *Further* led me and Maruti on our abbreviated tour, I found it difficult to accept that I was still on board a starship. Almost as difficult to accept, perhaps, was the fact that the robot probe Xerxes was there, idling at a table in front of the café, eir eyeless gaze fixed on the·small birds wheeling overhead, with something almost like a smile on eir metallic features.

THIRTY-TWO

"Xerxes 298.47.29A!" Maruti called out happily as we stepped out of the tram and onto the walkway leading to the café. "So nice to see you again."

The Exode probe glanced up—if a robot with no eyes can actually be said to "glance"—and the faint smile quickly faded.

"Maruti," Xerxes said with a faint sigh, nodding in Maruti's direction. Ey turned, and to me said, "Captain Stone."

The *Further* avatar alighted gracefully on my shoulder.

"And…?" Xerxes regarded the silver eagle for a moment, thoughtfully. "Ah. *Further*. I almost didn't recognize you."

"Astrogator," the avatar answered, inclining its head momentarily.

Xerxes had contributed a significant amount of power to the *Further* fund—the majority of the non-inconsiderable fortune ey'd amassed over the centuries by sharing Exode technology and science with the Entelechy—more than any but the Plenum, the Demiurgists, and the Pethesilean Mining Consortium and, as a result, was one of the leading voices in the crew. Ey'd accepted the role of astrogator, but more to stave off boredom than anything else, it seemed.

"Mind if we join you?" Maruti said, pulling up a chair before waiting for an answer. As the probe regarded him silently, the chimpanzee motioned the waitron over. At first, I assumed it was a subsentient drone, like the zookeepers who looked after the park animals, but as the server drew near, I saw it was flesh and blood, some sort of uplifted bipedal feline.

"Yes, gentles?" the cat-waitron purred. "Can I help you?"

"It's not too early in the ship's day for a cocktail, is it?" the chimpanzee answered and, when the waitron responded with only a confused look, hastened to add, "I'm sorry, an obscure joke. In our dear commanding officer's day, I've discovered, some cultures preferred to limit the ingestion of intoxicants to the later percentages of the day."

The cat, who I saw now was female, glanced at me, a somewhat suspicious look on her face. "Whyever for, Captain?"

I could only smile and shrug. "Things were different in primitive times, I suppose."

With a lingering confused glance my way, the waitron took Maruti's order, some strange beverage with an unlikely name. I joined Xerxes and Maruti at the table, as the *Further* avatar hopped from my shoulder to the back of a nearby chair, and then the cat turned her attention to me.

"And you, Captain Stone, is there anything you require?"

"No," I said, and then thought better of it. "Actually, you can answer a question for me, if you don't mind."

"Certainly," the cat said with a smile.

"I was just wondering…" I paused. "I'm sorry, what was your name again?"

"It hasn't been announced, but it's Ailuros, actually."

"I was just wondering, Ailuros, why choose to wait tables? When the work can be done by drones, I mean."

The waitron regarded me quizzically, her whiskers twitching. "You could just as easily ask why any of us do *anything*, sir. All of us on board the *Further*, as indeed all sentients throughout the Human Entelechy, perform functions that could just as easily be accomplished by subsentients, who would just as likely be more efficient and error-free in their work. So why bother, when we could be at our ease?"

I thought it over for a moment. "Well, from what I've seen, people still perform services in exchange for payment—power, I mean." I glanced at Maruti. "Don't you intend to give Ailuros a gratuity when she brings your order?"

"Naturally," the chimpanzee said in a broad gesture, pulling a cigar from a case in his smoking jacket and cutting off the tip. "Provided the order's right."

"So it would be easy to assume, Ailuros, that you work in exchange for power. Right?"

"Perhaps," Ailuros purred, her head tilted to one side, "until one took into account that, as an expert in the physics of the quantum vacuum, I could likely find more lucrative employment elsewhere. There are engineering firms who'd be willing to exchange more power for one day's work from me than I could earn in ten years of serving beverages."

"Fair enough," I said, nodding appreciatively. "In that case, my question stands. Why wait tables?"

"Because I like waiting tables." Ailuros, smiling, turned and walked away.

When she'd gone, I turned to the others, confused.

"If I'm too much the unfrozen caveman in your world, please forgive me, but there are still so many things about your society that I just don't understand."

"Don't worry, Captain Stone," Xerxes said in a tired voice, "there's much about them *I* don't understand, either. Like the reasons why so many biologicals feel the *desperate* need to unburden themselves to me. Perhaps it's something to do with my physiognomy, I don't know. But our server felt impelled earlier to tell me an abbreviated version of her life story, when all I wanted to do was watch the birds. She's contributed a hundred-thousandth share to the *Further* fund, I'm given to understand, and has a post working in drive engineering, but intends to spend her free time here, serving orders." Ey glanced the way the waitron had gone, and then back at me, and shrugged. "Your explanation for her actions is likely as good as mine."

"Xerxes," Maruti said, holding the end of his cigar in the flickering flame of a compact lighter, "you never struck me as a birdwatcher."

"In our brief, fleeting encounters, Maruti, I'm surprised that I struck you as anything at all."

Maruti took a long pull from his cigar. "Perhaps an interesting and unexpected benefit of our traveling together, a few thousand of us in such close quarters, is that we'll all learn things we never suspected about one another, becoming faster friends in the process."

The probe sighed and was silent for a long moment. "How... wonderful."

Less than fifteen minutes later, Maruti was shouting at him at the top of his lungs, and the chances of the two becoming fast friends seemed vanishingly remote.

THIRTY-THREE

"What do you mean, *deluded*?"

We were on the tram, continuing our tour of the ship. Xerxes, having nothing better to do, had opted to join us, and sat between Maruti and me while the *Further* avatar flew alongside.

"I don't mean to offend, of course, but it seems clear to me that you simply haven't applied any sort of scientific rigor to your unformed beliefs."

"*Unformed*?" Maruti's mouth opened wide, his lips pulled back vertically and teeth bared, his facial hairs erect. I was still learning to read chimpanzee expressions, but even I recognized this as aggressive.

As we descended the lift shaft, heading toward the lower hemisphere, Maruti had casually asked what Xerxes hoped to get out of his participation in the *Further*, and Xerxes said that he was mainly hoping to stave off boredom. The chimpanzee had then mentioned the desire of the Demiurgists to find definitive, incontrovertible proof of ancient aliens, and things had gone quickly downhill from there.

"Well, your ideas have scarcely reached the level of hypothesis," Xerxes went on, "and the scant data you've been able to gather, none of it statistically significant, can all be easily explained by a wide variety of far more plausible causes. I don't see the desperate need to cling to the myth of ancient non-terrestrial intelligences as anything but an irrational delusion, and I'm sorry if that offends you."

"'*If* that offends,' you say? As though such a casual dismissal of the work of thousands of sentients over hundreds of years can be anything *but* offensive?"

Xerxes shrugged. "I know that the fact that your life has, to date, been wasted must be a troubling one to accept, but that's hardly *my* fault, is it?"

"But *you* are the result of design and intention, just as much as I am. I find it impossible to believe that a being such as yourself couldn't accept at least the *possibility* that if my subsentient ancestors could be uplifted and dumb matter could be transformed into a consciousness such as yours, then the rise of life on Earth in the first place might not have been the result of an interfering intelligence, whether ancient alien or extradimensional being or what have you."

Xerxes let out a labored sigh. "And I suppose next you'll be claiming that rainbows are painted in the sky by fairies from underspace, no?"

Maruti, all sense of polite discourse forgotten, screamed wordlessly at the probe, teeth bared and hairy fingers curled into claws at his side.

The tram came to a stop in a large open space. "Ah," Xerxes said calmly, climbing to eir feet, "we seem to have arrived."

Ey strode away from the tram, pausing only to glance back and say, "Captain, Maruti, aren't you coming?"

I looked over at Maruti, who seemed more like a wild animal than I would have imagined possible, and suspected that even four cubic kilometers would seem too small a space if this disagreement continued much longer.

■ ■ ■ ■ ■

The *Further* had brought us to a large hold area, a vast cavernous space, where familiar shapes were being carefully arranged. As we climbed from the tram, a large black-and-white shape, trailed by a cloud of fine mist, came ambling over toward us, singing out a greeting.

"Welcome aboard, folks," called Arluq Max'inux, the towering cetacean. "Come down to make sure I'm not getting any scratches or dings on them?" She hooked an enormous thumb at the shapes hulking behind her, craft of various shapes and sizes. The far wall, with its slight curvature, was just within the outer hull, and bay doors could be opened to allow the craft to come in or out, the internal atmosphere kept in place by fields.

Two of the craft, in particular, were familiar—the replica of the *Orbital Patrol Cutter 1519* and the metric engineering prototype that Chief Executive Zel had displayed at the fundraiser. Arluq, who'd taken the post of ship's fabricator, had been overseeing the arrival of the various craft the *Further* would carry on board, and I'd insisted that the cutter and the prototype be among them. The prototype, which I'd asked be dubbed the *Compass Rose*—I couldn't conscience a ship that didn't have a name, no matter how small—seemed to me like it would make a useful shuttle or captain's gig. It couldn't reach superluminal speeds, but its metric engineering drives could generate internal gravity in the crew compartments, and it could land and take off from spaces that a torchship wouldn't be able to reach, much less a sailship.

"Looking good, Arluq," I said.

I followed the cetacean over to the *Compass Rose*, which sat flush on the deck, the size of a small house. One walked up any of the eight radiating points to the open hatch, looking for all the world like a flying saucer from an old black-and-white science fiction movie.

"I took her out for a spin before bringing her on board, RJ, and if the full-size model is anything like the prototype, we're in for quite a ride. I got her up to a quarter the speed of light in less than seven-thousandths of a standard day."

That was quick, a little under ten minutes. I was impressed, and I'm sure my expression showed it.

"What do you say?" Arluq's mouth spread in a wide smile, revealing wicked teeth. "Want to take a ride?"

I was deeply tempted, but before I could answer, the *Further* avatar interrupted. "Your pardons, but the first has requested that the command crew convene on the bridge. If you have no objections, I'm to escort you."

I looked from the silver eagle to the cetacean and sighed a bit wistfully. "Maybe another time, Arluq?"

"Sure," she answered with her vicious smile. "I'm not going anywhere. Or I guess I am, but we're all going there together, right?"

"True enough," I said. Except it wasn't. I had to go to the bridge and deal with the "first," while Arluq got to stay in the landing bay and play with the toys.

It hardly seemed fair.

THIRTY-FOUR

The bridge was designed like an amphitheater, concentric steps leading down to the control center, a wide circular table surrounded by seats at regular intervals. One seat was slightly larger than the others—the command chair.

Lit only by the glow of the smart displays on the table's surface, the rest of the room in shadows, Zel i'Cirea and the brothers Grimnismal were in close conversation when we entered the room, but as soon as we did, they fell quickly silent.

I stepped down into the center of the room, followed by Maruti and Xerxes, while the *Further* avatar winged overhead, coming to rest on a perch high on the wall. A long silence followed, broken at last when Zel finally spoke.

"Captain Stone." She paused again, her expression unreadable. "I believe this is yours."

She stood up slowly from the command chair and stepped to one side. The two corvids, shooting me looks, retreated to the far side of the table and slumped down side by side in a pair of seats, leaning close together like birds on a wire.

Zel had little love for me, I knew, but I didn't know why—not yet, at any rate.

"Thanks, First," I said, opting not to sit, but instead just leaning my hand on the seat's back. "Glad to be here."

■ ■ ■ ■ ■

One of the problems I ran into when agreeing to act as the Plenum's representative was that the *Further* wasn't originally part of any tradition of command and that there was no structure in place for how things were to be run. The only guide we had was that responsibility and authority, like any potential profit, was to be apportioned on a share basis, determined by the amount of power donated to the ship's construction. Almost like the old wet navies of earth, which divided spoils in equal shares among the crew, with the lowest-ranking crewmembers getting only fractional shares and the captain getting multiple shares, and everyone else falling in between.

In working up an organizational structure for the *Further*, then, each of the shareholders had a voice, but the principal contributors had the most influence. Shortly after Maruti had completed his rejuvenation and installed my interlink, the principals met to hammer out some kind of approach.

The principal shareholders of the *Further* are the Plenum, who ceded all right to contribute to the discussion to me, their sole representative; the Pethesilean Mining Consortium, represented by Zel i'Cirea; the Demiurgists, represented by Maruti Sun Ghekre IX; and Xerxes, representing himself. It took the better part of two days to work out an agreement, which seemed remarkably fast to me, but to those more accustomed to the speed of Entelechy, decision making was an eternity.

The organizational structure we ended up devising was a mélange of the lessons I learned in the Orbital Patrol and UNSA, Zel's experience with the solar sailships of the Pethesilean fleet, and as much authority and structure as the more lax Maruti and the more ordered Xerxes were able to agree upon between them. There were no ranks on board the *Further* as such—though some insisted on adopting their own, such as the Anachronists who prefered to pretend like they were in an antique wet navy or on board a ship of the First Space Age—but by consensus, it was decided that the commanding officer would bear the title of "captain." Most everyone else in the crew had been given titles describing their posts, such as Exobiolgist Maruti, Astrogator Xerxes, and Fabricator Max'inux. Zel i'Cirea, whose people are second only to the Plenum in the amount they contributed to the *Further* fund, was second in command and, in accordance with Pethesilean tradition, was referred to as "First."

Not all the members of the "crew," using the term loosely, had positions, with some of them acting only as passengers. And other positions were traded back and forth between the crew, at will, from time to time, whenever the mood struck; it would be complicated for an unaugmented organic mind like mine to follow, but the *Further* itself kept track of the crew and their responsibilities from instant to instant. In order for two members of the crew to trade positions, they needed only to inform the *Further* and it entered the record.

There were many times when I'd been tempted to offer the command chair to First Zel i'Cirea, if only to escape more of her withering stares.

· · · · ·

Zel was treating me to one such stare as we all stood around the control center in an awkward silence. There were politics at work I didn't understand, but I knew enough to recognize that the corvid brothers had sided with the Amazon in some sort of power struggle I didn't even know was taking place. I was on the other side, the hapless unfrozen caveman, unsure even how I'd managed to give offense in so short a time.

Xerxes, not standing on ceremony, took a seat and configured the table in front of em to display astrogation information. One of the corvids, Hu or Mu, I couldn't tell which, was occupying the next seat over and leaned over conspiratorially.

"My brother and I helped design the control interface, you should know."

"Did you?" Xerxes answered, sounding not at all impressed. "Well, be sure not to mention 'design' to our good physician"— ey nodded toward Maruti—"or else he's liable to respond with another of his irrational outbursts."

Before Maruti could respond, his teeth already bared, the entry to the bridge slid open again, and a pair of young women entered wearing matching one-piece suits of flashing green.

"Well, look," the two said in unison as they loped down the steps, "the gang's all here!"

"*Namaste*, Madam Jida," I said, pressing my hands together at my chest.

"Oh, don't be so formal," one of the two said, sliding into the seat beside me. "As ambassador extraordinary of Jida Shuliang to the universe at large, I suppose the correct term of address is 'Your Excellency.'"

"The rest of me is getting my quarters in order," the other said, dropping into the seat on my other side. "But I'm already unpacked and ready to go. So when do we launch, already?"

And that was that.

THIRTY-FIVE

There was one more member of our command crew I hadn't met yet, though I didn't know it until I reached my quarters and finally unpacked.

We had just left Ouroboros, powering away from the Entelechy at speed, the transition from normal space to the distorted bubble of space time that enclosed us entirely imperceptible. The only sign that we were moving at all, in fact, was the view beyond the hull as the stars in front of us slowly began to cluster closer together, their shades shifted toward the blue end of the spectrum, while the stars behind were red and drawing nearer one another.

I'd given the order to depart from the bridge, but once we were underway, there wasn't much to do or see for a few days. The metric engineering drives could maintain the distorted region of space around us for five standard days, during which time the bubble would be moving through normal space at a rate of ten light-years per day. At the end of five days, the bubble would collapse and we'd revert to normal space, after which the drive would recharge for another standard day, more or less. (The recharge cycle could be shortened by a few hours if we cut back on other power usage, but as that would mean shutting down gravity, environmental controls, and even life support, I doubted any of us would be in that much of a hurry.)

The *Further*, therefore, could average a maximum of fifty light-years of travel every six days. At top speed, it would take us just under one year to travel from one edge of the Entelechy to the other. For this first hop, though, we'd be taking a short shakedown cruise, journeying from Ouroboros to a planet called Aglibol, some forty light-years away.

For the next few days, then, we had little to do but settle in and wait. I had scarcely seen my quarters, stopping in only briefly after arriving to drop off my scant luggage, and with no responsibilities keeping me on the bridge and Zel and her corvid cronies still fixing me with hard stares, I decided it was high time to unpack.

The quarters I'd selected were simple, even Spartan compared to the opulence of the diamond house on Earth. A sitting room, a smaller room with a bed, a small kitchen, an office with a desk and chairs, and a washroom, all configured more or less to "Information Age standards," or so I was told. If that meant I could understand the functioning of the toilet without needing an expert's assistance, it was fine with me.

One wall slid aside to reveal a kind of wardrobe, and unpacking my bag, I hung the sherwani coat, white churidar pants, and juties up on hooks and, after taking out the rest of the contents, hung the empty bag itself on another hook. Then I returned to the sitting room, set the Space Man action figure on a place of honor on a shelf, put the handheld beside it, and then hung my holstered cap gun from a peg that helpfully protruded from the wall when I needed it. Then I was left holding only the diamond case Amelia had given me when we parted in Central Axis back on Earth. I sat down at the table and set the case down in front of me.

I looked at the case for a long while, thinking about my former crewmate. I understood her reasons for staying behind while I went off to the stars, but that didn't make her decision any less difficult to take. This was an amazing world in which we'd found ourselves, and it was a shame that we wouldn't be able to share it with one another—whether simply as friends or as something more.

What trinket could Amelia have given me that could possibly make up for her absence?

I slid the case open, and inside I found a signet ring, the color of silver, set with a red gem. The stone might have been a fire opal, and indeed, it seemed to glow with a kind of inner light.

An inner light that quickly spilled out into the room around it, glowing brightly.

"It's about time you opened that case," said a familiar voice. "It was getting stuffy in there."

Suddenly, on the table's surface stood a miniature holographic projection of a woman, no more than thirty centimeters tall.

"G'day," the projection said in Amelia Apatari's voice, winking. "Did you miss me?"

THIRTY-SIX

I think my heart stopped beating for a moment, and only my years as a battle-hardened expert in Interdiction Negotiation kept me from jumping up on the chair and screaming like a little girl.

"What's the matter, RJ? You look like you've seen a ghost."

"I…I…" was about all I could manage.

"Of course, technically, I suppose I *am* a ghost, come to think of it."

"But…but what…"

"If you don't unclench a bit, my dear Ramachandra, you're going to blow an o-ring."

I still held the signet ring in a white-knuckled grip, and when I looked down at it, I could see the lights dancing deep within the fire opal whenever the holograph moved. Startled, as though something I'd thought was a stuffed toy had turned out to be a live snake, I dropped the ring and sprang to my feet. To my credit, though, I *didn't* jump on the chair and scream, however tempting it might have been.

"What *are* you?" I said, and then followed quickly with, "Well, Amelia, obviously...but *how*?"

The tiny woman on the table sighed, a sympathetic expression on her delicate features. "Sit down, RJ. I'm supposed to help you, not give you a bloody coronary."

I found my way back onto the chair, regarding the ring I'd dropped onto the table warily, as though it might bite me.

"It's like this, mate. When I decided to stay in the Entelechy rather than come with you—that is, when *Amelia Apatari* decided to stay—she knew she'd be leaving you without any connection to your own world and time. And while I wasn't willing—while *she* wasn't willing to sacrifice her own dreams to come along with you, she wanted to do something to make it right."

It was strange, watching the little figure, the table faintly visible through her translucent body, who seemed to find it difficult to remember she wasn't the woman she so resembled.

"You remember Maruti saying that he'd reconstructed a more or less complete version of my consciousness and memory from my...well, from my 'remains,' right?"

I nodded numbly.

"Well, I asked Maruti if he could just update the copy with my recent memories and download it into something you could take along with you." She nodded toward the ring sitting on the table a short distance from her. "The ring was Maruti's idea. Stylish, don't you think? Complete with its own holographic projector."

"So you're...what? Some kind of...copy of Amelia?"

"Technically, I'm a digital incarnation of Amelia's consciousness housed in the ring. I can run as a virtual emulation inside the ring itself or interact with the outside world either by direct interlink communication or by holographic projection."

"Wait, I'm still not sure I understand. Amelia stayed back in the Entelechy, as we discussed, and you're a full copy of her mind. Does that make you…alive? I mean, are you sentient?"

The little holographic projection pursed her lips in an expression I'd grown to recognize in the years I served beside Amelia. It was the face she made whenever reminded of a fact she'd sooner forget.

"Well, *actually*, when 'Amelia' asked for the copy to be made, she insisted that Maruti keep it just below full sentience. I remember her being worried about creating a fully self-aware version of herself if it was only going to be, for all intents and purposes, someone else's property. But I don't know. Do I *seem* subsentient?"

I didn't have an answer for that, or even the faintest notion what one might be.

"I *feel* the same as I always have, if you ask me," the holograph went on. "So either sentience isn't all it's cracked up to be or that chimpanzee might have pulled a fast one."

I reached over and gingerly picked up the ring. Holding it up to my face, I peered into the depths of the gem, as though I might catch a glimpse of Amelia's mind somewhere in there. "It's been a while since Amelia gave this to me. What have you been doing in there all this time, anyway?"

The projection laughed, Amelia's laugh, familiar and throaty. "Well, it looks like cramped quarters, but there's quite a bit to be said for being a digital consciousness. Sure, I don't have a physical form, but I've got perfect recall and enough processing capacity to simulate any environment I choose. So I've been lounging around, rereading all of the *Taimi Taitto, Girl Reporter* graphic albums I loved as a kid, eating my favorite meals, and revisiting my favorite places. And even made a few new stops along the way.

Paris in the 19C was particularly nice, I thought. Honestly, if I didn't know I was an emulation, I'd never have guessed it."

Tentatively, I slipped the signet ring on the ring finger of my right hand.

"And you're just going to ride along with me, then?" I said, looking from the ring to the woman on the table.

"Sure," the projection answered, and I found I couldn't think of her as anything but plain old Amelia. "Just think of me as your personal advisor."

"I don't know," I said, shaking my head slowly but smiling all the same. "This is going to take some getting used to."

"Ah, what have you got to worry about? It'll be beaut!"

THIRTY-SEVEN

It was late in the ship's night, the percentage of the day when the lights in the corridor were dimmed and many of the biologicals in the crew let their bodies rest, and I was propped up in my bed, trying to read.

I've always been something of a bookworm. It comes from having a writer for a grandfather and a professor of English for a father, I suppose. Our house in Bangalore was always full of books. When I left home and moved to Ethiopia to start university, I brought a few of my favorite books along, many of them handed down to me by my grandfather—Robert Heinlein's *Space Cadet*, Cordwainer Smith's *Norstrilia*, Iain Banks's *Use of Weapons*. After graduating, when I signed on with the Orbital Patrol, mass restrictions meant that I had to leave all of the books behind, and so I brought digital copies along instead. I included my handheld in my mass allotment on board *Wayfarer One*, years later, and loaded onto it every book that I could lay my hands on, everything that I'd ever read and everything I'd never found the time to try.

Now, finding myself in the distant future in a rejuvenated body that, according to Maruti, need never age, I had all the time in the world. And since we were still days out from Aglibol and I couldn't sleep, I saw no reason not to catch up on my reading.

But my damned interlink kept getting in the way.

Perhaps I should explain. I'm fluent in several languages— English, Hindi, Kannada, and Amharic—and the books on my handheld are written in all four of those, with a sizable percentage in other languages I can't even read but that I thought the other members of the *Wayfarer One* crew might enjoy.

That night, propped up in my bed on board the *Further*, with Amelia entertaining herself in some virtual environment inside the ring sitting on the side table, I paged through the handheld's index, seeing if anything sparked my interest. I thought I might try something new, but then chanced upon something very old, indeed.

I'd been forced to memorize and recite whole stanzas of Goswami Tulsidas's epic poem *Ramacharitamanasa* in secondary school, and though I preferred other versions of the *Ramayana*, there was still something about this 16C Hindi version that reso- nated with me.

I tapped the title listing on the display, and the first stanzas scrolled on the screen, but I was immediately disoriented as the Hindi characters were completely obscured by glowing roman letters superimposed over them, a precise translation of the text into English.

Puzzled, I called up the handheld's menu interface but could find no settings that could account for the translation. I scanned a few more pages of Tulsidas's text and found the English translation superimposed across all of them.

I closed the file and called up a few more texts. All of the English texts displayed fine, but any other languages were obscured by the same superimposed translations.

It wasn't until I dropped the handheld onto the bed that I realized that the superimposed text was not on the display itself, but seemed to hover slightly *above* the display. I picked the handheld back up, turning it first one direction and then the other, and slowly began to understand what was happening.

The table in my sitting room was made of the same smart matter as the control center on the bridge, and with only a little effort, I was able to configure it into a touch-sensitive display. Using my index finger as a stylus, I wrote out a few simple words and phrases, in Kannada, in Amharic, even a few simple words I knew of Spanish, Dutch, and Russian. In each instance, as the words were completed on the display, the superimposed translation would appear—and, as with the handheld, hovering just above the surface.

It wasn't the displays that were providing the translations. It was *me*.

It had to be the interlink, of course. It interrupted the flow of sensory input from my ears to my brain and substituted my language of choice—Information Age English—for whatever language the speaker was using, provided it had the full grammar and lexicon in its stores. There was no reason it couldn't do the same with visual information. I was surprised not to have noticed the effect in the few days previous but, on reflection, realized that I'd seen very little in the way of written language since arriving. Perhaps a culture able to beam data back and forth directly between their heads had little use for the written word? Or was it simply a question of taste and style? Or had I just been unobservant?

Whatever the case, it was pretty annoying. I could see how instant translations could come in handy, but the inability to turn the thing off was just a damned nuisance.

Maruti would likely be able to tell me how to set the preferences on my interlink, configuring it to my liking, but it was late, and I had little desire to get dressed and traipse out into the darkened hallways. Was there some sort of communication or phone system I could use to call him?

And then I remembered that interlink communication didn't require line of sight. Maruti had explained that an interlink could connect to the infostructure, and though we were cut off from the datascape of the Entelechy, there was a smaller shipboard information environment that could serve the same purpose.

"Maruti?" I said out loud and then repeated, concentrating. ::MARUTI?::

::Can you *please* stop with the shouting, Captain?:: immediately came the reply, sounding as clear as if he were in the room with me.

::Sorry. I wasn't sure if this would work.::

::Well, clearly it has.:: Strangely, I got the impression of a sigh. Clearly, nonvocal communication could also be transmitted by interlink. I'd have to be careful about that. ::I'm quite busy at the moment, enjoying a glass of port with another of our crewmates, that delightful Ailuros from the café. Is there something I can help you with?::

::Oh, sorry,:: I replied. I hadn't even thought about what the chimpanzee might be doing when I "called," having been so eager to see if I could even make connection. ::It's just...I'm trying to read, and my interlink keeps tossing up unwanted translations.::

::Hmm. This text is in your language of choice?::

::No, it's not. Everything in English is fine, it's just everything else that gets stomped on.::

Again, I got the impression of a weary sigh. ::Well, *obviously* an interlink is going to translate any language that doesn't fit its profile, unless told otherwise.::

::Ri-ight. So how do I get it to stop?::

There came a long pause, and I wondered what sort of facial expression Maruti was sharing with the cat-woman. I couldn't help but think of someone holding a phone away form their ear and twirling their finger in circles around their ear, making the once universal sign of insanity. ::You simply *tell* it to stop. Now, is there any *other* burning question I can answer for you at this late hour?::

::Um, no?::

::Good night, Captain.::

"Good night," I said out loud, having already felt the connection to the chimpanzee drop.

I picked up the handheld and brought up a page full of Hindi text, obscured by English translation.

"Interlink," I said out loud, "stop translating the text."

Suddenly, the translation vanished, and the Hindi text was unobscured.

I tried another experiment. ::Interlink, start translating.::

Again, text floated in front of my eyes.

"Well, that was easy," I said.

I ordered the translation to turn off again and settled back onto the bed to read the story of my namesake trying to rescue his wife Sita from the demon lord.

And promptly fell asleep.

THIRTY-EIGHT

The next ship's morning, rested and refreshed, I bathed, dressed in a simple black coverall ship suit and slip-on shoes, and ate a quick meal of oatmeal and buna in my kitchen, chatting with Amelia, who projected herself onto the table and enjoyed an emulated meal of her own. After we'd finished, Amelia popped back into the ring for a while, and I decided to head to the bridge.

My quarters, like those of the rest of the command crew and most of the department heads, were on the same level as the bridge, and while I was sure I'd have been alerted if the ship had run into any problems while I slept, as captain I felt obliged to check in as a matter of course.

Stepping out into the now brightly lit corridor beyond my door, I was immediately brought up short by the unlikely trio standing just beyond. It was a woman dressed in the uniform of a Napoleonic-era British officer in Nelson's Navy; a man dressed in a red velour tunic with a gold star embroidered on the breast, black trousers that flared below the knee, and high black boots; and another man wearing a styled mid-20C-era dark-blue sailor's uniform, with a white "Dixie cup" hat and a red kerchief around his neck.

"O Captain," the woman in the Napoleonic uniform said in passable English, standing to attention, snapping off a crisp salute, "Midshipman Euphagenia d'Angelique Bibblecombe-Aldwinkle, reporting for duty. May I present Lieutenant Commander Rex Starr"—she indicated the redshirt and then pointed with her chin to the sailor suit—"and Chief Warrant Officer Donald Duke."

"Donald *Duck*?" I said.

"Duke, sir," the sailor suit said. "Donald Duke."

"Ah, of course. And, Starr, was it?"

The redshirt stood to attention, chin held high. "Yessir."

"I think you might have the wrong starship, friend."

"Sir?"

"Never mind." I surveyed the trio. When I'd first seen them outside the diamond house, they'd been a superheroine and a pair of zoot suiters, and later on Cronos, they'd been Scarlett O'Hara and the blue-and-gray brothers. The Anachronists had clearly found a new mode to explore. "So you're part of the *Further*'s crew, I take it?"

"Oh, yes, sir," the midshipwoman said, positively gushing. "When we heard that you were taking command, we couldn't resist."

"We've taken on new personas and everything," the redshirt added proudly. "Do you like them?"

"They're...they're just splendid. Glad to have you on board." I paused, considering. "Um, if you don't mind me asking, what positions have you taken in the crew, come to that?"

"I'm in astrometrics," the sailor suit said, "and Rex and Gina—"

"Euphagenia d'Angelique Bibblecombe-Aldwinkle!" the midshipwoman said hastily, interrupting.

"Right, sorry. Rex and Euphagenia d'Angelique Bibblecombe-Aldwinkle are helping out in industrial fabrication."

"Any post is fine with us," the redshirt said. "We couldn't pass up the chance to experience what it must have been like for the ancient explorers of your time."

"And you all have adopted ranks, I see."

"Oh, naturally," the midshipwoman said, shoulders back. "It wouldn't have been an authentic primitive experience without them."

"Quite right," I said, nodding sagely. "Well..." I waved my hands in absent motions. "Erm, carry on the good work?"

The three beamed. They stood to crisp attention and snapped off salutes, then turned on their heels and marched off down the corridor.

· · · · ·

I continued on toward the bridge, exchanging nods and pleasantries with every manner of biological, synthetic, and mix of the two along the way. But before I reached the entrance to the bridge, I heard a voice calling my name.

"Captain Stone, do you have a brief percentage of the day to spare?"

I turned and saw First Zel i'Cirea standing in an open doorway, dimly lit rooms beyond. Her dark-blue hair was pulled back into a tight knot at the back of her head, the sapphire-colored eye patch over her left eye in stark contrast to her alabaster skin.

"Certainly," I said, a bit warily, and walked over. "What can I do for you?"

"I have something to show you." She stepped to one side and motioned to the rooms beyond the door. Her manner was unusually solicitous, and I couldn't help but be suspicious.

"Is there something wrong, First?"

"No, nothing like that," she said, a faint smile on her lips that didn't reach her eye. "I just wanted to get your opinion on something."

I shrugged. "I'm in no particular hurry."

As I stepped into the room, it took a moment for my eyes to adjust to the gloom beyond. There was someone standing in the far corner in the shadows, a low couch, and a pair of chairs.

"Do come in," Zel said as the door closed behind me. "Captain Stone, I believe you'll recognize my guest?"

The figure stepped out of the shadows. As the light fell across his features, he stood revealed as an old man in his late seventies, if not older, hair white and thin against dark skin, shoulders slumped and knees slightly bent.

It was me. Or rather, the me I'd been just a few days before.

THIRTY-NINE

"What is this?" the old me said angrily. He took a few steps forward and pointed an arthritic finger in my direction. "Who the hell is *he* supposed to be? What kind of game are you playing, lady?"

"My questions exactly," I said. It was disorienting, hearing my voice come out of another's mouth, much less someone who looked exactly as I had only a short time before. I turned to Zel. "What's going on here?"

"Oh, I'm sorry," the Amazon said with a faint smile. "Perhaps you prefer *this* model?"

She glanced at the old man, who seemed to waver for a moment like an image reflected in a rippling pool. When he steadied again, he now appeared to be about thirty, in the prime of life, looking so much like me that I could have been gazing into a mirror.

"Look," the other me said, as though nothing had changed, "I've played along this far, but I think I deserve some answers. Where am I? What's going on?"

"All of your questions will be answered in time," Zel said serenely, "but first, I have a question of my own. Who are you?"

The other me straightened, forcibly controlling himself. "Captain Ramachandra Jason Stone, UNSA, commander of *Wayfarer One*. Now, I demand to know where I am."

"What's the last thing you remember, Captain Stone?" Zel asked.

"Going into cryogenic suspension on board my ship," he answered dismissively. "Now, who *are* you people? Where's my crew? Where's my ship?"

Ignoring the other me, Zel turned and looked my way. "Go ahead, ask him a question, if you like. As many questions as you feel are necessary to establish his identity."

I narrowed my eyes and looked hard at my second-in-command. Her words were friendly enough, but there was a hard edge to her voice, and I didn't like the way things were heading.

"It's a holographic projection, isn't it?" I asked.

"Well, naturally," she answered, "but I could just as easily have fabricated a physical body, if I'd so chosen. There are no extant samples of R. J. Stone's genetic material in the historical record, but I'm sure we'd have been able to cobble together a reasonable facsimile that would stand up to any rigorous examination."

"What are you people talking about?" the other me said, his tone growing angrier by the moment. "I demand to speak to someone in charge!"

Zel shrugged, casting a sidelong glance at the other me. "His speech is more than a little clichéd, I'll admit, and I have him speaking and understanding Common and not Information Age English, but his personality template was a rushed job, and I'm hardly an expert at this. If I'd had time to bring in someone with the appropriate experience—a dramatist, perhaps—the dialogue would doubtless be improved. But this is good enough to prove my point, I think."

"What point?" I demanded, growing a bit hot myself.

"Ask him a few questions, Captain Stone, and *then* I'll tell you."

I stood, fixing her with a hard stare.

"*Fine*," she said with a sigh. "I'll start. Captain Stone"—she turned to the other me—"when and where were you born?"

"March 2, 2136 CE, Bangalore, India," the other me answered, with pause.

"I included a compulsion to answer questions," Zel said in an aside to me, "just to speed the process along, but if you prefer to read in a lengthy delay and a bit of back-and-forth, that's perfectly fine." She turned back to the other me. "And who were your genetic donors." She paused, and then added, "I'm sorry, who were your *parents*?" She glanced my way. "It's sometimes hard for Pethesileans to keep the facts of sexual reproduction straight, I'm afraid."

"My father was Jonathan Stone, and my mother was Sanjoevani Pilot."

"What's this supposed to prove?" I asked impatiently.

"Patience, Captain. Now, what was your favorite entertainment as a child?"

"*Earth Force Z*," the other me answered. "And *The Adventures of Space Man*."

"Who was the first female you ever loved, aside from your parent?"

"Vijaya Nelliparambil."

"What's your favorite curse?"

"*Madar chowd*."

"What pastime do you enjoy but not find enough time to pursue?"

"The game of Go."

"Where did you learn the game?"

"From Eiji Hayakawa, my commanding officer on board lunar buoy tender *Orbital Patrol Cutter 972*."

"How did you...?"

"OK, OK," I said angrily, raising my hands. "This is a great trick—you two must be loads of fun at parties. Now, what's this all about?" I thought of the digital copy of Amelia Apatari, currently residing in the signet ring on my finger. "Did you get hold of a copy of my mind?"

"No," Zel said in a clipped tone. "I've not once referred to any of the recordings done of your connectome or genome, either those done by the crew of my mining ship or the ones carried out by Maruti Sun Ghekre the Ninth." She drew her mouth into a tight, hard smile. "Next theory?"

"Look, I'm getting tired of this!" the other me shouted, taking a step forward. "If I don't get—"

"Enough," Zel snapped and, with a wave of her hand, froze the other me in his tracks. He was struck silent, and absolutely immobile, like a paused playback. "He was getting a bit tiresome, don't you think?"

I stepped forward, leaning in to examine the holographic projection more closely. Seen from a distance of only a few centimeters, I noticed that the fine details were wrong. A meter or two away and it looked just like me, but on close inspection, the nostrils were a little too flared, the eyebrows slightly the wrong shape, the lips not quite full enough.

"All right, I give up." I straightened, and turned to face Zel. "What's this supposed to prove?"

Zel fell into one of the nearby chairs, legs folded and arms arranged gracefully across her chest. She motioned me toward the other chair with an incline of her head, but I preferred to stand.

Zel motioned to the frozen holograph. "It took me only an insignificant fraction of a day to draft our friend this morning. And he's able to answer any number of questions put to him about the private life of Ramachandra Jason Stone. Correct?"

"Yes, but—"

"And his general appearance is consistent with recorded images of Stone that survive to the present as well, yes?"

"I don't know," I said tiredly. "I haven't seen any."

"Well, *I* have. I've been studying them, in fact, ever since your ship was 'discovered.' I've been studying everything I can find about the life of Captain Ramachandra Jason Stone. And do you know what I've discovered?"

"No. What?"

"That everything about you is in perfect accord with history's record. And do you know what that fact suggests to me?"

I took a labored sigh. "No," I said through clenched teeth. "What?"

"I'll put it simply, Captain Stone," she said, all trace of warmth or humor gone from her voice. "I think that you're just a better version of our somewhat repetitive subsentient friend here."

"*What?*"

"I don't think that you're real." Zel spoke slowly, enunciating broadly, as though talking to a child. "You are nothing more than a constructed personality in a well-crafted suit of flesh, passed off as a figure from history and legend."

I blinked, slowly, unable to believe what I was hearing. "You think I'm a *what*?"

"A simulation, a copy, a replica. An artificial personality constructed from everything that's known about the historical Stone, drawn from diaries, journals, biographies, government records, what have you. A pawn in someone else's game."

"I'm a…In whose game?"

"Well," Zel said calmly, "let's examine the facts, shall we? Who has the most to gain by passing you off as the genuine article? And, more importantly, who has the resources to do so?"

"I don't…" I trailed off and found that I was pacing the room, my hands twisted into white-knuckled fists at my sides.

"I'll tell you," Zel went on, not waiting for me to continue. "The Plenum. After all, *they* were the ones to authenticate the age of the derelict craft, remember? And after shepherding you around the Entelechy, showing you off in a few crowded locales, they suddenly decide to contribute to the *Further* fund, which hasn't interested the AIs in the slightest in a hundred years. And who do they pick as their sole representative in the crew?"

"Look—"

"And when one of their number volunteers to act as the governing intelligence of the *Further*, it just *happens* to be built on the template of the same AI who was your nursemaid and guide? Doesn't that seem somewhat unlikely?" Zel stopped and fixed me with a hard stare, one eye narrowed, the sapphire eye patch glittering over the other. When she spoke again, her voice was cold and sharp, like a knife made of ice. "Doesn't it?"

"Hold on a minute," I said, raising my hands before me. "You've asked a hell of a lot of questions, so give me a chance to answer, all right?"

Zel drew her mouth into a tight line, but kept silent.

I couldn't help but think about Amelia in her ring, unable to tell whether she was sentient or not. I found that the only answer that occurred to me was the same answer she'd come up with as well.

"Look, I can't prove that I'm real, I suppose, if you're capable of doing"—I waved toward the holograph—"all of that. The only thing I can tell you is that I *feel* real. You might be able to program a simulation into saying it remembers my parents, but I actually *do* remember my parents. There's a difference."

"Is there? Suppose you're only telling *yourself* that you remember them? And even if you *do* remember them, that memory could have been lathed out for you by an AI dramatist, for all you know. Memory is hardly infallible."

I shook my head wearily and started for the door. I'd had enough of this line of discussion for one morning.

"Well, then I guess I'll just have to keep on acting as if I'm real until proven otherwise."

"Captain Stone," Zel called out as the door slid open in front of me. "Don't you want to take your new friend with you?" She motioned toward the frozen holograph.

I forced a smile on my lips, without any trace of humor. "He's all yours, First."

The door slid shut behind me, and I was once more alone in the corridor.

I could feel my pulse racing, and as I continued on toward the bridge, I steadied my breathing, following the pranayama exercises my mother had taught me.

But *had* she taught me? Had the mother I remembered ever even existed? Was I, was Amelia, were all of us, just simulations, merely pawns in some complex political maneuvered going on far above my head?

I didn't know. I *couldn't* know, I realized. All that was certain was that I didn't *feel* like a constructed personality.

But it was all academic, right? I was real.

Wasn't I?

FORTY

When I reached the bridge, there was no one present but the ship's avatar up on its perch. I was too worked up to stroll back out, though, and found myself pacing in a wide circle around the control center, trying to burn off the excess energy. My confrontation with Zel had shaken me, and I wasn't sure yet what I thought about all of it.

"Captain?" the avatar finally said, having remained silent until then. "You seem to be somewhat preoccupied. Is there something I can help you with?"

Yes, I felt like saying. *Did your friends in the Plenum cook me up in a Petrie dish to pull one over on everyone?*

But I bit back the words. To even ask the question would be to admit that some part of me believed that the second-in-command had been right, and I refused to accept that. Besides, it was ridiculous. Far more likely was the idea that Zel i'Cirea had been trying to rattle me, and had picked a remarkably effective means of doing so.

"*Further*, just what *is* Zel's beef with me, anyway?"

"Sir?" The silver eagle cocked its head quizzically to one side.

"Sorry, idiomatic expression. What I mean is, the second-in-command seems to bear some animosity toward me, and I don't have any notion why."

"Have you asked her?" the avatar asked simply.

"No," I said, feeling foolish. "But then, our last conversation got away from me a bit, I think."

"Well," the avatar said thoughtfully, "perhaps she resents you for taking command of the *Further*."

"Wh..." I began, and then the penny dropped. "You mean *she* was going to be captain?"

"Of course, sir. First Zel i'Cirea has spearheaded the *Further* project since its infancy, more than a hundred years ago. It was always her intention to be the commanding officer of the completed vessel."

If it had been a snake, it would have bit me. Repeatedly.

"And the Grimnismal brothers see me as some kind of interloper, too."

"Perhaps, sir. It isn't surprising if they do. The drive engineers have been First Zel's associates for a number of years."

I slumped into the command chair, feeling like an idiot.

"So what *else* don't I know about this ship I'm meant to be commanding, *Further*?"

"Oh, a great many things, I'd imagine, sir. I don't believe you're familiar with the ship's armament, for example."

I sat upright, looking up at the eagle on its perch. "Armament?" I'd been thinking of the *Further* in terms of my last command, *Wayfarer One*. And while I'd brought along my cap gun on the journey to Alpha Centauri B, *just in case*, the boffins back in Vienna had never for a moment considered outfitting the ship with weapons. Why would it need them? "What sort of armament?"

"I have been designed to accommodate a wide range of possible scenarios, including engagement with hostile forces. In the interest of the ship's safety, I have been equipped with launchers, emitters, and an inverter."

I leaned forward, my elbows on the table, fingers steepled. "Run that by me again, *Further*. And slowly, if you don't mind."

"Certainly, sir. Our primary offensive weapons are the launchers. Integrated into my metric engineering drives, the launchers are essentially barrels in which small regions of extremely high gravity can be induced. Matter is placed in one end, gravity is momentarily induced at the other, and the matter accelerates to terrific speeds in an extremely short amount of time. The far end of the barrel opens onto my outer hull, and the matter continues at its high velocity until it strikes its target. The energy costs of the launchers are relatively low. The projectiles can be anything that fits into the barrel; though, most often, the raw material kept on board to be used in fabricants is utilized. In certain circumstances, the projectile is configured to deliver an explosive charge at the target, but most often, the projectiles are nothing more than inert 'slugs.'"

"OK," I said thoughtfully. "That's the launchers. What about the emitters?"

"I am also equipped with emitters, particle beam weapons capable of firing beams of accelerated protons. Extremely effective in certain circumstances, though shielding can diminish their impact."

"And the...inverter?"

"Yes, sir. I have one field inverter, which redirects the metric engineering drive's field to create a region of altered space, similar to the 'bubble' that surrounds me under propulsion but directed outward. Within this inverted region, the characteristics of space can be altered at will: Time can run faster, gravity can increase to near infinite, etc. This can have a devastating impact on a target, but the use of the inverter can leave me defenseless and without power, even without life support in extreme circumstances."

I whistled low. "Just what is it you people expect to find out there?"

The eagle waggled its head from side to side in a shrug. "That is the question, now, isn't it, sir?"

In the brief silence that followed, I wondered how far other technologies had evolved while I'd slept. As much as I loved the cap gun hanging from a peg on my wall, I wouldn't want to walk into a firefight having no notion what the black hats were packing.

"What about personal armament, *Further*? What are our options there?"

"I'd be happy to configure a testing range, if you'd like to see for yourself."

I couldn't help but smile. I might just have found a way to work off that excess energy, after all.

FORTY-ONE

I didn't realize, until the *Further* fabricated a projector for me, that so many of the people I'd seen walking around the worlds of the Entelechy had been armed.

"Projectors have manifold uses," the *Further* explained as I picked up the sleek arc, looking for all the world like a golden wrist cuff about seven centimeters wide, inset with a small hemisphere of what looked to be obsidian. "It is principally a personal multifunction tool for energy manipulation, and its use as a weapon is only one of its possible applications."

I snapped the cuff onto my right wrist, and it conformed immediately to my forearm. "How do you control it?"

"There are a variety of control options, but in your case, direct interlink integration would likely be the most efficient."

We were in a long gallery, which just a few moments ago had been part of a larger storage space but the ship had reconfigured into a separate firing range. At the far end of the room floated a pair of spheres, one white and one black—my targets, I presumed.

"There are as many types of projectors as there are individual configurations," the avatar went on, "but this is the standard model, whose functions include a flashlight, a cutting tool, a plasma discharge, and a limited-use defensive force field."

I nodded, holding my arm up, inspecting the cuff.

::Flashlight,:: I thought, and a blinding white ray of light leapt from the obsidian hemisphere, shooting right in my eyes. Squinting, I shouted, "Off! Off!"

The light blinked off as quickly as it had come on.

"There are safeties built into the projector that prevent you from accidentally discharging a plasma round or injuring yourself with the cutting tool. You could disable the precautions, if you preferred, but in most circumstances, I would recommend—"

"No, no," I said quickly, rubbing my still-watering eyes, seeing spots. "I'm quite happy with the safeties, thank you."

The silver eagle nodded, satisfied.

"So the projectile is plasma, you say?"

"Yes, projectors fire toroids of charged plasma. But a projector of this sort holds fairly limited—however, efficiently compressed—reserves of charged gas and is primarily intended for short-term use."

I turned my wrist back and forth, looking at the smooth unbroken line of the cuff, which felt almost weightless on my arm. "How is it powered?"

"Projectors of this sort are rechargeable and draw energy from the ship itself. However, a projector can be configured to absorb any energy in the appropriate bands of the electromagnetic spectrum in order to recharge, a capacity that can even be adapted in the field to drain energy from other devices. Similarly, a projector can be used to manipulate external electromagnetic fields, though to a limited degree."

I glanced at the spheres floating at the far end of the gallery, more than a hundred meters away. "Mind if I give it a try?"

"By all means," the avatar said, hopping out of the way and taking up a position behind me. "I've cleared the area and reinforced the walls, ceiling, and floor of this chamber so that any errant shot need not cause any damage."

"You have that much faith in my marksmanship, do you?"

The avatar waggled its head in a shrug. "Merely a precaution, sir—no value judgment intended."

"Hmm," I humphed, but smiled.

I held my arm straight out in front of me, my hand curled in a fist and pointed at the targets.

::Fire.::

I might have had time to blink, but I doubt it. As soon as I'd thought the word, there was a brief flash, and then there was only one sphere floating at the end of the gallery, the other drifting slowly to the floor in a cloud of dust.

"Just point and shoot," I said. "Seems pretty simple to me."

"Quite impressive," the eagle said with a sigh, and I got the feeling I was being patronized.

I glanced from the eagle to the target and back. "Well, we're just getting started. Now let's make it a little more interesting. How fast do you think you can get one of those spheres to move?"

FORTY-TWO

It was past midday, with fewer than two standard days until we would reach our destination and the end of our shakedown cruise. I was in the bridge with the brothers Grimnismal and one of the Jida emissaries. I sat in the command chair, while the two corvids, the *Further*'s drive engineers, gave me a tutorial in wormhole engineering and the possible benefits of faster-than-light travel. The Jida emissary, draped gracefully over one of the chairs at the control center, listened in with a bemused expression.

The walls and ceiling of the bridge consisted of an unbroken dome, which had been coded to display a real-color image of the exterior view of the ship so that it seemed like four of us sat in the midst of a great expanse of empty blackness, with the stars before us shrunk almost to a single red point, the stars behind a small cluster of blue.

"OK," I said as confidently as possible, "the basics of thresholds have been explained to me. They're initiated with both ends in one place, and then one end is dragged to its destination at slower-than-light speeds. But one can transit the threshold at any point throughout the process, right?"

"Well, naturally," one of the corvids said, as though there were something terribly wrong with me for having to say it out loud.

"Though," the Jida emissary said, "in some instances, the threshold's journey *is* the destination."

I gave her a confused look, at which the corvids exchanged weary glances and sighed.

"There are sailships that have thresholds as permanent onboard fixtures," she went on. "Some carry exceedingly small ones, capable of sending only information back and forth but that allow those on board to remain connected to the infostructure—a tremendous expense, but worthwhile for some, I suppose." She gave me an odd, unreadable look, which suggested I should have been reading more into her statement than I obviously was. "And some cruise ships are equipped with even larger ones, capable of allowing a sentient to travel through bodily; these cater to those who enjoy the romance of traveling between the stars but who prefer not to spend decades or centuries on board. They pay hefty sums of power, step through the threshold, enjoy the rugged shipboard life—from the comfort of their staterooms, naturally—and then return home at their leisure. Their clientele may be somewhat select, given the enormous costs, but even so, it's an extremely lucrative business." She smiled slyly. "I've been known to make a fair amount of power off my cruise line investments, myself."

"In any event," the other corvid said impatiently, "you are quite right, Captain Stone, that thresholds must be maneuvered in place at sublight speeds, and given that the fastest subluminal ships can accelerate to speeds no greater than half that of light, the installation of a new threshold can be a time-consuming procedure."

"And my brother Hu fails to mention," said the other, who I guessed must be Mu, "the problems associated with the cosmic string material that is the fundamental component of a threshold construction."

"Too true, brother, too true." Hu nodded eagerly. "I'm sure, in your primitive era, that such things were scarcely dreamed of, but the fundamental principle of threshold engineering is negative mass."

"Yes," Mu put in, "negative mass is required to stabilize the wormhole mouth, and before the discovery of a cosmic string in interstellar space, thousands of kilometers long but only a proton in diameter, thresholds were only theoretical. The creation of the first threshold, the moment from which their calendar is measured, was the true birth of the Human Entelechy."

"A cosmic string is a topological defect in the fabric of space time," Hu said, interrupting his brother. "They form when different regions of space time undergo phase changes, resulting in domain boundaries between the two regions when they meet. This is somewhat analogous to the boundaries that form between crystal grains in solidifying liquids, or the cracks that form when water freezes into ice."

"Precisely right, brother. Extremely thin and with a diameter on the order of a proton, they nevertheless have immense density and represent a significant source of gravity. As a result, the transportation of cosmic string material through normal space can be a very time-consuming and costly task as well, undertaken only by those—like our erstwhile employer *First* Zel i'Cirea—who are quite experienced in such matters."

"But why wouldn't you just transport the cosmic string frag-ments through existing thresholds like everything else?" I asked. "Why do they have to be transported in normal space?"

The two corvids glanced at one another, shaking their heads sadly. "Haven't you heard *anything* we've said? Cosmic string frag-ments have negative mass, correct? And so any attempt to trans-port it through a threshold destabilizes the support and causes the wormhole to collapse."

"And you couldn't transport it aboard a faster-than-light ship like the *Further* for the same reason?" I asked.

"Hardly the 'same reason," Mu said, his tone scornful, "but such a childish analogy will suit for your purposes, I suppose."

"The gravitation effects and negative energy characteristics of the comic string could collapse the local distortion of the quan-tum vacuum," Hu added slowly and simply, as though talking to a simpleton or a child.

"Which is, of course," the Jida emissary said, her eyes nar-rowed but her tone playful, "where *you* two come in, no doubt?"

The two corvids paused for a moment, seeming to swell with pride, lifting their beaks higher and straightening their rounded shoulders. "As you say, Madame Jida," said Mu.

"As you should know, Captain Stone," Hu explained, "my brother and I have hypothesized the existence of a novel form of exotic matter, one that would have negative energy characteristics similar to cosmic string material and would likewise be able to stabilize and sustain thresholds, but that could be transported at faster-than-light speeds via a metric engineering drive."

"Expansion in the Entelechy," his brother declaimed, "has always been limited by the time needed to transport cosmic string material to one terminus of a new threshold, the creation of the threshold, and then the transport time as the other ter-minus is moved into position. With distances of hundreds, even thousands, of light-years, this means that the rate of expansion is slow, to say the least."

"If our predictions are correct," Hu said haughtily, "and we're able to locate a transportable form of negative matter, then we might even be able to design new forms of thresholds, themselves capable of being moved at faster-than-light speeds. And *then* humanity would be free to expand throughout the galaxy at unimaginable speeds."

"Throughout the galaxy?" Mu scoffed. "Throughout the *universe!*"

"And," Jida said, smiling sweetly but with an edge beneath her voice, "I imagine you boys will make them pay dearly for the privilege, won't you?"

The two corvids only exchanged a quick glance and grinned hungrily.

FORTY-THREE

To be "commander" of the *Further* was a somewhat nebulous concept, I quickly discovered. As the spokesperson for the majority shareholder, I was able to make decisions—or at least cast a tie-breaking vote—on large-scale decisions affecting the ship as a whole. On the small scale, though, the various departments and groups that made up the ship's crew were functionally autonomous, essentially their own little fiefdoms. So long as they carried out their designated role, the departments were free to govern themselves however they saw fit. Most had adopted a more or less strict hierarchical structure, individual workers reporting to supervisors, who themselves reported to department heads, with the department heads themselves directly answerable to me. But a few of the departments, particularly those that constituted only a handful of sentients, had adopted more novel organizational approaches.

Astrogation was, so far as I was aware, made up of only three individuals. The department head, and member of the command crew, was Xerxes. Ey was assisted by two others, though it was some days into our shakedown cruise before I discovered who. At first, all I knew was that Xerxes didn't appear to be terribly busy and that ey could often be found in the Atrium watching the birds.

It was there that I found em, with still a day's journey ahead of us before we reached Aglibol.

I had been rambling around the ship, trying to familiarize myself further with its layout, and been stymied by the fact that some of the corridors and compartments had been restructured even since I had passed them last, only a few days before. In the end, all I really managed to do was tire myself out and make the nodding acquaintance of a hundred or so of the crew I'd not previously met. At the end of a few hours of that, I was ready to get off my feet for a while.

A short tram ride carried me to the Atrium, where I knew, if nothing else, the large-scale structures would have remained principally unchanged, I could find a place to sit, and someone might be willing to bring me something to drink. I was right on all three counts; though, since my last visit, the café appeared to have shifted a few meters to one side to make room for a collection of chairs that seemed to be some sort of virtual reality parlor or gaming area, those in the chairs connected via interlink in a simulated sensorium.

Picking up a tall glass of ice-cold water from the café, I wandered into the park to find a comfortable place to rest my legs, and chanced upon Xerxes, sitting on a bench, head titled back, eyeless gaze fixed on some point high above. I looked up and saw a small flock of birds wheeling overhead.

"You're not disturbing me, Captain, if that's the reason for your hesitation."

I'd been standing behind Xerxes, some meters off, and as ey had said, I'd indeed been hesitant to approach, reluctant to interrupt what seemed to be a private moment.

"Thanks," I said simply and, closing the distance to the bench, settled down beside em. "I keep forgetting that you see in all directions."

"Any light that hits my surface registers," Xerxes said, sighing, "though I find I only pay attention to a small percentage of the visual information at any given time."

I glanced at the flock overhead, which seemed to shift and move like a single organism as it swooped and dove back and forth above the treetops, darting first one way and then another. "Birdwatching again, eh? Is it a habit of yours, if you don't mind me asking?"

Xerxes shrugged. "I suppose—that it is a habit, that is, and not that I mind you asking, which I don't. A few incarnations ago my signal was intercepted by a planet colonized in the later days of the so-called Diaspora by sentients descended from uplifted terrestrial avians."

"Bird people?"

"Precisely. And in the years I spent with them, observing and cataloguing their culture, I was forever amazed to find preserved in their habits the biological imperatives of their subsentient ancestors."

"Such as?"

"Well, flocking behavior, principally. Whenever they moved from one population center to another during their seasonal migrations, they would spread out over the landscape like black clouds, tens of thousands of flightless individuals in any given cluster, and yet without any central authority or guiding intelligence, they still managed to move essentially as one, maintaining set distances each from another, the mass moving almost as a single organism."

"Just like a flock of birds," I said, watching the cloud of birds darting back and forth overhead.

"Exactly like a flock of birds," Xerxes agreed. "The scientists and sociologists of the avian culture had spent generations studying their own inborn imperatives, and had developed whole classes of mathematics devoted to continuum dynamic predictions and the analysis of the effects of individual fluctuations on group movements, and in the end, the only result of the countless years of labor was a single, simple statement."

Ey paused thoughtfully.

"Well?" I asked, at length. "What was it?"

Xerxes turned eir eyeless face to me. "We are animals, and we do as animals must."

I took a long sip of my water. "That seems somewhat...bleak."

"Only if one finds the notion of being an animal as something to be avoided. If anything, the avians found it to be a tremendous comfort."

"They were...comforted? By someone saying that they were no better than animals?"

Xerxes shook eir head. "They wouldn't have said 'no better,' and I won't, either. It assumes some hierarchy with an animal at one extreme and the speaker at another, and is suggestive of nothing so much as the ancient notion of a 'great chain of being,' in which organisms were ranked by how closely they approached some divine ideal." Ey paused and looked at me. "You are not a holder of an irrational belief in some divine, are you, Captain Stone?"

I took another sip of water, thoughtfully. "If you mean do I believe in a god, or gods, some supreme intelligence that exists outside the observable universe, then the answer would be no. However, by the same token, I can't say to you definitively that none exist. We simply lack substantial evidence to make a decision one way or another."

Xerxes gave a small nod, pursing his metallic lips. "A supremely defensible position, Captain. And one that goes to support the avians' contention." Xerxes glanced around, a gesture that was clearly for my benefit, to indicate the variegated crewmembers who were scattered through the Atrium. "The Human Entelechy takes great pride in its name, and in the notion that it has extended the franchise of 'humanity' to all of the children of Earth—biological, synthetic, and otherwise. The avian culture among which I lived came to a related, but opposite conclusion. Rather than saying that all sentients were humans, as no clear dividing line between animal and human could be drawn, the avians concluded that all sentients were animals, though with varying levels of sophistication and degrees of expression. There was no ideal to which they were evolving, no divine atop a great chain of being, but rather an accumulation of instinct and tradition carried down to them by their forebears. And as such, there was no shame in recognizing that, as animals, there were certain biological necessities that were their inheritance and that they would no sooner escape than you could the need to consume quantities of hydrogen hydroxide."

I lifted my glass in a mock salute and took another long swallow. "And that's why you watch birds?"

Xerxes shrugged. "No," ey said simply. "I watch them because I find it difficult to predict what they'll do next, and that helps me pass the time."

FORTY-FOUR

On the morning of the fifth day out from the Ouroboros ship-yards, the command crew gathered on the bridge to watch as the bubble of distorted space around us collapsed, and the *Further* dropped back into normal space.

Before us hung the purple-and-green world of Aglibol, an Entelechy world some forty light-years away from our starting point. Instantly reconnected to the infostructure, we were flooded with congratulations, queries, and well wishes, and we paused to bask for a moment in the knowledge that our shakedown cruise had been a complete success.

Things wouldn't be that easy again for a long, long while.

FORTY-FIVE

Celebrations, both impromptu and planned, sprang up all over the Entelechy as word of our successful voyage rippled outward. Interest in the *Further* had been limited for decades, even longer, and it had taken my unexpected return for Zel and Maruti and the others to whip up enough support to complete construction. Now, countless citizens of the Entelechy were regretting their decision not to take part, and the intelligence of the *Further* reported that it was fielding an unending series of requests by individuals, groups, and worlds to take part in the project.

That night, a dinner and reception was held aboard the ship itself, in a grand ballroom configured especially for the event. It was like the night of the *Further* fundraiser, but on a much grander scale, as dignitaries transited in from all over the Entelechy to attend.

There was the kind of aimless, shuffling meet and greet that seems to cross cultures and eras, and I was introduced by any number of crewmembers to an endless parade of names and faces I'll never recall, whether family or friends or fellow members of whatever group or culture or doctrine the crewmember represented. It reminded me of nothing so much than an open house at a secondary school, parents, students, and teachers mingling uneasily, and as I wandered the grand room with a glass of some spirit or other, smiling politely and trying to tune out the underlying buzz of interlink communication that whispered at the edge of hearing, I wondered how my father, not a gregarious man by nature, had weathered so many years of such gatherings at the National Public School.

Finally, bells chimed from somewhere high above us, and the throng reconfigured as tables and chairs rose from the floor. Dinner was about to begin.

I found myself sitting at a round table with faces familiar and new. To my left sat one body of Jida Shuliang, who was temporarily reconnected via interlink to the rest of the legion while the ship was back in real-time range of the infostructure; her other two bodies were positioned elsewhere throughout the room. To my right sat Maruti and his guest, and opposite sat Zel, flanked by a pair of statuesque women.

Amelia Apatari had declined the invitation to attend, and I could understand her wanting to avoid any awkwardness, but the Amelia emulation in my signet ring had chosen the opportunity to mingle and had projected herself onto the table to take part in the discussion. Sitting primly on a little holographic chair, she was dressed in an elaborate high-waisted skirt and jacket that she assured me was a perfect replica of that worn by one of the heroines of *The Chronicles of Zenna*, a seemingly endless series of fantasy novels she'd devoured as a kid, all about a pair of girls, one a Kiwi and the other a Brit, transported to a strange world of magic. Amelia confessed that she felt not a little like Melanie and Kate these days, herself.

"So, Captain Stone," the woman to Zel's left said as subsentient drones set drinks and starter dishes on the table in front of us, "I imagine it must be difficult for a man with your…limitations to be thrust into such a challenging role, no?" She smiled, and her tone was all sweetness and light, but I could feel the edge of a knife beneath her words. Introduced to me as Cirea t'Stralla, Executive Emeritus of the Pethesilean Mining Consortium, she could have been Zel's twin but that she had green hair instead of blue, and had both eyes intact.

"Well, Cirea," I said with a smile, "my mother always said that limitations are hurdles, not walls, and that it's best to jump right over them instead of worrying about climbing."

Cirea exchanged a glance with the woman on Zel's other side, who chuckled ruefully. She'd been introduced as Renwa t'Dianor s'Foian ch'Girasil, the Pethesilean Mining Consortium's chief strategist, and though she'd not spoken a word to me yet, I got the distinct impression that she was carrying on a lively conversation with the other two Pethesileans via interlink. From the glances she kept shooting my way and the cold smiles that spread occasionally across their faces, I decided it was probably best I wasn't able to hear her comments or jokes or whatever they might be, since I doubted seriously they were terribly flattering to me.

"What in the Demiurge's name is a hurdle?" burbled the individual sitting beside Maruti. Apparently genetically engineered to live in a heavy-gravity environment, his wattled skin a shade of green that suggested photosynthesis might be part of his diet, the Demiurgist, introduced to me only as Hierocrat Nmimn, looked like a cross between a sumo wrestler and a toad, and wouldn't have been out of place if cast as a monster on an episode of *Doctor Who*.

"An ancient sport," Maruti explained, gesturing slightly with his glass. "Primitives set up obstacles and raced each other while running and jumping over them, sometimes on foot and sometimes riding on the backs of enslaved subsentients."

Nmimn rolled his bug eyes at me and took a few gasping breaths. "Your mother seems to have employed cruel metaphors, Captain Stone. She delighted in the enslavement of subsentients, I take it?"

"Horses weren't slaves," Amelia chimed in. "It was more like a symbiotic relationship, I'd say. I was no fan of steeplechase, myself, but then, I didn't much care for boxing, either."

::What do you know about horses?:: I subvocalized, my words sent only to Amelia, the interlink equivalent of whispering behind my hand.

::Only what I learned from reading *Taimi Taitto in the Wild West*,:: Amelia replied with a nonvocal smirk. ::But I'm getting tired of this whole more-evolved-than-thou routine from the Amazon Triplets and Mister Toad, aren't you?::

::Just a bit.::

Jida seemed to recognize our mounting discomfort and, as a product of an earlier era herself must have sympathized, because she quickly came to our rescue.

"Surely," she said, her tone casual, "accusations of enslavement, perhaps unfounded, are not relegated to the distant past. What about the self-proclaimed Subsentient Separatists?"

Nmimn harrumphed, his thick jowls shaking, and Maruti took a long sip of his drink, while the three Amazons bristled visibly.

"Separatists?" I asked.

"They're what your era would call a 'fringe group,' Captain," Jida explained. "They're a loose confederation of individuals who claim that all cognition, even the low-level processing of a subsentient drone or insect, is sacred and that the Entelechy's use of drones for menial labor amounts to nothing more than slavery. They're known for declaiming that the Entelechy is built on the back of subsentients and that we should shut down the threshold network and return to some imagined pristine existence, in harmony with all cognition."

"They're lunatics," Cirea said dismissively.

"They're a menace," growled Nmimn.

"Yes," Jida said, nodding slowly, "but it's important to remember that…"

She trailed off, her mouth hanging open and her eyes widening as something across the room caught her attention. I looked in that direction and saw a pair of strangely dressed figures entering the room. With rows of horns on their heads and their skin coded jet black, they had some sort of symbol on their foreheads—three interlocking circles in a triangle—and were wearing floor-length white robes and heavy black boots.

I watched as the two waved to someone off to my left, and then saw the answering waves from the three Anachronists I'd run into earlier in the corridor—the midshipwoman, the redshirt, and the sailor suit. Were the horns and jet-black skin another historical "re-creation"?

"I…" Jida began. I glanced back her way and saw that her face had frozen in a mask of anger and hatred. She sat so rigid her blood might have turned to solid ice in her veins. "You'll have to excuse me," she said hastily, and then stood up quickly, the chair flowing seamlessly back into the floor at her feet. "I've suddenly lost my appetite."

She strode quickly away in the opposite direction, her foot-falls sounding like gunshots on the floor, and I could see the other two Jida bodies following closely after, their expressions just as grave.

"What was *that* about?" I said, looking from Maruti to Zel.

"Damnable poor taste, if you ask me," Maruti said, shaking his head.

"Iron Mass," Zel said simply, her gaze flicking over to the table where the two horned figures were now sitting. "As though these *Anachronists* weren't noisome enough with their childish playact-ing, they chose to re-create true horrors as well."

I'd remembered what my escort had told me about the Iron Mass. I knew that they'd been "bad neighbors" but still didn't have a clear idea of what they'd done that was so horrible. "They were a 'lost culture,' right?"

"Not the first," Cirea said thoughtfully, "but certainly one of the worst. The Iron Mass was formerly a planetary culture of the Human Entelechy whose threshold was dismantled when they proved to be habitually antisocial. Their misguided beliefs led them to reject all digital consciousness and artificial life of any kind."

"Yes," thrummed the toad-thing Nmimn. "But while their strange customs were tolerated so long as they were harming no one but themselves, with the rise of the one known as the Scourge of the Divine Ideal, and the bloody holy war they called the Second Lesser Effort, they brought pain and suffering to count-less millions of Entelechy citizens, after which the threshold to their world was permanently dismantled, and they were cut off forever from the rest of the Entelechy."

"Most of us know it only from history, of course," Maruti said, "but Jida was alive in those days, some five thousand years ago. Can you imagine what it must have been like to live through those times?"

I thought about the rogue nations of the 22C, those who refused to join the world community and continued to wage wars fought by their ancestors centuries before, all in the name of one myth or another. "Yes," I said sadly. "I'm afraid that I can."

■ ■ ■ ■ ■

After dinner, everyone gathered in an adjacent auditorium, where a group of dramatists were staging a play to commemorate the *Further*'s successful maiden voyage. While I'm pretty sure that Gilbert and Sullivan hadn't intended *HMS Pinafore* to be set on a solar sailship of the 27C, nor for Captain Corcoran to be portrayed by the descendant of uplifted meercats, I think they would most likely have been pleased by the production.

FORTY-SIX

The next morning, I gathered together the command crew representing the principal shareholders. With nothing to see from the bridge but the slowly turning Aglibol, and nowhere to go until the ship's stores of energy were resupplied, I suggested that we meet in the café overlooking the Atrium.

"Well, troops," I said, setting down my cup of buna, while the others settled into chairs at the surrounding tables, "where are we going next?"

With the shakedown cruise successfully completed, the *Further* was ready for its first new mission.

"Isn't that really up to you, Captain Stone?" Xerxes said. "After all, as majority shareholder in the *Further*, the Plenum is in a position to select whatever destination it likes, with the wishes of the other shareholders following in subsequent missions."

"True," I said. "And since I'm the sole Voice of the Plenum on the ship, the decision is mine, and I'm deciding to open the floor for suggestions. So"—I glanced around the room—"any suggestions?"

The responses were hardly surprising, given our previous discussions. Zel and the brothers Grimnismal wanted to search for their exotic matter and had laid out a list of likely places to begin looking. Maruti, for his part, wanted to search for proof of the Demiurgist doctrine and suggested that we journey to a particular planetary nebula, some distance from Entelechy space, that early reconnaissance probes suggested had some interesting characteristics. Even our waitron Ailuros had a contribution; though, given her brief history with Maruti, I understood her suggestion that we seek out a possible home for feckless chimpanzee philanderers to be an unsubtle jab in his direction, to which Maruti only shrugged, a halfhearted expression of apology on his face.

With Ailuros's suggestion as a possible exception, all the recommendations were precisely what I would have anticipated. But when all the other principal shareholders had voiced their suggestions, Xerxes had so far remained silent, sitting near the open window, eir attention on birds in flight.

"Xerxes," I said, calling out, "what was that pulsar you told me about the night we met?"

Ey turned eir eyeless face to me, a gesture entirely for my benefit. "The binary pulsar we discussed on Cronos, do you mean?"

I nodded.

Ey sighed. "The pulsar is part of a binary system, four hundred and sixty light-years from Sol, a little under fifty light-years from our present position. It was known by scientists in your era, Captain, as PSR J0437-4715. With a period of only five-point-seven-five milliseconds, it is the nearest and brightest millisecond pulsar to Sol. The rotating neutron star is about one-point-three-five solar masses, and its white dwarf companion is point-one-three solar masses, and the system has an orbital period of five and a half days. Five billion years old, the neutron star consists of two components, a nonthermal power-law spectrum generated in the pulsar magnetosphere, with a photon index of about two and a thermal spectrum emitted by heated polar caps, with a temperature decreasing outward from two MK to half an MK. The neutron star surface is covered by a helium atmosphere. Unlike other pulsars, it lacks a synchrotron pulsar wind."

The other command crew began shifting, restless.

"Um, yes, OK, thanks, Xerxes," I said. "Now, could you tell us *why* this particular pulsar interests you?"

"Ah." Xerxes nodded. "Yes. Well, the details of this binary pulsar have been well established since the Information Age, but in recent years, the periodicity of the pulsar has changed slightly—no more than a few hundred thousandths of a percent—but the orbital period and radial velocity of the binary has slightly increased, suggesting that the mass of the system has changed."

"That's impossible," Zel said dismissively.

Xerxes shrugged. "I'll allow that it is definitely improbable, First. But impossible? Through natural mechanisms, certainly. Neither the Exode nor the Entelechy know of any means through which such a system could lose mass so quickly, which suggests an intelligent agency."

"And how long would it take to get there?" I asked.

"From our present location? Travel time would be five days, the maximum distance the *Further* can travel before needing to stop and allow the metric engineering drives to recharge. But we wouldn't be able to leave for the better part of a day while the drives recharge."

I clapped my hands and rubbed them together. "I think we have a winner, folks," I said, smiling. "We're going there."

I climbed to my feet as the others raised their voices in protest, all but Xerxes, who turned serenely back toward the window.

"Ailuros," I said, waving to our waitron. "I've been thinking about taking a tour of the drive engineering decks, and this seems as good a time as any. I hate to drag you away from waiting tables, but if you're not terribly busy, would you mind giving me a brief tour?"

The cat shrugged out of her apron. "Why not?"

I followed her toward the door, the complaints of the others drifting after me. "Don't worry," I said, glancing over my shoulder. "We'll get to all of your ideas, sooner or later. But I left Earth to explore, and I'm damned if I'm not going to do a little *exploring*!"

I still wasn't sure why the Plenum had picked me as their representative on the crew, but I wasn't about to look a gift horse in the mouth. Since I'd stepped through the threshold onto Alpha Centauri, completing in a few strides the journey I'd dedicated my life in the 22C to accomplishing, I'd been unsure what I would do next, what frontiers there might remain for an explorer like me to visit.

Now we would see.

FORTY-SEVEN

Leaving the café, Ailuros and I boarded a tram, which whisked us off toward drive engineering.

"I'm somewhat surprised you haven't toured the drive engineering section previously, sir."

"I wanted to do so," I answered, "but I think that I wore out my welcome a bit with the brothers Grimnismal the other day, when they were giving me a tutorial on wormhole engineering. I didn't get the impression that they'd be eager to chauffer me around their deck on a sightseeing tour."

"Well," the cat said with a slow blink and a nod, "the corvid brothers are known for getting on the nerves of others, so it probably served them right. Believe me, I work in drive engineering because I love my generator, not because I hold any especial affection for the Grimnismals. At least waiting tables in the café

I'm likely to be acknowledged for my efforts on occasion, perhaps even thanked. The brothers view everyone as a potential audience for one of their self-aggrandizing lectures about their personal brilliance and how the exotic material whose existence they've predicted is going to revolutionize the Entelechy."

"Do you really think that stuff exists?"

"A completely unknown type of material that will allow us to maneuver thresholds anywhere in the galaxy at faster-than-light velocities?" She smiled, eyes half-lidded, an expression I recognized from any number of housecats I'd had as a kid. "Well, it would be nice, wouldn't it? But I wouldn't hold your breath waiting for it, sir."

In a matter of moments, we'd reached drive engineering, the central deck of the ship. It appeared to be one immense space, some two kilometers across, the ceiling overhead twenty meters above the ceiling below. The tram stopped near a network of gantries halfway in between, with a sphere a short distance meters away connected to the walls in all directions by a network of thick pipes or cables.

"Careful climbing out of the tram, sir," Ailuros said, vaulting out ahead of me. "Step too far and you'll end up bobbing up and down at the change point, and that can be pretty unsettling to the digestion, I assure you."

At first, I had no idea what she was saying. Then I stepped out onto the gantry and looked down to see a pair of crewmen walking upside down on the *other side*. It was then that I understood that I was standing precisely at the central plane of the *Further*, the level to which gravity in both hemispheres pointed and that the "floor" ten meters below me was another ceiling in the opposite direction.

It was a strange sort of vertigo, standing at the edge of the walkway and looking down, with nothing but empty space before me, but I understood what Ailuros had meant. *Down* as a concept ended somewhere just a few centimeters beneath my feet, so if I fell over the side, I'd be falling *up* for a moment, then down again past the center point, then up, then back down, yo-yoing back and forth across the center plane of gravity until I burned off enough momentum of air friction that I just hung motionless in the middle, my head and feet both attracted "down" to my waist. I could see that it would be a bit upsetting to the stomach, to say the least, and was glad I hadn't had a large breakfast that morning.

Ailuros had already set out across the gantry, heading to the sphere in the near distance. I hurried after her, careful to keep well away from the edges of the walkway.

I caught up with the cat as she stopped a few meters from the sphere. Standing so close to it, I realized it was much bigger than I'd earlier guessed, at least nine meters in diameter, and that it had only seemed small when seen against the vast stretch of the two-kilometer-wide space.

"That's the power generator," Ailuros said proudly, and I could hear the faint rumble of a contented purr beneath her words.

"It's pretty big," I said, with a low whistle.

The cat nodded. "Couldn't be any larger and still be able to maintain the necessary negative energy state in the interior, couldn't be any smaller and still be able to contain a sufficient region of quantum vacuum. It sits at the exact center of the ship's central sphere, which is some two kilometers across." She pointed to the network of pipes and cables radiating out from the sphere toward the walls, a kilometer away in every direction, making the generator look like a spider sitting at the center of its web. "Those run to the drive elements in the ring, which extend another kilometer beyond the hull." She looked over at me, smiling. "Did you know that if the generator were a scale model of Sol, then the ring begins roughly where Earth's orbit would be located?"

I allowed that I didn't, as a matter of fact.

"As I'm sure you're aware, unlike convention craft or planet-side structures, the *Further's* power generator draws its energy directly from the quantum vacuum itself."

"Right," I said, nodding. To prove I wasn't a completely ignorant primitive, I added, "In my day, it was sometimes called zero-point energy, since it's the energetic ground state of empty space."

The cat nodded appreciatively. "A fairly apt name, I suppose. I'm a bit surprised to discover that the quantum vacuum was known about, even in ancient times."

I smiled slightly. "Well, it wasn't all stone axes and mastodon hunts, I assure you."

"Oh, no disrespect intended, sir," Ailuros said hastily. "It's just that I've been studying the quantum vacuum for three life-times now, and only now do I feel like I've even begun to grasp the essentials. I was formerly a philosopher of sorts, I suppose you could say, but my research led me to an analysis of physics, which led me to the study of the quantum vacuum, which led me ultimately to the *Further*. The corvid brothers may be more interested in the metric engineering capacity of their drives"—she gestured toward the outer hull and the equator of dark machinery that circled all around—"if not the sound of their own voices, but my passion is reserved only for the power generator itself."

A wide platform circled the sphere, which lay half in one hemisphere and half in the other. I circled slowly around the sphere, which seemed an unremarkable ball of dark, gray metal. "Something confuses me, Ailuros. If the quantum vacuum represents an essentially inexhaustible supply, why aren't similar generators more widely used? And especially given that the Entelechy uses power as a means of exchange. Why don't planets or habitats build similar engines to supply power for themselves?"

"I've been arguing that for years," she said, somewhat sadly, "but I'm afraid the economics simply don't bear out. The energy required to construct the generator in the first place far outweighs its capacity to generate more. It simply isn't a cost-effective solution as a means of power generation for a world to adopt as a source of power."

"Ah. There were similar issues in my day, I suppose. Gold was a valued commodity, because of its rarity, but anyone could generate more gold if they wanted to do so by transmuting platinum into gold by bombarding it with neutrons, but the cost of the production was more than the result was worth."

"Mmm. Alchemy." She nodded knowingly. "I knew that was practiced by the ancients. Well, the whole system costs an arm and a tail just to keep running. Every time the drives create a bubble of distorted space, it costs roughly the entire energetic output of a developed world over the course of a standard day, and that's after pouring the equivalent of a planet's energetic output for one hundred years into building them in the first place. That's why you're not likely to see many habitats and ships using metric engineering to induce artificial gravity on board, when you can just use centrifugal spin at an infinitesimally small fraction of the cost."

Out of the corner of my eye, I saw another tram lower down through the ceiling and come to rest on the gantry. A pair of unlikely looking creatures stepped out and started for us. It was the Ganesh, Vinayaka, and the blue-skinned, four-armed Sarasvati, the Vedas who'd visited me on Earth and who'd hosted my brief visit to their habitat, Thousand-petaled Lotus. I'd glimpsed them the night before in the reception but had just assumed that they were visiting dignitaries. All the dignitaries had left the ship overnight, though, so the fact that they were still on board meant that they were actually part of the crew.

I felt a bit guilty to find myself so uncomfortable at their approach, but as nice as they were, I wasn't at all used to being worshiped as a god and didn't much care for the idea.

"*Namaste*," I said, bowing slightly, with my hands pressed palm to palm.

"I bow to the light in you," said the elephant-headed Vinayaka, echoed by Sarasvati, her bright-orange areolas like late-stage main sequence stars in a bright-blue sky.

"Sri Rama," the blue-skinned woman said, her red hair hanging around her head like a fiery sunset, "we bear greetings to you from the well-traveled Exode probe, Xerxes 298.47.29A, our superior, who bid us relate to you the news of our impending departure."

"Superior?" It took me a moment to parse that. "Are you posted to astrogation, then?"

"That felicity is ours, Sri Rama," the elephant-man said. "And our superior Xerxes has instructed us to inform you that the course to your wisely chosen destination has been laid in and that the moment the power generator has finished its worthy task of recharging the ship's drive the *Further* will be in a state of readiness to depart."

"If you don't mind me asking," Ailuros put in casually, "why didn't Xerxes just interlink the captain himself?"

Sarasvati's cheeks went slightly purple, and I realized she was blushing.

"We requested the task," Vinayaka explained, "having not yet been presented the opportunity to visit Sri Rama since boarding his vimana."

"Well, um, thanks?" I said, unsure what the appropriate protocol might be. "I, uh, don't have to remind you that I'm not Rama, right? That I share a name with the mythical figure, and that's all?"

"Ah," Sarasvati said, with a broad wink. "It is just as you say."

"Yes," the Ganesh nodded slowly, his tone deliberate, "we would certainly not gainsay the *commanding officer* in front of his crew, 'Captain Stone.'"

"No, you are certainly not Sri Rama, the delighter of all, whose graceful form is an embodiment of bliss and is dark as a rainy cloud." The blue-skinned woman pressed her hands together and inclined her head.

"But if you were he, and not mere *captain*," Vinayaka said, "the praiseworthy lord of Sita, the chief of Raghu's line, rich in splendor and ever propitious, then we would endlessly praise your name."

With that, the pair bowed deeply again and quickly retreated back toward the tram.

I could only sigh.

"I don't know, sir," Ailuros said, watching them go. "Suddenly, the corvid brothers don't seem so bad. At least they've never tried to *worship* me."

FORTY-EIGHT

Since we had hours—or a nontrivial percentage of standard days, I suppose—to go before the drives finished recharging, I figured it was time to take Arluq Max'inux up on her offer of a ride in the *Compass Rose*. If nothing else, I wanted to learn my way around the controls if we were going to be using it as a landing craft.

I called ahead by interlink so that, when I reached the landing bay, Arluq had the *Compass Rose* prepped and ready. The bay doors were already open, the interior atmosphere held in place by fields, and beyond I could see part of the green-and-purple curve of Aglibol and the starry skies beyond.

"You ready to get going, Arluq?" I called out as the tram that had brought me backed away to some other destination.

"Sure thing, RJ, but put this on first." She held out what appeared to be a wide belt, just long enough to fit around my waist.

"What's this?" I took it from her and held it up to the light. It was a dull-gray color and was smooth and cool to the touch, but surprisingly heavy, weighing maybe four or five kilograms.

"If you can't swim, you've got to wear protection when you get in the water, right?" Arluq produced another belt, almost identical to the first, if not perhaps a bit longer. In a swift movement, she wrapped it around her waist, and when the two ends met, they joined seamlessly. "Same idea, but a mantle is good for all kinds of environments."

I shrugged and did as she'd done, and found that the two ends fused as soon as they touched without any assistance from me. "A mantle, eh?"

"Right. It's keyed to react automatically to changes in the environment, but it responds to manual interlink commands, too. Give it a try, why don't you?"

I looked down at the wide gray belt around my middle, and looked up, feeling a bit lost and helpless. "Give *what* a try?"

"This," Arluq said, and suddenly, the wide belt began to flow and change. In the blink of an eye, it had spread out so that, instead of a wide gray belt, Arluq was now wearing a gray one-piece bodysuit that covered her from thick neck to the tips of her fingers and toes, leaving only her head exposed. "Mine's got more reserve mass than yours, naturally, because I'm a pretty big girl, but I could probably make do with one as small as yours in a pinch."

"What…what just happened?"

"The mantle's made up of a network of nanoscopic robots and smart matter. It can go from completely transparent"—suddenly the gray suit turned completely transparent, visible only as a

glassy sheen over the clothes underneath—"to entirely opaque"—
and now it went jet black, soaking up all light around it—"from
flexible as silk to solid as fullerene. It can maintain internal pressure and temperatures at optimal levels, whether the exterior of
the suit is hitting a hard vacuum or open flame." She stepped over
to a low shelf rising up out of the deck and picked up a greenish-
gray lump. "Go on, RJ. Just tell it to reconfigure into a suit."

::Make a suit?:: I subvocalized.

It felt like being suddenly immersed in warm water for a split
second, and then it was over, and I was dressed from head to toe
in gray metal. Literally from head to toe, I discovered, reaching
up to my face and finding it completely covered by the material
of the mantle.

"Arluq?" I tried to say out loud, but only managed a grunt.
::*Arluq*?:: I subvocalized, panicking.

"Relax, RJ. Just tell it to roll back and expose your face, is all."

I did as she said, and an instant later, my eyes, mouth, and
nose were uncovered, though the mantle still covered my neck,
ears, and hair.

"Don't go doing that for too long without a supply of raw
matter, OK?" Arluq stepped over and slapped the greenish-gray
lump on my back. When she pulled away, it hung there across
my shoulders like a small backpack. "The mantle can convert this
into breathable atmosphere and liquid for hydration, using the
waste heat of the nanofacture to warm the suit's interior. It can
run for a while on its own reserves if you just have the mantle
on you, but once it starts cannibalizing its own material to produce air and water for you, the lifespan of the mantle gets cut to
a fraction of a percent. With enough raw matter on board, it can
sustain you indefinitely."

"That's amazing!" I said.

"You think so?" Arluq said, unimpressed. "I don't know. I'm working on a model that doesn't need to haul around all this raw stuff, but for the time being, this bulky thing's going to have to do."

• • • • •

Arluq refused to believe how impressed I was when, a short while later, after navigating the *Compass Rose* out of the landing bay into empty space and then engaging the metric engineering drive, we traveled a million kilometers in a matter seconds.

"We didn't even hit a quarter-light yet," she said dismissively as we dropped back into normal space after the brief hop.

When I asked if there was time for an EVA, for me to test the mantle against hard vacuum, she just shrugged.

"Whatever you say, RJ," she said, shaking her massive head. "When you get done playing in the shallow end of the ocean, though, let me know, and I'll open this thing up and show you how it can *really* move."

FORTY-NINE

The drives finally recharged, the *Further* left Aglibol behind, once more losing connection with the infostructure, cut off from the rest of the Entelechy. But the last time we'd been cut off, we'd been traveling toward another Entelechy world, secure in the knowledge that, if our shakedown cruise was successful, we'd shortly be back safely in reach of the threshold network, tied once more into the data sea of the infostructure. This time, though, bound for a binary pulsar never visited before by anyone from the Entelechy, and unsure what we'd find or where we'd be going from there, it was unclear when we'd once more be in contact with the rest of civilization. As a result, where our first voyage was one of excitement and anticipation, this second journey seemed to take on a more somber, even melancholy tone, though no less expectant.

There was little to do for the next five days but kill time. Amelia quickly got bored of talking to me about old times and retreated back into the signet ring for a few days to catch up on the twelve thousand years of history she'd missed. She told me that she'd been learning to fly all sorts of strange craft in emulations she'd pulled from the infostructure or from the *Further*'s memory archives, indulging her love for flight whenever or however the mood struck, in often strange combinations, flying 24C hovercraft over medieval France, a Sopwith Camel over the ice volcanoes of Titan, Diaspora-era reaction rockets in close orbit over a terraformed Mars, and on and on.

I tried to distract myself with reading but found little enthusiasm for it. I was anxious to see what we'd discover when reaching this pulsar of Xerxes's, fully aware of the fact that we'd be the first living eyes—for varying definitions of "living"—to lay eyes on the system from close up. I'd left Earth behind in the 22C to explore, and this was my first opportunity to go anywhere that those before me hadn't already gone countless times before.

On the second day of our journey to the pulsar, I ran into Maruti in the Atrium and discovered by chance that he and I shared a hobby, a passion for a game that was ancient even in my day.

The game of Go had been more than two thousand years old when Eiji Hayakawa, my commanding officer of *Orbital Patrol Cutter 972*, taught me the rudiments of the game. So I was amazed to discover that it had survived more or less unchanged into the modern day.

"I remember countless games with my Uncle Cornelius," Maruti said as he arranged the board and pieces between us. He'd fabricated a nineteen-by-nineteen grid, just like the one on which I'd learned the game, and invited me to his quarters to pass the time with a game. "Now, *there* was a chimp who knew the value of a fine cigar."

I took black, and Maruti white, and then we began to play as the chimp launched into a seemingly endless—and seemingly pointless—anecdote about his uncle. As the game wore on, though, and the stones were slowly categorized as dead, alive, or unsettled, Maruti's story finally drew to a close, and we chatted aimlessly for a while about past games and the men who'd taught us. Finally, though, our concentration on the game won out, and our conversation became more and more desultory and brief.

"Atari," I said at length, breaking the silence.

Maruti looked up, startled, his expression confused. "What did you say?"

"Oh, I'm sorry." I grinned sheepishly. "Old habit." I pointed to his white stones remaining on the board, which I'd been gradually encircling with black. "Those stones have only one liberty, and a single move could capture the whole group. That condition used to be known as being in 'atari.'"

"Ah," Maruti said, thoughtfully puffing on his cigar. "My uncle Cornelius had a name for it, too. He called it 'about to get screwed.'"

I goggled.

"I'm sorry," the chimpanzee quickly added, "that's an idiomatic expression that might not translate too well from Cercopean to Information Age English. It means to—"

"No, no," I said, laughing. "I got it just fine."

Maruti sipped his glass of port. "But why, Captain, did you opt to alert me to the fact?"

"Well, that's the old habit part. The man who taught me the game insisted on observing an antique custom, abandoned even in my time, in which the instigator says the word out loud to call their opponent's attention to the potential danger. It's a courtesy, really, nothing more."

"Mmm." Maruti nodded thoughtfully and then plopped a white stone down on the empty juncture, my advantage lost. "Thanks for that, then, Captain. Your move, I think."

FIFTY

As the ship prepared to drop back into normal space, rather than watching from the bridge with just the command crew and department heads, I asked everyone who was interested to join me in the Atrium. The *Further* avatar perched on my shoulder as more than a thousand crewmembers crowded into the park, lining the walkway, spilling over the bandstand and theater shell. Some lay on the grass, propped up on their elbows, watching the domed ceiling high overhead. I'd asked the *Further* to configure the ceiling to display a real-time, true-color image of the hull's exterior view.

We were approaching our destination head-on so that the north pole of the *Further*'s main sphere was pointed directly at the binary pulsar. Only moments remained before the bubble of distorted space collapsed, but we'd already been slowing for hours.

The stars, which had been crowded only a short while before into a red dot directly overhead, were gradually shifting down the scale, spreading apart, barely pinked by our accelerations.

With the crowd around me, the only light that of the pinkish stars overhead, I was reminded of my grandfather's stories of his childhood in America and Independence Day celebrations. The illusion was strengthened when Maruti ambled over, wearing a top hat and tails, drinking some sort of a frozen cocktail.

"I thought I'd dress for the occasion," the chimpanzee said, smiling. "Not all of us opt to wander around stark naked at all hours like Xerxes." He glanced around. "Where is that dour robot, anyway? It's his bloody pulsar we've come to see, isn't it?"

"I didn't realize it was in your purview to deed ownership of stars, exobiologist," said a voice from behind him, "but if that power is yours, I'll happily accept."

Maruti sighed dramatically. "Good ship's evening, Xerxes."

Ey joined us, and the robot, the chimp, and I looked overhead as one, all of us eagerly anticipating our arrival in our own way.

"Just another moment, Captain Stone, and we'll be arriving," said the silver eagle on my shoulder.

"Did I miss it?" chimed the voice of Amelia, projecting onto my other shoulder. "I got caught up in learning to navigate a sail-ship and lost track of time."

"No, little ghost," Xerxes said, "but we'll be there momentarily."

A short distance off, the cetacean Arluq lounged in the bowl of the fountain, luxuriating in the cool water. The brothers Grimnismal were perched on a nearby bench, in some sort of disagreement with the cat Ailuros.

"Shouldn't those two be down in drive engineering?" I said, pointing toward the corvids, asking no one in particular. "Shouldn't someone be looking after the operations?"

"I have things well in hand," the *Further* said, "but if anything should arise, I assure you I'll alert the drive engineers immediately."

"They're busy arguing about Ailuros's proposal to reconfigure the power routing system when we arrive," said Chief Executive Zel, walking over to where we stood. "Ultimately, I think it'll be a question for the principals to decide, since it doesn't look as though they're going to reach an accord anytime soon."

"Captain," said the voice of three Jida bodies in unison, approaching from the other side, "this is probably the best idea you've had yet. We need to have these sorts of gatherings more often. I'm having the *best* time." A pair of escorts walked with them, each flanked by Jida on either side—one a space-adapted anthropoid male who stood almost as tall as Arluq, the other a whip-thin artificial being of some sort who looked to be made of flowing quicksilver and whose laughter was like tinkling bells—and from the gentle caresses the Jidas bestowed on arms of muscle and quicksilver alike, it wasn't terribly hard to imagine what sort of time Jida was having.

"We're almost there," the *Further* said.

"Xerxes," Zel said, "what can we expect to see when we arrive?"

"The display above us is coded to the visual spectrum, blocking out any harmful X-ray radiation or the like coming from the rotating neutron star."

"Yes, but it'll just be two small stars, yes?"

"Essentially," the robot said with a sigh.

"Captain?" the *Further* said. "We are there."

Somewhere between the words "are" and "there," it happened. The stars, now only vaguely pinked, shifted once more in position before freezing in place, once more startling white, and the binary pulsar hung above us.

The *Further* was capable of fairly limited maneuvering in normal space, and so it had brought us in fairly close to the center of the system so as to be in an optimal position. Directly overhead, a pole star to our night sky, hung the pulsar. Somewhere off in the night was a tiny white dwarf companion, only about forty-three thousand times more massive than Earth. Just as had been expected.

What hadn't been expected, however, was that the pulsar might have an asteroid belt, much less a planet.

But this particular pulsar appeared to have both.

"Didn't see *that* coming," Maruti said, doffing his top hat respectfully.

FIFTY-ONE

A short while later, as automated subsentient probes shot out from the *Further* toward the planet and the asteroid belt, the command crew gathered in the bridge, where Xerxes shared eir thoughts on the unexpected appearance of a planetary system.

"Planetary formation around pulsars is rare," ey said, "even exceedingly rare, but not unknown. This pulsar was the result of a core-collapse supernova. Formerly a massive main sequence star, it gradually worked through its available supply of fuel, fusing hydrogen into ever-heavier elements—oxygen and carbon, at first, and then neon, magnesium, silicon, and iron—each time liberating energy released in the form of light and heat. Once the heart of the star began to produce iron, though, fusion gradually slowed, as iron requires more energy to fuse into heavier elements than is released in the process. When the fusion shut off entirely, the enormous outward pressure of heat energy likewise ceased, and the star's own massive gravity caused its core to collapse in less time than it takes to say, condensing from an object roughly the size of Earth to one less than twenty kilometers across—a neutron star.

"This rapid collapse forced together the subatomic particles of the atoms themselves, fusing electrons and protons into electrically neutral neutrons and neutrinos. In the blink of an eye, the huge numbers of out-rushing neutrinos and neutrons collided with the in-rushing outer layers of the star with such force that it rebounded the outer layers back into space, while at the same time fusing them into still heavier elements—zinc, gold, silver, platinum, cobalt, and uranium. And in the example of this star, with temperatures of over one billion degrees Kelvin and neutron densities in excess of 10^{20} cm^{-3}, r-process nucleosynthesis would even have been possible, the fast neutron capture and beta decay producing a whole range of transuranic elements.

"Typically, this debris is ejected from the star at escape velocities and travels out into space. In some cases, of which this was evidently one, the debris fails to escape the dead star's gravity and forms a disc around it. Much like the debris discs surrounding young stars at their birth, this matter has the potential of accreting into larger masses, eventually resulting in planetary formation."

Eir brief lecture ended, Xerxes stood patiently and waited, as everyone sat in silence. I wondered if, like me, they were still parsing out all of the facts ey'd just thrown at us.

"I followed very little of what you just said," Maruti said, breaking the silence, "so you'll have to tell me...Did you happen to explain *that*, by any chance?"

Maruti pointed an unlit cigar at the smart display on the control center, and I leaned forward in the command chair to see for myself.

X-ray emissions bleeding from the pulsar had interfered with extraship communication, meaning that only line-of-sight communication was possible, so the signals the *Further* was receiving were the first since the probes had been launched.

"Um, what are we looking at?" I said. Even the suspicion had sent my heart into my throat, and my hands were gripping the armrests of my chair in vice grips.

"That is the surface of the pulsar planet," the *Further* said.

"No," Maruti sang, and pointed at neat rows of stone structures, like towers or cairns. "I think the captain means, what are *those*?"

FIFTY-TWO

Opinions were sharply divided, but that was hardly surprising.

"And I say that the cairns are undoubtedly the result of alien intelligence!" Maruti shouted.

"Would that it were so," Xerxes answered in a calm that clearly infuriated the chimpanzee, "as it would earn me a signal honor among the Exode to be the first to discover incontrovertible proof of nonterrestrial intelligence, but it simply isn't possible. The simplest solution is that these are purely geological formations, nothing more. We should, instead, be focusing our attention on the missing mass I mentioned previously, which is doubtless a more fruitful avenue of investigation."

"Could life have even evolved in this kind of environment?" I asked.

"Hardly," Zel said, shaking her head. "Any life in the vicinity of the star would have been incinerated when it went supernova, and the level of X-ray radiation from the neutron star would eliminate the possibility that even unicellular life would arise in the aftermath."

"So who built cairns?" Hu Grimnismal asked.

"No one built them, brother!" Mu said, exasperated. "Didn't you hear the robot? They're geological."

"Really?" Hu asked.

"I don't know," the Jida emissary said, lounging in her chair, "they look like the result of architecture to me, however primitive."

"Look," I said, jumping out of the command chair and holding up my hands. "This is getting us nowhere." I turned to the ship's avatar, sitting on its perch on the wall above us. "*Further,* how much power remains in the metric engineering drives?"

"Only a fractional supply, Captain. Not enough to create a bubble of distorted space, I'm afraid."

"But you're able to maneuver a bit in normal space?"

"I have small reaction drives at strategic locations in the outer hull, yes, though their range and use is limited."

I glanced at the image of the planetary system projected on the walls and ceiling around us. Just to my right, the pulsar rotated, while straight ahead, the planet slowly spun.

"Well, one way or another, we're going to that planet. I could take a landing party over in the *Compass Rose,*" I said, "but communication between the shuttle and the *Further* would be spotty at best, right?"

"Correct, sir."

"Are the reaction drives enough to get us there, in that case?"

"Yes," the *Further* answered, "though just barely. Once in place, we'd have to wait until the power generator cycles for a standard day to make any additional maneuvers."

"That's good enough for me. Shall we go?"

The *Further* cocked its head to one side, regarding me with silver eyes. "Sir, might I suggest first sending down additional probes in order to get a better picture of what we might encounter?"

"Come all this way and not get my feet wet? No way, *Further*. I'm seeing this with my own eyes."

"Oh," Jida said, sitting upright excitedly. "I haven't set foot on a completely new planet in *centuries*. Can I come?"

FIFTY-THREE

By the time the *Further* had maneuvered into orbit around the pulsar planet, it was all worked out. The landing party—consisting of Maruti, Xerxes, one of the bodies of the Jida emissary, a planetary scientist named Zaslow, an expert in geodynamics named Bin-Ney, and me. Zaslow was some blend of biological and synthetic, his frame that of a natural-born anthropoid, but his sensory organs were replaced with artificial enhancements, his skin with some form of smart matter, and likely more augments and enhancements that weren't as obvious. Bin-Ney was an anthropoid like me, and I recognized him as one of the Anachronists who'd attended the reception at Aglibol dressed as an ancient killer. Jida shot him angry glances, but he was out of costume, as it were, his skin coded a pale shade of blue, his head completely hairless, wearing a nondescript suit of gray, so she didn't make an issue of it at the moment.

Arluq got the *Compass Rose* ready for takeoff, and the landing party was outfitted with mantles and wrist-mounted projector cuffs. The projectors were intended for use as general multi-tools, not as weapons, but when everyone gathered in the landing bay, I had my cap gun holstered at my side.

"Captain Stone," Xerxes said, a puzzled look on his metal features, "we'll be landing on an uninhabited world in orbit around a dead star. Why could you possibly need to go armed?"

"If I learned anything in the Orbital Patrol, it was that it's always better to walk into an unknown situation and discover the sidearm you brought along wasn't needed than walk in unarmed and discover that it was."

I didn't know how right I was. If I had, I would have brought a hell of a lot more firepower with me.

. . . . .

The *Further* was forced to adopt a non-geosynchronous orbit, since the planet rotated so slowly that a geostationary orbit would be too far away to remain within the planet's gravitational sphere of influence, and the ship couldn't remain stationary with the metric engineering drives, which couldn't draw on enough power to fire up a bubble of distorted space. The X-ray interference of the pulsar meant that only line-of-sight communication would be possible, so the *Further* would only be in range for brief periods.

"Though the planet is somewhat smaller than Original Earth," the *Further* explained via interlink as the landing party and I boarded the *Compass Rose*, "it is denser, with roughly the same mass, meaning that gravity at its surface is roughly one standard gravity. We're currently orbiting at a distance of a few hundred kilometers from the surface, making a complete rotation every ninety and fifty-two hundredths of a minute, by your reckoning,

Captain. Communication will be possible only for roughly ten minutes at a time, followed by eighty minutes of silence before communication is regained."

In other words, once we were on the ground, we'd be on our own for long periods of time. I wasn't bothered. We were all grown-ups, after all, and could look after ourselves. Besides, what was the worst we'd find down there?

We had no idea.

FIFTY-FOUR

I brought the *Compass Rose* down to land on a narrow valley, its bottom featureless and flat, surrounded by ridges and promontories on all sides. The ship had a pretty clever subsentient intelligence driving it that was probably smart enough to take off and land without any help from me, but ever since Arluq had shown me the ropes, I'd been aching for a chance to get the ship out and try her for myself.

"OK," I said, cycling the atmosphere once we'd all climbed inside the airlock, our mantles configured to offer each of us little habitable environments within, all but Xerxes, who could walk out under the light of the dead star as naked as ey did through the corridors of the *Further*. With the air cleared from the lock, no sound traveled, and our voices carried only by interlink. ::Does everyone remember where we parked?::

The others shot me confused looks through the mostly transparent faceplates of their mantles, and I shook my head, the gesture muted by the gently sliding fabric of the mantle, but clear enough to get the point across.

::Never mind. But I'll have you know, in the twenty-second century, that would have been *hilarious*.::

■ ■ ■ ■ ■

Crossing the ridge to the north of the landing site, we found ourselves looking out over a field of cairns. They were arranged in low rows, looking like a plantation or a neatly arranged forest.

::It's just breathtaking, isn't it?:: said Jida.

I had to agree. We skidded down the scree on the north side of the ridge and approached the near edge of the cairn forest.

::Look!:: Maruti sent. ::They're laid out in a grid, like a Go board.::

::That's a pretty damned big game, Maruti,:: I said. ::The towers look to be spaced about three meters apart, and the whole thing must be half a kilometer to a side, at least.::

Xerxes skirted the forest edge to the left, while Bin-Ney and Zaslow hurried ahead, eager to analyze the towers close up. Jida and I approached the nearest of the structures.

::They looked so much smaller on the screen.:: I walked up to the cairn, reaching out to touch its surface. The mantle communicated the texture to my fingers, and I found it was bumpy and irregular, like coral.

::And the robot thinks *these* are just a geological formation?:: Maruti said, coming up to join us.

Each of the cairns stood about twice my height, maybe four meters tall. A slightly darker shade than the surrounding rock, they were wider at the top than the bottom, tapering outward slightly as they rose. Ridges ran along the ground, connecting each cairn to those around it, seemingly made of the same dark-gray material as the cairns themselves.

::I don't know, Maruti,:: Jida said thoughtfully. ::I've seen similar formations in caverns that were the result of nothing more mysterious than dripping water.::

::But laid out with this kind of regularity?:: Maruti waved his arms, indicating the ordered rows of towers. The lines were hardly precise, but they were undeniable. ::And it isn't as though there's any water here, Madam Jida.::

· · · · ·

::Captain Stone,:: Xerxes called from a hundred or so meters away, approaching the ridgeline to the west. ::I believe I've found the mouth of a cave. I think I'll investigate.::

::Go ahead,:: I answered. ::Over these distances, we should be able to maintain contact with one another even if we're not in visual range.::

::Oh, that robot isn't going alone,:: Maruti said, charging after em. ::If anyone's going to find proof of alien intelligence, it's going to be *me*.::

The robot and the chimpanzee disappeared one after the other into the cave mouth, and the rest of us continued to the north, moving slowly through the cairn forest.

::Capt...:: crackled a voice in my head, broken with static. ::This...Zel...the *Further* says that we're about to pass out of... sighted a ship...approaching...::

"Zel, repeat!" I shouted aloud, and then, ::Zel! Can you hear me?::

I turned to Jida, who was just rounding a cairn a dozen or so meters ahead of me.

::Jida,:: I subvocalized. ::Did you make out any of that?::

::Captain…!:: Jida began, raising her arm and pointing at something out of my line of sight, but by the time I realized she was aiming her projector, it was too late. We were under attack.

FIFTY-FIVE

Our attackers must have lain in wait, hidden behind the towering cairns. When Jida stumbled upon them, they'd chosen their moment to fire. The initial barrage of particle beams and larger projectiles rendered our mantles completely rigid and almost entirely opaque so that we were all momentarily trapped and immobile inside our shells. When we'd regained mobility, we'd been dragged together to the edge of the cairn forest and disarmed, our projector cuffs taken, my holstered cap gun with them.

We were surrounded by a dozen or more figures, all armed with some sort of bladed weapons, all wearing segmented pressure suits that looked as though they were made of black iron, giving them the appearance of large insects. But the voices shouting at us over the radio waves, harsh and hate filled as they sounded, were all too human.

I was on my knees, Jida to my left, Zaslow and Bin-Ney to my right.

::What are they saying?:: said Zaslow. We'd scarcely exchanged five words, but I could tell he was close to some sort of breakdown.

::I don't know,:: I said, trying to sound braver than I felt. Our interlinks were struggling to translate whatever language our attackers were broadcasting to us, without much success.

::I swear I've heard that language somewhere before,:: Bin-Ney said.

Through the interlink, I could sense Jida's sudden gasp, and when I looked over, I saw that she'd lifted her hands to her throat, defensively, though she'd seemed unharmed just a moment before.

::Oh dear,:: sounded her voice in my head.

::What is it?:: I asked. ::Are you hurt?::

::I know what they're saying. I know who they are.::

Jida looked at me, and though her faceplate was partly opaque in the hard X-ray glare, I could still see terror behind her eyes.

::The Iron Mass.::

PART THREE

FIFTY-SIX

I was never military. But for a while I was a cop.

In her former life, before being reborn in the Human Entelechy, Amelia Apatari had been a soldier-flyer, a volunteer with the United Nation's standing army, the Department of Peacekeeping Operations. As a Peacekeeper, she'd been trained to fight, trained to kill. Of course, all she really wanted to do was to fly, and to see new places, but she'd had the training, if needed. And she'd needed it, on occasion.

Me, I'd signed on with the Orbital Patrol because I wanted to go into space, and it seemed to offer the best chances. A division of the Department of Outer Space Affairs, the Patrol had been chartered for emergency response and search-and-rescue operations under the original draft of the Outer Space Treaty, before it was revised and ratified in the early 22C. The 1967 draft of the

OST was pretty down on the notion of any militarized use of space:

> *The moon and other celestial bodies shall be used by all States Parties to the Treaty exclusively for peaceful purposes. The establishment of military bases, installations, and fortifications; the testing of any type of weapons; and the conduct of military maneuvers on celestial bodies shall be forbidden.*

Needless to say, that language got tweaked a bit once extraplanetary colonies started declaring themselves sovereign nations—to say nothing of the growing numbers of "pirate kingdoms" based in the asteroid belt, the Jovian moons, or wherever smugglers and thieves could lay their hands or equivalent cybernetic appendages on a bit of real estate. In short order, the idea that space was solely for peaceful purposes seemed quaint, like steam trains or poodle skirts.

The Peacekeepers, who to that point had been limited to strictly terrestrial operations, were given expanded operational authority to allow them to deal with brush wars and border skirmishes on the colonies, belts, and elsewhere. That just left crime to contend with.

So while the Orbital Patrol hadn't been chartered for law enforcement, by the time I was a kid it'd been given limited jurisdictional authority. But there were still old guards in the General Assembly who weren't crazy about the notion of an interplanetary police force, and so the UN only granted interdiction authority to a small subset of Orbital Patrol officers.

When I'd signed on board *Cutter 972*, I'd been tapped as an Interdiction Detachment. As with most ID officers, I'd had secondary responsibilities as a crewmember, but when circumstances demanded, I was authorized to board other craft. Most every patrolman got trained in Interdiction Negotiation, a multi-disciplinary approach incorporating elements of psychology, military strategy, negotiation tactics, and martial arts, even if only ID officers ever used the training, just like all patrolmen were trained marksmen even though ID officers were the only ones authorized to use energetic firearms in the field.

A few times, after boarding smugglers' ships or pirate vessels, just me with no backup but my cap gun and the jurisdictional authority of an Interdiction Detachment, I'd found myself taken prisoner—a crook had gotten the drop on me or managed to disarm me, or whatever the case might have been—and a time or two, I wasn't sure I was going to make it out alive. But I'd never been completely without hope, had never given up on the notion of escape.

It had taken twelve thousand years, and an exiled group of genetically engineered religious fanatics, but I was coming close to breaking my streak.

FIFTY-SEVEN

I expected the Iron Mass simply to end us, there in the shadow of the cairn forest. From the tone of their voices and the words our interlinks were quickly learning to translate, it certainly sounded as if they had the will to do so. But for reasons of their own, they limited themselves to hurling invective at us, brandishing their strange long-bladed, long-handled spears. The handles of the spears appeared to be extensible so that they looked like scimitars with the handle collapsed or like Japanese *naginata* when at full extension. There were no signs of any other weapons, but the fact remained that they'd hit us with *something*. For all I knew, they had something like a projector built into the carapaces of their black insect armor.

They had no interest in our weapons, whatever the case, dumping them unceremoniously into some sort of mesh bag, which one of them then slung onto his back. Or her back. Or eir back, I suppose. In the armor, it was impossible to say, and after the last few weeks in the Entelechy and on board the *Further*, I wasn't about to hazard a guess.

I tried to interlink Maruti and Xerxes to tell them to keep out of sight, but we'd apparently moved too far away for the signals to carry, or the cairns and caves were producing more interference than I'd anticipated. Still, our captors didn't show any indication that they were aware of the chimp and the robot, so for the moment, they seemed to be safe. The same, I'm afraid, couldn't be said for the rest of us.

After a while, the attitude and postures of our captors seemed to shift, and one of them stepped forward—the leader, I assumed. The others fell silent, and without saying a word, only using broad gestures, the leader indicated that we should stand up.

::What should we do, Captain?:: Bin-Ney sent.

::At the moment?:: I answered. ::I think we should stand up.::

When we were on our feet, the Iron Mass leader pointed at us with his weapon's blade, turned, and started walking. The Iron Mass behind us and to either side gestured angrily with their own spears, and it didn't take too much to work out that we were expected to follow him.

• • • • •

Our captors outnumbered us more than two to one, and were armed. We were hardly defenseless, our mantles capable of withstanding a considerable amount of damage, but the Iron Mass's first attack made it clear that they could immobilize us with little effort. If we tried to run, we wouldn't get three steps before the Iron Mass shot our legs out from under us with particle beams—but from where? Were there beam weapons incorporated into the handles of their spears? And besides, as amazing as our mantles were, I didn't fancy testing their ability to withstand a continuous barrage of firepower from twelve angry attackers.

I'm not sure how long we walked. I suppose I could have instructed my interlink to display a counter in my field of vision, or recite the time for me, but it couldn't have been more than thirty or forty-five minutes. It seemed longer, though, an interminable death march—to what destination, we didn't know.

Finally, we arrived at the edge of what appeared to be an enormous canyon. It was impossible to get a sense of scale, but it seemed at first glance large enough to rival the Grand Canyon on Earth, or even Valle Marineris on Mars. It was colossal, mind-numbingly big. In the base of the canyon below us, something large and dark and metallic lumbered, like a giant scorpion.

The sides of the canyon sloped down at a steep grade, and as the Iron Mass forced us at the point of their spears to climb down, we had to struggle to maintain our footing. As we slid down, kicking up scree as we went, I realized that the sides of the canyon were grooved, tiered like shallow stairs. It wasn't a naturally occurring formation, but was man made.

As we neared the base of the canyon, which was covered in the same grooves as the canyon walls, I got a better look at the giant scorpion-looking machine, which was producing enough noise that I could feel the vibrations even through the thin atmosphere of the pulsar planet.

The machine was almost a kilometer wide and seemed a strange assemblage of different elements. A wide platform perched atop a central pole, which appeared to be driven deep into the surface. Beneath the platform, a long armature extended from the pole out to a distance of more than half a kilometer, from which a giant hunk of machinery descended, digging down into the surface, spinning at a high rate of speed like a drill bit.

Above, on the topside of the platform, there was a central dome of some opaque material, with a large rectangular structure on one side and an upright, slender, cylinder-looking edifice, almost like a large cannon, on the other.

As we approached, heading for the central post underneath the enormous structure, in the sickly green illumination of lights running on the platforms underside, I saw that the giant drill at the end of the armature was slowly moving from the end of the arm toward the center.

This was a drilling platform the size of a small city. And this enormous valley was one gigantic strip mine.

The Iron Mass had been on the pulsar planet for some time, it was clear. And they had been busy.

FIFTY-EIGHT

A lift in the central post carried us up, where our captors ushered us into a cramped, darkly lit room, which I assumed was located in the dome atop the platform. The others and I kept our mantles in complete extension, covering our whole bodies, but once we were inside the pressurized dome, the Iron Mass began to remove their black insect suits, keeping watch over us in shifts.

I got my first glimpse of an Iron Mass, and it was a sight I won't soon forget.

The Anachronists with poor taste who'd impersonated the Iron Mass at the *Further* reception had gotten no nearer the mark with those re-creations than the zoot suiters had gotten to 20C clothing. They had been cartoons, broad caricatures, but seeing the real thing was something else entirely. The Anachronists had seemed faintly silly with their black skin and horns. But seeing the Iron Mass, their hair engineered to grow into a series of small horns from their foreheads to the napes of their neck, like cornrows of rhino's horns, their skin coded jet black to make them more resistant to radiation, the effect was quite arresting.

The Iron Mass were anthropoids like Jida and me, but deeply engineered. They had spurs growing from their knuckles, and one on each elbow, doubtless for use as weapons. And when they blinked, a third inner eyelid slid momentarily over their catlike piercing blue eyes, a nictitating membrane. They were surprisingly short and compact, the tallest of them coming roughly to my chin, the shortest several centimeters shorter than Jida. But they were broad shouldered and thickly muscled, with no hint of body fat. These were stripped-down, streamlined biological machines designed for survival.

The Iron Mass believe that evolution will one day produce God, whom they call the "Divine Ideal." If the Iron Mass's morphology is any kind of indication of what their God will look like, I'm in no hurry to see Him for myself.

FIFTY-NINE

Our captors had hardly spoken to us since we left the cairn forest, but once they'd all gotten out of their pressure suits, dressed now in high black boots, loose-fitting white trousers, and sleeveless white tunics, their leader turned once more to address us. She was a woman, as it happened, but there was little that seemed feminine about her.

"You!" She pointed at us, her finger tipped with a talon-like nail. "You will to remove protective."

Our interlinks had managed to compile a workable lexicon of Iron Mass words, but were still struggling with syntax and usage.

::Captain?:: Zaslow sounded as uncertain as I felt.

::Hold on, crew,:: I said. ::Let's see where this goes.::

"Remove protective clothing," the Iron Mass woman repeated, her piercing blue eyes flashing. "Now!"

The others glanced at me, and I faced the woman and said, "We'd rather not, if it's all the same to you."

Our mantles were our only defense, the only thing standing between us and the points of the Iron Mass's spears, and I wasn't about to give them up.

The woman shook her head angrily and motioned to one of the other Iron Mass. "Bring it!"

Two of the Iron Mass hurried out of the room, leaving the others and me to exchange confused glances. In a moment, they returned, carrying a large cylindrical mechanism of some sort, like a bazooka with a battery pack strapped to it.

"You will remove your protective clothing," the woman said, her lips pulled back over pointed teeth, "or suffer consequence."

I glanced at Jida. "I think that we're still—"

"Fire!" the woman shouted, and a gout of light leapt from the end of the cylinder, hitting Zaslow squarely in the chest, blasting through his mantle, through his chest, finally shimmering on the wall behind him.

The planetary scientist looked down at the gaping hole in his chest, circuitry and biological visceral incinerated in an eyeblink.

:: Zaslow!:: I shouted.

"Oh..." he said, and then collapsed in a heap on the ground—dead.

The woman motioned, and the cylinder was swung around and pointed at my chest now.

"You will remove your protective clothing."

It didn't make much sense to argue.

SIXTY

The three of us—Jida, Bin-Ney, and me—were marched through narrow corridors to an even smaller room, dimly lit by a strip of some green luminescence on the floor. We were shoved unceremoniously through the hatch, which was then shut behind us, closing with a resounding clang.

Zaslow was dead. And all I'd ever really known about him was his name. If I'd been quicker on my feet, if I'd been faster with a response, would he still be alive?

I swallowed hard. There'd be time for self-recrimination later, if I were lucky. For now, I had the surviving members of the team to worry about—let the dead worry about themselves, for the time being.

"Are you two all right?" I asked, looking to the others.

Bin-Ney nodded, but Jida kept silent, her attention fixed on the hatch, her hands clutching at her throat.

"Jida, are you hurt?" I asked.

She turned to me, as though startled to hear her name, and for a moment, she stared at me with blank confusion. Then she slowly lowered her hands and shook her head. "No, I'm not hurt. But I'm afraid we're all far from all right."

■ ■ ■ ■ ■

"I was still in my original incarnation," Jida said, her voice sounding small and faraway in the dimly lit room, "with only a handful of bodies comprising my legion, when the Iron Mass was sealed off forever from the Entelechy. It's been more than five thousand years since any of us last had contact with them, but that clearly wasn't long enough."

"What can you tell me about them, Jida?" I asked. "They're some sort of religious zealots, right? They believe in a supernatural creator?"

Jida shook her head. "The deity of the Iron Mass, which they call the 'Divine Ideal,' is not the creator, but rather, the created. The universe, the Iron Mass believes, is evolving into a unified consciousness, and all life that has ever arisen in the universe is a part of that process. The symbol of the Iron Mass is the triumvir—three interlocking circles within an equilateral triangle, representing mind, body, and soul—and all individuals bear a responsibility, which the Iron Mass calls the 'great effort,' to improve themselves on all three axes, to help give rise to the Divine Ideal. However, the Iron Mass believe that if any of the three aspects of being are neglected, it is an offense to their deity. So an uploaded consciousness represents the reduction of body and soul in the interest of preserving the mind, while an artificial intelligence is a perversion of the three. The Iron Mass have no objection to genetic engineering, which they consider a vital aspect of the Divine Ideal's development, just as much as is evolution and pro-creation, but they reject anti-senescence, believing that aging and death are a necessary aspect of being."

"Wait," Bin-Ney said, disbelieving. "They let themselves *age*?"

Jida nodded. In the low light, I could see her shooting a hard look at Bin-Ney. I knew she was remembering the time only a few days before when Bin-Ney had disguised himself as an Iron Mass as a re-creationist game. But I doubted that Bin-Ney thought history quite so romantic, quite so worthy of idealized re-creation, when staring it right in the face.

"For centuries," Jida went on, "the Iron Mass were considered little more than cranks, more or less harmless with their strange notions. And since their beliefs were all inwardly directed, con-cerned with their own bodies and minds, they posed no nui-sance to their neighbors. But then a charismatic leader arose from among their ranks who came to be known as 'Scourge of the Divine Ideal and Unconquered Master of the Infinite Worlds, Lord-of-the-Fortunate-Conjunctions Zero Perihelion Iridium.' It was said that he'd been born with blood filling his palms, a sign that blood would be shed by his hand."

Jida paused and looked down at the palms of her hands, her thoughts momentarily a million miles—and five thousand years—away.

"Zero Perihelion Iridium preached that not only were digi-tal and artificial intelligence perversions, and an offense to their deity, but that if the three aspects of being were thrown out of balance on a universal scale, then the Divine Ideal would never arise at all. As a result, Iridium urged the Iron Mass to adopt what he called the 'lesser effort.'"

The way that she intoned the last words spoke volumes about her thoughts on the "lesser effort," the syllables dripping with venom.

"The First Lesser Effort, led by Iridium himself, was the cause of the threshold to the Iron Mass's home world being temporarily isolated. Members of the Iron Mass spread throughout the worlds of the Entelechy, preaching their peculiar brand of hatred, staging protests, and harrying synthetics, digital consciousnesses, and others of blended provenance. When the Iron Mass refused to stop harassing other citizens of the Entelechy, the Consensus convened and quickly decided to isolate the Iron Mass for a probationary period, their threshold enclosed in fullerene-reinforced diamond."

Jida sighed, and her left hand fluttered briefly to her neck for only an instant, like someone suddenly afraid she'd lost a treasured necklace. But her fingers found nothing there, and she slowly lowered her arm.

"Fifty years later, the probation was lifted, and the threshold to the Iron Mass world was again opened. Time had not mellowed their tempers. Zero Perihelion Iridium had been a young man when the threshold was isolated, and as the result of the Iron Mass's rejection of anti-senescence, he was now of advancing years. The Iron Mass had prepared themselves for the reopening of their threshold, and with their way to the Entelechy reestablished, Iridium launched what he prosaically called the Second Lesser Effort."

The last words were choked out, like they were barbs caught in her throat, ripping her mouth as she spoke them.

"The Iron Mass managed to kill nearly a billion citizens before they were finally stopped. Nearly all of those who were killed were restored from backups, but as the Iron Mass had destroyed their interlinks along with their corporeal forms, there was a tremendous loss of memory. And the…the trauma…for those who survived the attacks was considerable and…lasting."

"That's…" Bin-Ney began, struggling to find the words. "That's…I studied the Iron Mass, but only in popular dramas. I didn't know about…"

Jida's glare was so hot and intense I was surprised it didn't bore a hole through him, like poor Zaslow.

Bin-Ney averted his eyes and said, his voice low, "I just found their aesthetics appealing, is all."

Jida ignored him. "The Consensus needed little time to deliberate. Once the Iron Mass were forced back through the threshold to their home world, the threshold was permanently closed, the stabilizing arch dismantled, and the juncture allowed to evaporate. That was the last recorded contact anyone had with the Iron Mass."

Jida's hands had drifted back to her neck, her fingers wrapped around her throat on either side, almost like she was trying to choke herself. Or hold something in.

"Jida," I said softly, carefully, "what happened to you when the Iron Mass attacked the Entelechy? How were you hurt?"

She looked at me, her eyes wide, as though she were seeing past the millennia, as though it were happening again, right in front of her.

"I was….*she* was…" Jida paused and straightened her shoulders before continuing. "One of my bodies was there when the door to the Iron Mass home world was opened. I was curious to see what would happen. I was…"

She trailed off for a moment, seeming out of breath.

"It's OK, Jida," I said. "It was a long, long time ago."

Jida nodded slowly, but her expression looked unconvinced.

"My interlink was active when it happened, of course. So what happened to my body in front of the Iron Mass threshold was experienced by the entire legion. The Iron Mass had these hooks and these knives, and they..."

Her hands were wrapped so tightly around her neck now that her voice sounded choked off, her air passages constricted. I leaned forward and gently pried her fingers away from her neck, having to labor to lower her strong arms to her sides.

"They gutted me," Jida gaped, wide eyed, teeth bared. "They ripped out my throat when I started to scream, and then opened me up with their knives, and then..." She squeezed shut her eyes, misted with tears. "I wanted to shut that body out, close down the interlink to the rest of the legion, but I couldn't look away, couldn't leave her alone...couldn't leave *me* alone like that. I've lost countless bodies to accidents, to age, to misadventure, but that was the first and only time I'd lost one to pure, unreasoning hatred. I couldn't leave that part of me to look into those unfeeling eyes alone. So that part of Jida Shuliang died with my words of comfort in her mind. And I've lived all the days of my life since with her screams of horror and pain in mine."

SIXTY-ONE

I'd long since lost track of time, but the voice of Zel i'Cirea meant that eighty minutes must have passed.

::Captain Stone, can you hear me?::

::Loud and clear,:: I subvocalized, on the chance that the Iron Mass might be listening in—and in the hopes that they hadn't detected the interlink communication frequencies. Anyone looking in would see three people sitting quietly, their expressions carefully blank and affectless.

::We've sighted a ship that we believe, based on its markings, to be from the lost culture of the Iron Mass.::

::We've done more than *sight* them down here, I'm afraid.::

::What is your condition, then?::

::Jida, Bin-Ney, and I have been taken prisoner. Zaslow's been murdered.::

::And Maruti and Xerxes?:: Zel asked.

::We're right here, sirs,:: came the voice of Maruti.

::Perhaps if you defined 'here' it might be more informative, mmm?:: added Xerxes.

::We're still investigating the cave systems. We tried to interlink you a short while ago but just assumed that we were out of range. We didn't even know you folks were missing.::

::Well, we *were*,:: put in Jida.

::All right, settle down,:: I said. ::We've got a lot of people on the line. I'm guessing that the *Further* being in orbit is acting as a relay so that we can communicate on the ground, even if we can't interlink point to point.::

::So it would seem,:: Zel answered.

::Which means we've got just a few minutes before we all lose contact again, and a long while before contact is reestablished. Let's make it count. Zel, you say you've sighted a ship. What's it doing?::

::After first sighting, it began to adjust its orbit and is now nearly alongside us. So far, though, they've not responded to any communications, whether radio, or pulsed light, or any other mechanism we have available to us.::

::But they haven't made any overtly hostile gestures.::

::No.::

::Captain,:: cut in Maruti, ::we just *have* to tell you about this remarkable discovery we've made.::

::It'll have to wait a moment, Maruti,:: I said. ::I'm afraid we're a little preoccupied at the moment.::

::Should we send down reinforcements, Captain?::

::Thanks for the offer, Zel, but I'm not sure it would do much good. These guys are pretty well entrenched. And since the Iron Mass ship in orbit is obviously watching you, any move to rescue us could force their hand, which could end badly for us down here.::

::To say the least,:: Jida said humorlessly.

::I prefer to keep our options open, for the moment, and watch for any opening.::

::Sir, about our findings…:: Maruti began.

::Not yet,:: I said. ::*Further*?::

::Yes, Captain Stone?:: came the voice of the avatar in my ears.

::What's the state of the drive? Could you get away if you needed to?::

::Sadly not, sir,:: the *Further* answered. ::We drained the reaction drives in moving into orbit around this planet, and we won't be able to use the metric engineering drives for another point-nine-two standard days.::

::OK. So there's no rush, but if you get charged and ready, and there's still no sign of us getting free, I want you to fire up the metric engineering drives and get back to Entelechy space. If nothing else, we need to warn anyone else away from this rock and let everyone know that the Iron Mass don't appear to have been sitting on their hands the last few thousand years. They've been mining this planet for years, it looks like, but mining what, and what they've been doing with it, I haven't got a clue. As for the Iron Mass ship in orbit, so long as it doesn't make any aggressive moves, just keep your distance.::

::And if it *does* make any aggressive moves?:: Zel asked.

::In that case,:: I answered, ::I trust you to do whatever's necessary to safeguard the ship and her crew.::

::Captain Stone, I must insist…:: Maruti said.

::Maruti, you and Xerxes continue your investigations. If you happen to find anything that's going to get Jida, Bin-Ney, and me out of this fix, and all of us back on the ship, you let me know. Otherwise, keep out of sight, for the time being.::

::But what about—::

And then the connection was broken, the *Further* rotating once more out of range.

SIXTY-TWO

The most profound silence I ever experienced was drifting in cis-lunar space inside the belly of an empty cargo tank. It's a long story, but the short version is that I was in a shuttle mishap, without a functioning pressure suit, and had to eat a vacuum to get from the damaged control module to the cargo bay, where luckily one of the tanks was intended to transport livestock and so was pressurized and heated. With the engines offline and the radio out, there was nothing to do but sit and wait—a few thousand cubic meters of air and me, surrounded by reinforced ceramic and steel. At least inside a pressure suit I'd have my own breath and heartbeat sounding in my ears, but the vast empty space in the tank ate up any sounds echoing back from the far walls, so it was just me and silence.

Until *Cutter 972* had appeared on the scene like the proverbial cavalry and saved my hide, I'd thought for sure that was it for me.

The aching sensation of helplessness in my gut was much the same, sitting in the dimly lit cell on the Iron Mass mining platform, but the difference was that there was nothing like silence here: the constant rumble of the drill down below, moving back and forth on an arm spinning slowly around in circles, the drill describing an ever-increasing spiral, the source of the grooves on the canyon floor and walls; the rumble of life-support systems, clanking fans somewhere far off in the walls, echoing through the air vents; and the occasional heavy tread of Iron Mass moving back and forth outside our windowless door. The air in the room was hot and close, and in the dim light, we could barely see one another, but we didn't have to look to know what expressions we all carried—uncertainty, dread, and fear.

Time moved at a snail's pace as we sat, unmoving, on the floor of our cell.

Finally, there came a shuffling sound on the far side of the door, and with a deafening clang, the hatch swung open.

An imposing figure stood in the doorway, horns longer than those on any of the Iron Mass we'd seen so far, a wicked scar down the left side of his face, his right ear missing its lobe. He was no taller or broader than the rest, on reflection, but something about his posture, about his bearing, suggested a much larger man. He glared down at us, his ice-blue cat's eyes narrowed to slits, and something like a smile curled his lip.

"Before you stands Commander-of-the-Faithful Nine Precession Radon, House of the Ideal's Pure Expression, leader of these men. You will dine with me."

SIXTY-THREE

Having heard Jida's story of the Iron Mass and what had happened the last time anyone from the Entelechy had laid eyes on them, I wasn't sure what to expect next. But whatever possibilities might have crossed my mind, being on the receiving end of an attempted conversion was not one of them.

"Our creed requires us to give every organic a chance to embrace their destiny and join us in working toward the birth of the Divine Ideal."

We were seated on thin cushions around a low table, the man called Nine Precession Radon at the head and me at the other end, Jida and Bin-Ney on either side. Small cups of some strong spirit were in front of us, but so far, only Radon had taken a sip, the rest of us watching warily.

"I remember the last time the Iron Mass spread their creed," Jida said, eyes half-lidded, teeth clenched, "and you got yourselves exiled from civilization in the bargain."

"*Civilization?*" Radon laughed, a startling, barking sound. "Exiled, do you say? Ha! It was the greatest blessing ever to befall my people that we were excised from your so-called *Human Entelechy*. We should never have submitted ourselves to be ruled by a consortium of mechanical miscengenists and disembodied digital ghosts."

::I hope he doesn't mean *me*,:: chimed a voice in my ear.

I struggled not to react, but to keep my expression neutral.

::Amelia?:: I subvocalized.

::Sorry I've been gone, but I got distracted catching up with old movies and lost track of time. Did you know they made holographic adaptations of *The Chronicles of Zenna* in the twenty-third century?::

::Amelia, we're a little busy here at the moment…::

::I know, RJ, I'm just kidding. I seem to have missed a lot of the plot, huh? Who's the fruit bat?::

::Keep quiet, will you? We'll talk later.::

I turned my attention back to Radon, trying not to glance at my signet ring, which I'd forgotten was still on my finger, and thinking about ways having Amelia on our side might work to our advantage.

"The people of the Entelechy are weak and complacent," Radon went on. "There is neither fire nor passion in them. And only a hand that can grasp a sword may hold a scepter."

"Is that why you attack the first people you see after five thousand years of isolation?" I said, keeping my voice level. It was too early to say which Interdiction Negotiation strategies might apply in these circumstances, if any, but I saw no reason to aggravate matters until I had a better picture of what we were dealing with.

"The first people? Oh, no, my dear boy," Radon said, smiling broadly. "We might not have had any contact with the Entelechy before now, but we've encountered countless other outposts over the millennia, cultures scattered out like seeds during the Diaspora. And all of them have either come to accept the wisdom of the Divine Ideal or paid the price for their misbelief."

A pair of Iron Mass entered the room, carrying trays of food. As they set them down at the center of the table, one of the servers started coughing and didn't stop as he retreated to the corner of the room. Finally, he stopped and, at a glance from Radon, muttered a sputtering apology.

"W-what price is that?" Bin-Ney asked.

Radon ladled a mound of grayish-green gelatin off one of the trays onto a plate before him, and smiled wistfully. "Death, of course. Though, some serve their purposes, even after their life is terminated." Radon glanced to one of the two servers, a woman, and said, "Fluorine. Do you recall the stories of our forebears launching the severed heads of their enemies as missiles against their brethren?"

The woman—Fluorine, evidently—smiled and nodded. "What about Oxus, Commander-of-the-Faithful?"

Radon clapped his hands, almost gleefully, like a kid opening a present to discover precisely what he'd ask for.

"Oh, Oxus," he laughed, slapping the table's surface with the palm of his hand. He turned to me and grinned, as though eager to share a favorite joke. "On the planet Oxus, you see, a woman begged to be spared when her colony was put to the sword for refusing to accept their place in the divine order. She told my brothers that she had swallowed a data crystal and that the information on it would be invaluable to them. After ripping her open and removing the crystal with his own two hands, the leader of the house ordered his men to disembowel every captive to see what they might have secreted away." He guffawed loudly. "What do you think of that, eh?"

The male server coughed again, a long series of convulsions wracking his chest.

"You seem very powerful," I said, applying a bit of Interdiction Negotiation technique, trying to find some leverage with our captors. "I imagine most people who meet you are very frightened."

"Powerful?" Radon shook his head. "I am merely a servant of the Divine Ideal and accrue no power to myself. Now, tell me…"

The server's cough became much more violent, until finally he doubled over, hacking up a huge wad of bloody sputum that thwacked into the floor at his feet.

"Is he OK?" I asked.

"Psht," Radon said dismissively. "He merely has the sickness—or one variety of it, at any rate. The ships of the Iron Mass use fission engines, leading to high rates of radiation-related illness among us, but since members of the Iron Mass seldom live longer than one hundred years anyway, we don't consider it a major cause of concern."

He glanced over as the female server helped the other, first to his feet and then to stagger out of the room.

"Besides, we live for the world that is to come, not the world of the moment." He leaned forward on his elbow and looked from me to Bin-Ney to Jida and back. "Now. Are you prepared to accept your personal role in the evolution of the divine?"

SIXTY-FOUR

Nine Precession Radon rambled on, talking about the glorious plans of the Divine Ideal, the god who waited for humankind at the end of time, and how every living being—excluding those who didn't fit the Iron Mass definition of "living"—had a place in the grand scheme, if they so chose.

I could tell Jida was not weathering all of this terribly well, but she managed to keep quiet through most of it. Bin-Ney, for his part, looked like a deer caught in headlights, his mouth hanging open, his thoughts on something terrifyingly unpleasant. I'd been trained to resist any number of different varieties of torture as part of my Interdiction Negotiation instruction, but listening to Radon, I was reminded of nothing so much as the four days I spent ferrying a pair of religious missionaries to Mars; they'd seen the *Cutter 1519*, with its close quarters, as a perfect opportunity to refine their proselytizing skills before spreading the good word among the red planet's colonists.

Radon had the same manic zeal, the same true-believer glint in his eye. That he had red horns instead of hair, and wicked spurs on his elbows and knuckles, and wasn't dressed in a short-sleeved white button-down shirt and black tie were about the only things that differentiated him from them—that, and the fact that the missionaries hadn't, at any stage, held my life in the palm of their hands.

Given Radon's stories about what had happened to misbelievers, I figured it was in our best interests to feign curiosity in his nonsense screed until some possibility of escape presented itself. So I nodded politely, made appropriate noises, and prodded him with questions a time or two, when he seemed to suspect our interest was on the wane.

The meal of green-gray goop was tasteless but fairly filling, and when the female server had returned—with no sight of her coughing companion—and cleared away the table, it seemed that our audience with the commander-of-the-faithful had come to an end.

Radon called for guards to usher us back to our cell.

"We'll continue these discussions at a later hour, so in the meantime, you can contemplate your place in history. Later, we'll test your resolve, to see whether you are truly prepared to accept the Divine Ideal as your personal destiny."

I didn't like to imagine what a "test" of our resolve might involve, and didn't ask.

■ ■ ■ ■ ■

A quartet of spear-wielding guards led us through the cramped corridors, taking a different route than we'd previously followed.

After a few twists and turns, which I imagined might have been intended to keep us disoriented about the internal layout of the dome, we came to a juncture barred by a closed hatch. Three of the guards kept us under careful watch, while the fourth went to a panel set in the wall, touched a series of flickering lights, and then the hatch opened.

We went through, and I saw that there was an identical panel on the other side of the hatch. Going down a long corridor, we took a turn to the left, another to the right, and then found ourselves back at our cell.

The guards shoved us through the open hatch and then closed it behind us. We were back in the green-tinged darkness, as far from freedom as we'd been before. Or so it might have seemed.

::RJ,:: came the voice of Amelia in my ear. ::I think I have a plan.::

SIXTY-FIVE

The first steps of the plan were so simple, so clichéd, that I felt a little embarrassed even attempting them. But after considerable deliberation, no other options presented themselves. Besides, I figured, fads and fashions being what they were, maybe after twelve thousand years the oldest trick in the book could be new again.

I positioned myself by the hatch, leaning against the wall, looking as casual as possible in case there were cameras or other viewing devices secreted around that we couldn't see—and since they could be virtually nanoscopic, or the walls themselves could be transparent from the other side, it was no stretch of the imagination to think that there were. Then Jida lay on the ground, her legs doubled up to her chest, and began moaning softly. Bin-Ney took up position over her.

We waited until we heard the tromp of boots outside the door, then I motioned to Bin-Ney, and he went into his act.

"Help!" he shouted as loud as he could. "I think there's something really wrong with her! She might be"—and here he paused unnecessarily for dramatic effect, the back of his hand to his forehead, looking almost like he might swoon—"*dying!*"

I stifled a sigh. I knew I shouldn't look to an Anachronist for verisimilitude, but I hoped his hamming wouldn't get in the way of the plan.

The tromping boots stopped at the door, and I heard a muffled exchange. Then, with a groan of metal on metal, the hatch slid open.

"Oh, *thank* you," Bin-Ney swooned, while Jida groaned loudly. "She's really, really sick!"

"Quiet in there," came the barked voice from the other side of the hatchway. Positioned where I was, hidden by the side of the door, I couldn't see out, but I could tell from the Iron Mass's tone, and the fact that they weren't coming through the door, that they weren't exactly buying it.

Jida moaned, howling loudly.

"Keep it quiet," said another harsh voice, "or you'll soon have something to moan about."

This wasn't working. I wasn't surprised. It was time for something a bit more direct, and a great deal riskier.

"Hey, where's the other one—"

Before the Iron Mass had completed his question, I'd jumped to one side, landing right in front of the open hatch in a crouch, and launched myself at them, barely even taking time to gauge their distance and position.

The Iron Mass were both armed with spears, as I'd anticipated, but hadn't had them at the ready. If they had, I doubt I would have lasted three seconds. As it was, I managed to tackle one of the Iron Mass to the ground before the other had a chance to respond.

The force of my blow knocked the air out of the first Iron Mass, which gave me a split-second advantage. While his companion lunged at me, swinging his weapon downward in a wide arc, I grabbed hold of the spear of the Iron Mass beneath me. Both hands on the fully extended handle, I yanked it back and to the side, forcing the spear's blade up behind me with all my strength.

As I rolled to the side, the spear pulled from my hands, its tip buried in the abdomen of the attacking Iron Mass. Strangely colored blood flecked the corners of the attacker's mouth, and his own spear clattered to the ground as he looked in confusion at the weapon protruding from his belly.

The Iron Mass on the ground scrambled to get up, swinging his arm to one side, the spurs on his elbow clawing across my calf, but I kicked out and caught his jaw with the heel of my boot, and he fell back to the floor, groaning.

Shouts of alarm sounded from down the corridor, and I knew I didn't have time to stop and pick up one of the weapons as a trio of Iron Mass barreled toward me, only meters away. I took to my heels, running the other way. I reached the end of a short corridor, jogged left, then took a quick right. I sprinted, running as fast as I could, but the footfalls of the pursuing Iron Mass came closer and closer.

At the end of the corridor was a closed hatch, the same one we'd come through when returning from our dinner with Radon. On the wall beside it was the control panel—my goal.

I reached the control panel of twinkling lights only steps ahead of the Iron Mass. I held my hand up and laid my palm against the cool, smooth surface, hoping against hope that this worked. Only an eyeblink later, the three pursuers caught up with me. The one in the lead swung his bone-spurred fist at the side of my head, the impact sufficient to jar my teeth and sending lights fireworking across my vision. Somehow I kept on my feet for an instant longer, my hand still held to the control panel.

The next Iron Mass raked his elbow spur across my back, cutting my shirt to shreds and opening huge gashes in the flesh beneath. The third knocked my knees out from under me with the butt of his spear's handle, and I went down like a marionette with its strings cut.

I lay on the ground as the three stood over me, taking turns getting their kicks in, occasionally leaning down and pounding my face or body with their spurred fists. My mouth filled with blood, and I could feel myself losing consciousness.

Just before I fell away into a bloodred darkness, I could hear a tiny, distant voice in my mind.

::OK,:: Amelia said. ::I'm in.::

SIXTY-SIX

Amelia had noticed the interface when we were marched back to our cell.

From the signet ring, and using the evidence of my senses routed through the interlink, she'd been able to work out that the control panel was slaved to the local area's security and environmental controls but that, in addition to manual input, the controls received commands from farther up the hierarchy of the mining platform's computer network. Since the network would have to register any manual changes made—such as opening a secured door with a pass code—that meant that communication between the interface and the network was somehow bidirectional. It might only have been a small back door, and it might have been closed and locked, but hidden in that bit of twinkling lights was a route into the master controls of the mining platform.

The broadcast range of the signet ring was pretty short, not much longer than the length of my arm, and was pretty low bandwidth, at that, so she wouldn't be able to gain control of the computers from within the signet ring, but Amelia thought that she could reconfigure the holographic projectors to download her source code into the platform's computers. From within the system, she'd hopefully be able to work out how to open the doors remotely, locate our weapons, and help us escape from the platform.

I'd asked whether she couldn't just download a *copy*, and not her operating code, but Amelia explained that it didn't work that way. A mind, even a digital one, wasn't just software. An emulated mind mimicked the cellular basis of an organic brain, the structure of the synapses replicated digitally. That was why the first artificial intelligences, millennia before, had been based on uploaded human minds and not engineered from scratch.

As a result, Amelia couldn't just duplicate her files and dump them into the computer; if she did, she'd only succeed in planting a copy of her memories, lacking any conscious awareness. In order for her to be of any use, she'd have to move her entire source code into the computer, lock, stock, and barrel.

The plan had been for me to get the signet ring close enough to the interface for the transfer to take place. And, of course, to keep it in place long enough for all of the data to download. Amelia's voice, broadcast from within the network to my interlink, was proof that it had worked.

The only problem was the next part, with me recaptured after an apparent escape attempt and Amelia stuck inside the platform's network, unsure how to work anything but the most rudimentary communications systems.

I just hoped that I survived long enough for the effort to have done any good.

SIXTY-SEVEN

I was stripped to the waist and bound hand and foot in some type of shackles fixed to the wall. What it suggested about our captors that they already had a room equipped with shackles on the walls, I chose not to contemplate any longer than was absolutely necessary.

I was in bad shape, to be sure, but didn't feel nearly as horrible as I should have, given the abuse my body had already taken. I couldn't know for sure, but I guessed it had something to do with the medichines Maruti had injected when rejuvenating me. They couldn't keep me from getting injured, but they seemed to be speeding my healing processes considerably. I was still bruised and bleeding, but I'd more or less been able to retain consciousness, blacking out only a time or two.

Amelia was able to remain in intermittent contact and reported in as often as she was able about her progress. She'd been able to get access to the communications network as soon as she entered the local circuit of the network, and had successfully maneuvered her source code from the terminal into the network itself, but so far, she'd succeeded in little else. She knew the general layout of the platform and could tell me anything I wanted to know about the production quotas, but that was about all.

As a pair of Iron Mass bruisers worked over my kidneys, taking turns pounding their spurred fists into my sides, though, I welcomed any distraction she could provide.

::OK,:: Amelia said as she snaked her way through the network, trying to find the security controls, ::the big rectangular box outside the dome, on the west side of the platform…Did you see that coming in?::

I tried to subvocalize an answer to say that I had, but couldn't concentrate enough to form the words in my head.

::Well,:: Amelia went on, taking my silence for assent, ::that's the refinery. These guys are digging up transuranic ore from the planet's bedrock, refining it down to the useful elements and discarding the rest, and then using the mass launcher—that's the cannon on the east side of the platform—to send shipments up into orbit. What they do from there, your guess is as good as mine. Do they use it on the ship? Package it up and send it somewhere else?::

::Who,:: I managed to subvocalize, just barely, ::knows?::

That I managed to follow it with a nonverbal shrug, I consider a testament to my willpower, if nothing else.

::The network's software defenses haven't noticed my intrusion just yet,:: Amelia continued, ::but I'm guessing it's just a matter of time. Don't worry, though. I'll find your gear and the security controls, and we'll get out of here.::

I moaned, rolling my head from one side to the other. My captors chuckled and took a step back to regard their handiwork. I looked down and saw the raw, bloody mess they'd made of my chest and abdomen.

::H-hurry?:: I managed.

::Hang tight.:: I could hear the strain in Amelia's voice, and the fear. ::We'll both get out of this, you'll see.::

Neither of us knew it then, but she was wrong.

SIXTY-EIGHT

I must have drifted off, or blacked out, because when the voice woke me up, I opened my eyes to find that I was alone in the room. Still hanging from the wall, one giant throbbing pain from the top of my head to the tips of my toes, it took me a few moments to be able to parse out the sounds I was hearing as words and then to recognize the voice that was speaking.

::Captain Stone. Are you receiving me? Captain Stone?::

"Zel," I said out loud, forgetting myself. Then I blinked hard, concentrated, and subvocalized, keeping my face as expressionless as possible. ::Yes. I'm here. I'm just a bit…I'm *just*, is all.::

::You don't sound good, Captain, if you don't mind me saying.::

::No, Zel? Well, you should see how I must *look*.:: I took a deep breath, collecting myself and trying to pull up as straight as possible in my restraints. ::How long since our last contact?::

::Just a bit over point-zero-five-six-two standard days.::

Eighty minutes. Had it been that short a time?

::OK, where do we stand?::

::The Iron Mass ship has approached to just a few kilometers but appears now to be holding position. The *Further* has continued to receive information from its probes, though, and a clearer picture of what's going on in this system has emerged.::

::Captain,:: sounded the voice of the *Further*, ::it appears that the asteroid belt we sighted on first reaching the pulsar system was originally another planet, identical in composition to the one below us. However, nearly all traces of any transuranic elements appear to have been removed from the debris. Geodynamics could not account for the planet's apparent destruction, much less for the absence of such a large percentage of its constituent matter, so the only conclusion we can draw is that it was deliberately done.::

::They mined the other planet out, obviously,:: came the voice of Xerxes, ::and when they'd removed all deposits of the heaviest transuranic elements in reach, they exploded the planet to access the final deposits hidden deep in the planet's core.::

::That's borne out by the evidence of my other probes,:: *Further* answered. ::The probes sent down to the planet ahead of the landing party have reported back that, beneath the surface, the planet is riddled with bored mines. I can only imagine it's just a matter of time before this planet follows its former sibling into oblivion.::

::At least some percentage of the mined ore,:: Xerxes said, ::must have been transported elsewhere, outside the system, which would account for the alteration in the pulsar binary's orbital period.::

::You damnable machine!:: howled Maruti in frustration. ::I've been patient like you asked, but I cannot believe that you'll patiently talk about mined ores and orbital periods in the face of what we've discovered.::

::Which is?:: I asked, mindful of the moments slipping past, of the window of communication slowly closing.

::It's simply remarkable, Captain,:: Maruti said, and I could hear the excitement in his words. ::These cairns aren't geological at all!::

::Nor are they designed as such,:: Xerxes objected.

::But they are the result…Oh, never mind your ridiculous objections. Captain, these structures are secreted by anaerobic bacteria, which are able to metabolize the simpler minerals of the planet. Much like the stromatalites that once were found on Original Earth, the cairns are digestive effluvia, if you will, the waste products of the bacteria after they have drawn whatever sustenance they can out of the inert materials of the planet's thin atmosphere itself. As they continue to consume and excrete, the towers grow wider and taller.::

I couldn't help but sigh. ::So the things that brought us down here in the first place are nothing but towers of dung piled up under unicellular eating machines?::

::Yes. That is, no. That is…:: Maruti was stumbling over himself, too excited even to form a response.

::What my overzealous companion is trying to communicate, Captain, is that the arrangement of these stromatalite-like cairns is not random. Though the individual organisms we've analyzed appear to be nothing more than 'unicellular eating machines,' as you put it, the question remains whether they might not have collectively developed some level of intelligence.::

::What?:: asked Zel. ::Some sort of hive mind?::

::Exactly!:: Maruti shouted.

::Perhaps,:: Xerxes put in, eir tone much more measured. ::We have detected the presence of organic molecules in the environment that could be functioning as a kind of rudimentary signaling system. Terrestrial bacteria use such signal molecules, called autoinducers, in a process called 'quorum sensing,' to regulate population levels, respond to external stimuli, and...::

::So the eating machines could be talking to one another, then?:: I asked wearily.

::Essentially, yes,:: Xerxes said.

::Isn't that remarkable?:: Maruti chimed in.

::You'll have to forgive my lack of enthusiasm,:: I said, ::but I've had other pressing concerns.::

I caught them up to speed on our status as quickly as I was able. I had to assume that the Iron Mass weren't monitoring our interlink communication, or they'd long since have discovered Amelia prowling around their computer network, so I felt free to tell the others the details of the plan, such as it was.

::So you allowed yourself to be captured and tortured?:: Zel asked, a disbelieving tone creeping into her words.

::It was the only way to get Amelia into position.::

::Well...:: Zel trailed off for a moment in a thoughtful silence. ::I hope that doesn't prove to have been an unwise strategy.::

::You and me both,:: I said. Then I felt the interlink connection break, and I was alone with my thoughts once more.

SIXTY-NINE

When I was a kid, I joined the Bharat Scouts. Then I fell in a hole and decided I'd had enough of scouting for a while.

I'd earned the rank of Rashtrapati Scout and moved up to the Rovers and was going for my Rambler Badge. My crew had already been drilled on first aid and survival techniques, and all that was left was to complete a four-day journey, organized by me and approved by the rest of the crew. The trip could be by land or water, and by foot, vehicle, or vessel, which meant we could have sailed or flown ultralights or any number of other options. Me? For some reason, I opted to walk. We'd go trekking in the hills of Meghalaya, four days and nights.

The journey had to present a "definite test of endurance," and "bring out qualities of self-reliance, initiative, determination, and leadership."

Right. Some leader I turned out to be.

Four of us set out on foot from a village in the East Khasi Hills district. My dad had been our escort from Bangalore, but he'd be sleeping in a hotel bed in Shillong, while we kids slept rough under the stars. I hadn't told the adults, but I'd planned our route to increase our chances of getting to spend the night along the way in one of the little villages of the hill tribes, where we'd have a better chance of a comfortable bed—though still a pretty slim chance, at that.

I had a satellite phone with me in case something went wrong. But aside from getting blisters on our feet and aching calves and backs, I couldn't imagine what could possibly happen.

Then, before we'd even gone a full day's trek, the earth opened up and swallowed me whole.

There were caves all over the Khasi Hills, among them the deepest and longest in all of South Asia. People had been coming to Meghalaya to chart and explore caves for centuries, and if you'd asked me at the time, I would have figured that every cave that could be discovered had been discovered. And then I fell into one that no one seemed to have found before.

One of the other kids fell in with me, but the other two managed to scramble back out of the way quickly enough not to get dragged down as well. Apparently, we'd stepped where no one else had stepped, in the history of forever, because the roof of the cave was separated from the ground above by a layer of dirt and gravel only a few centimeters thick, and with our weight on it, the whole thing just gave way.

Vikram was knocked unconscious by the fall, but for all I knew, he was dead. It was almost pitch black, with only a hazy light streaming down from the hole we'd made far overhead. I'd landed at a bad angle, my legs tangled up in stalagmites, both of them broken in multiple places and my left arm pulled out of its socket. Only my right arm could still move at all, but any attempt to drag myself across the floor sent waves of nausea and pain ripping across my body, so I quickly decided to give that a rest.

I had the satellite phone in my pack, but after spending long, bone-grinding minutes digging it out, I discovered that it didn't work, the signal blocked by the ceiling of rock and dirt overhead. Sanjay and Arati shouted down that they were going to go for help, and I discovered that one of my lungs must have punctured in the fall, since I couldn't catch enough breath to shout up that one of them, at least, should stay behind.

They both ran off back the way we'd come, and I was left down in the darkness, with the unconscious Vikram and a body racked with pain.

Then night fell.

I'm not sure what was worse—the pain or the waiting. Waiting, not knowing whether Sanjay and Arati would bring back help in time, or if they did come back, whether they'd be able to find the site of the cave-in again. Waiting, not knowing whether I was bleeding internally, and not sure how long I'd last if I were. Waiting, unsure whether I'd ever see daylight again. But ever present, and inescapable, was the pain.

That's what it was like, bound to the wall in the Iron Mass mining platform. Senses numbed with pain, waiting for the hatch to open again and for new torments to begin. And I felt the same, dull ache in the pit of my stomach now as I did then, the same sick sense of expectation and anticipation.

The only difference was, this time there was no chance that my dad would show up in the morning to rescue me.

SEVENTY

I'm not sure how long I was alone in the room. Amelia's attentions were elsewhere, trying to navigate through the network's defenses, so she had time to do little more than ping me on occasion to make sure I was still alive. The Iron Mass left me alone for a long time, no doubt to give me time to contemplate what abuses they might deliver when next the door opened, and I'm not too proud to say that I did just that. I had little to do, in fact, but contemplate abuses and watch as the invisible machines silently knitted my battered body as best they could. Serious injuries slowly became only grievous wounds, and my abdomen slowly shifted from a pulpy, raw, red mess to a spread of yellowish-green bruises. My breathing became slightly easier as time went on, suggesting that I might have had broken ribs along the way that the medichines were gradually patching up. I was far from fine, but I wasn't at death's door—at least not yet—so for that, if nothing else, I was grateful.

Finally, the hatch swung open, and the commander-of-the-faithful himself stood revealed, Nine Precession Radon. Apparently, it was time for my conversion to continue.

. . . . .

"You thought to fool me, feigning interest in the Divine Ideal, no?"

The Iron Mass leader leaned in close, shouting in rage, his spittle spattering against my nose and cheeks.

"Please forgive me," I said, falling back on Interdiction Negotiation training. "I'm not as strong as you are, and in my weakness, I thought I could escape."

Radon laughed, a sharp, barking nose.

"Don't try to soothe me with your honeyed words," he snarled. "I'm no imbecile to be coddled with simple flattery."

I chanced a smile. "Are you sure?"

"Quiet!" Radon bellowed, and then began pacing across the room. "Why? Can you explain it to me? You seem a reasonably intelligent sentient, for all your misbelief, so maybe you can explain what no one before you has."

I narrowed my eyes, watching him pace back and forth in front of me, a strange expression on his jet-black features.

"Why do unbelievers so willfully refuse to accept the truth?"

Surprisingly, the Iron Mass's tone wasn't one of hatred or anger, and he didn't seem to be taunting me, either.

"Do you really want to know?"

Radon drew up short in front of me and turned, his piercing blue eyes wide open and soft. "Yes!" he pleaded.

I was taken aback. He actually seemed to be sincere. Not only curious, but *concerned* about those who refused to convert.

"Could it be because what you profess is immaterial when judged against what you *do*? And what the Iron Mass *does* is kill and destroy everything that comes in its path that doesn't bow down and worship the god of your choosing."

"But the Divine Ideal is *real!*" he said, imploring.

"I'm not arguing that with you. I've got no proof one way or the other. All I know is what is in front of me, and what's in front of me is the kind of man who gleefully fires the heads of innocents back at their grieving families and who cuts open living beings to see if they've swallowed valuables and who guts a woman in front of her eyes or blows a hole through an innocent man for moving too slowly. So why *should* anyone listen to what you have to say?"

"But we do it for your own good," Radon said, drawing himself upright, teeth clenched. "We're purifying the universe. Those lives you mention were without purpose, without meaning, so what matter is it if they end now or later? But if just one comes to the full knowledge of the Divine Ideal through our efforts, and the birth of the Ideal is brought any nearer to the present, then it all will have been worth it."

"Will it? And how many have come to that full knowledge, I wonder."

Radon looked at me, eyes narrowed, and then turned his gaze away. "Too few," he said. "Always too few."

"So my friends and I, if we refuse your teaching, you'll kill us as well. And you'll go on digging holes in this planet as though nothing had happened. But what about this planet, anyway?" I gestured with my scraped chin, indicating the world beyond the platform's walls. "When my crew and I landed, we found cairns that looked like they might be the result of some sort of bacterial intelligence. Don't they get a chance to accept your god's love? Or will you just plow through them as well, as you've done with so many others?"

"Life? Here? Psht." Radon waved his hand dismissively. "Earth was the cradle of life, from which the seeds of the Divine Ideal sprung. No unicellular organisms of other provenance have any place in universe's destiny, merely flotsam along the way."

"So you'll continue to mine the planet until it's a cloud of rubble in space, then?"

"Of course," Radon said, as though it were the most obvious thing in the world. "We will complete the great work begun by our ancestors who came to this system centuries ago, and move onto the next system."

I eyed him thoughtfully. "Just what *is* this great work of yours, anyway?"

"Why, to fuel the Iron Mass expansion, of course. The results of our mining efforts are dispatched in unmanned rockets to the various houses spread throughout this part of the galaxy who themselves send out the fruits of their labor, as needed."

"You send it to..." I stopped, trying to puzzle it out. "How do you coordinate something like that over such vast distances? Are your ships equipped with faster-than-light drives?"

"Superluminal? Ha! That's a myth. No, each houseship of the Iron Mass carries its own microscopic threshold, too small to allow matter to pass, but sufficient to allow communication back to the Temple."

I wanted to ask more to try to draw him out. Like any good James Bond villain, now that he had me trussed up, he seemed more than willing to share all sorts of secrets. But before I was able to speak, a sound chimed, and Radon's attention was turned back to the hatch.

"Commander-of-the-Faithful," said the Iron Mass whose head appeared in the open hatchway. "There's a communication for you from the homeship."

Radon sighed and started toward the door. Before he reached it, he looked back over his shoulder. "I am truly sorry for you, you know. If I could somehow make you see the truth, I would do it in an instant."

He paused at the hatchway, a sad expression on his face, and then closed the hatch behind him.

::OK,:: said the voice of Amelia, sounding closer than ever, ::I think we're in business.::

SEVENTY-ONE

While I'd been trussed up, beaten, and lectured by a proselytizing zealot, Jida Shuliang had been going through a crisis of her own.

I don't think I realized how difficult it was for her, being cut off from the rest of her being. It's impossible for someone who lives only in one brain to imagine what it must be like to be part of a distributed consciousness but isolated from the rest of your mind. It must be something like being lobotomized, but rather than being spared the pain of all you've lost through the expediency of imbecility, you'd be completely aware of everything you could no longer touch, think, and feel.

It must have been difficult when the Jida emissary first came on board the *Further*. I'd never given it a second thought. Jida was a charming, even effervescent, fixture of Entelechy life, and the trio of Jida Shuliang bodies that boarded the *Further* above the Ouroboros shipyards seemed every bit the same woman as the one who I'd met at the *Further* fundraiser only days before. Except she wasn't. Not really. She was *part* of the same woman. A subset that shared the same general features of the whole, that seemed identical at a distance, but on closer examination, she lacked detail, like a fragment of a broken hologram, a reflection of the whole at a lower degree of resolution.

It was harder still, then, for a single body of the Jida emissary to come down to the pulsar planet with me, cut off from the rest of her mind back on the *Further*. She knew it would only be for eighty minutes at a time and must have thought it a small price to pay to set foot on a virgin world. But that was before we knew about the Iron Mass and what would come after.

So Jida, the five-millennia-old memories of her last death at the hands of the Iron Mass still fresh in her mind, sat alone in her jail cell with Bin-Ney and her memories, disoriented to be alone in her head for so long a time.

Then Amelia gained control of the security systems, and with the communication systems at her command, she'd created our own encrypted interlink network, connecting me in my torture chamber to Jida and Bin-Ney in their cell. And then Amelia told us where our weapons and mantles were being kept. And then Amelia opened the door to the cell.

::All right, then.:: The voice of Jida in my head sounded like a fist of iron gloved in velvet. ::We're getting our gear. Then we're coming to get you, RJ. And then we're getting the hell out of here.::

:: W-what about the guards?:: I heard Bin-Ney ask.

::What about them?:: Jida asked, fire beneath her words. ::These sons of bitches aren't killing me again.::

Suddenly, Jida didn't seem so disoriented anymore.

SEVENTY-TWO

Shackled to the wall, I felt more helpless and anxious than I had in all the time I'd hung there, knowing that Jida and Bin-Ney were free, sneaking through the cramped corridors of the habitat dome, trying to avoid running into any Iron Mass—at least until they retrieved our weapons and defenses. So close to freedom, the thought that I'd not live to see it was suddenly inescapable.

So when the hatch started to move, accompanied by the squeal of metal on metal, I breathed a sigh of relief.

::It's about time you showed up, Jida,:: I subvocalized, smiling slightly. ::I was beginning to worry.::

The hatch started to swing open.

::Um, RJ?:: came Jida's reply. ::We just reached the stores where our gear's being held. We're not *there* yet.::

The hatch swung all the way open on its hinges, and a pair of Iron Mass stood on the far side, a man and a women, each armed with their long-bladed weapons, the handles collapsed.

"The commander-of-the-faithful regrets that he has not been able to lead you onto the path of destiny," said the woman, stepping into the center of the room, the lines of her skull marked out by lines of thin scarlet horns. I recognized her as the leader of the group that had captured us in the cairn forest and brought us to the mining platform.

"He has conferred with the Temple and has been instructed to abandon the attempt," the man beside her said, his blue eyes narrowed.

The pair of Iron Mass drew closer and shifted their weapons in their hands. At some unseen signal from them, some hidden motion, the handles extended so that they now resembled long-bladed spears instead of swords, *naginata* instead of scimitars.

"Look," I said, trying to sound as calm as possible, "there's no need to give up hope yet, is there? I still could be made to see reason."

The pair lifted their weapons, pointing the blades' tips toward my chest.

"Would that it were true," the woman said sadly.

A faint humming filled the air, and their weapons began to glow faintly, the light emanating from the place where the blade met the haft.

::Jida?:: I subvocalized.

"Those who don't serve the purpose of the Divine Ideal hinder its coming," the man said. "And obstacles must be cleared aside."

The humming escalated, swelling in pitch and volume, and the glow from the weapons grew brighter.

::Guys?::

There was no answer on the interlink. Had something gone wrong? Had the others run into opposition?

"Your blind faith has made murderers of you all," I said hotly, abandoning any attempt to sway them. It went against the precepts of Interdiction Negotiation, but they'd served me not at all the last few hours, so there was little reason to continue backing a losing horse. "Will you just keep on killing and destroying until there's nothing left of the galaxy but you lunatics?"

The woman scowled, and the man's mouth drew into a tight line.

The thrumming hum of the weapons grew to a fever pitch, and the glow was almost blinding. Whatever they were about to do, they would do soon.

"I pity you," the woman said, bitter but sincere. "Your life, and death, will have no meaning."

"That depends entirely on your perspective," came the voice of Jida from the doorway.

Toroids of plasma leapt from the projector cuff on Jida's wrist, slamming into the back of the male Iron Mass, and a split-second later, Bin-Ney fired a stream that caught the woman in the back of the head.

The Iron Mass collapsed, plasma wounds blossoming on their backs as they spun around, and their weapons suddenly discharged, torrents of white light gouting out. One struck the ceiling, harmlessly, but the other intersected the wall only centimeters from my left hand. I could feel the singeing heat of the blast on my skin, and the small hairs on my forearm and the back of my hand were burned away in an eyeblink.

Stepping over the lifeless bodies of the Iron Mass, Jida hefted a mantle belt, a projector cuff, and my holstered cap gun. She and Bin-Ney wore their mantles completely covering their bodies from head to toe, entirely opaque except for a transparent faceplate.

"Well," Jida said, "what are you hanging around for, RJ? Let's get out of here."

SEVENTY-THREE

When they'd got me down from the wall and I stood on my own feet for the first time in what seemed an eternity, it took me a moment to recover my equilibrium.

"Are you going to be able to travel, sir?" Bin-Ney asked, reaching out a hand to steady me.

"Well, I don't see that we have much choice, do you?" I said, trying to sound good natured.

"Here," Jida said, reaching out and wrapping the mantle around my waist. "You get suited up, and then we'll go." I signaled to the mantle with my interlink, and it began to flow up and down, covering my body. "These two were the first Iron Mass we've run into, so there's a chance they don't yet know we're free."

Jida snapped the projector cuff onto my left forearm, and then I strapped my cap gun's holster around my waist. Unbuckling the strap securing it into place, I slid the cap gun out, the weight of it reassuring in my grip.

"With any luck, then," I said, "we'll be able to make it out of the platform without running into any interference. Then we make for the *Compass Rose*, pick up the chimp and robot, and get out of here. But first, we need to get Amelia back out of the network."

. . . . .

::What do you mean you aren't coming?:: I subvocalized as we hustled through the corridors heading toward the dome's center, trying to make as little noise as possible.

My plan was to find a computer interface on the way to the central elevator, yank Amelia out of the network, then hop the lift down to the surface. I had a stitch in my side, and my legs were already aching, but I plowed ahead, knowing that I'd have time to rest and recover if we managed to make it off the pulsar planet alive.

::I'm the only thing keeping the Iron Mass off your back at the moment,:: Amelia answered. ::I'm futzing with their security monitoring systems and suppressing some automated alarm systems. If I left the network, the entire mining complex would be at your throats in a matter of moments.::

::So we'll just take you out right before we get to the lift, and then we hightail it out of here.::

::No good, mate,:: Amelia answered, her tone resolute. ::The security systems will shut down the lift as soon as the alarms hit, and you won't be able to get down. Besides, with me here running interference, I'll be able to keep the platform from using its stationary weapons systems against you while you're heading for the ship. Otherwise, they'd just pick you off with a couple of well-placed particle beams.::

I kept hustling through the corridors, but my heart had sunk in my chest and my legs felt like they were made of lead.

::But....:: I began. ::I can't just *leave* you.::

::RJ, you big sook,:: she said, using the tone of voice she employed only when she thought I was being particularly oblivious. ::I'm a digital incarnation of a woman who's been dead and revived once already.:: She paused, and then added in a voice that was not as brave as I knew she'd hoped, ::What's the worst that can happen to me?::

■ ■ ■ ■ ■

We reached the lift, and I tried once more to convince Amelia to come with us, but she refused. As the doors of the lift cage slid shut, her voice became faint and laced with static.

::Be careful out there, RJ,:: Amelia said, sounding distant and small. ::And for God's sake, hurry!::

The lift stopped moving, and the doors slowly slid open.

::We've made it!:: Bin-Ney said before the energy blast from the Iron Mass spear sent him falling back to the floor, his mantle completely immobile.

SEVENTY-FOUR

A quartet of Iron Mass stood directly in our way. They seemed as surprised to see us as we were them, only faster than us on the draw.

"Damn it!" I swore. My cap gun was already in my right fist, and I aimed it at one of the Iron Mass and the projector cuff on my left arm at another, and as I leaped to one side, I opened up with both.

Jida jumped to the other side, firing off rounds of plasma toroids, catching one of the Iron Mass squarely in the chest.

Bin-Ney still lay on the ground, immobilized by the first blast, and while Jida and I plugged away at the Iron Mass before us, one of them lurched forward, driving the tip of his spear toward Bin-Ney's chest. Before I could react, the spear struck home, the blow stopped by Bin-Ney's mantle, but the force of the impact keeping him pinned to the ground.

One of the Iron Mass collapsed in a heap, a hole blown in his black insect pressure suit. Though the stuff was armored, the projectors were able to penetrate it, but it was taking repeated shots in the same general location to pierce the surface.

I took a shot to the knee, freezing my leg from the hip down, and Jida was spun momentarily by a shot that connected with her shoulder, but both of us were able to continue firing.

The Iron Mass continued to hammer at Bin-Ney's mantle with his spear, and while he hadn't broken through yet, I didn't like the idea of waiting to see how much abuse a mantle could take. Continuing to fire with my cap gun at one of the standing Iron Mass, I had my projector emit a cutting arc, which shot half a dozen centimeters from my wrist like a knife of flame. Lurching to Bin-Ney's side gracelessly, my leg frozen like a cast beneath me, I sliced down through the handle of the Iron Mass's spear, cutting it in two, and then backhanded the projector up and across the Iron Mass's chest and neck, opening up the armor and depressurizing the suit.

The other two Iron Mass finally fell, irregular holes blown in their carapaces, and only Jida and I were left standing.

We helped Bin-Ney to his feet and instructed our mantles to go flexible again. Then we headed for the canyon wall as fast as we could.

■ ■ ■ ■ ■

The climb was long and difficult, scrambling over the scree, but at length, we finally reached the top. Ahead of us in the distance, we could see the edges of the cairn forest and knew that the *Compass Rose* lay just beyond.

::Ha!:: Bin-Ney shouted in triumph. He turned and looked back toward the mining platform below. ::You thought you could stop us, but you—::

His words were cut off as a gout of blinding white light slammed into his chest, cutting through his mantle and the body beneath, blazing up and out his back into the twilit sky.

I grabbed Jida's arm and dragged her to the ground beside me. Peering over the edge of the canyon, we could see a number of Iron Mass pouring from the door of the lift beneath the platform, those in the lead hefting the large cannon that had ended Zaslow's life only a short while before.

::Come on,:: I said, scuttling back away from the edge, dragging Jida with me. ::We need to get out of here.::

When we'd gone beyond the line of sight of our pursuers far below, Jida paused just long enough to cast a glance back at the lifeless body of Bin-Ney on the ground. ::Assuming we get back to the *Further* and Bin-Ney is restored from backup, I need to make a point of telling him to keep his damned mouth shut when escaping from overwhelming odds. He's just tempting fate, and clearly fate can't resist the challenge.::

SEVENTY-FIVE

We hauled across the lifeless wastes of the pulsar planet as fast as we could go. Though we had a head start on our pursuers, they vastly outnumbered us, and we'd nearly exhausted our projectors' reserves of plasma and the capacitor charges of my cap gun. If it came to another firefight, we wouldn't last long.

On we raced under the gray sky, the dead star circling slowly high overhead. Somewhere up there the *Further* drifted in her orbit. Had she come under attack by the Iron Mass's "houseship" yet, or did they still keep their menacing distance?

Ahead of us loomed the cairn forest, the orderly rows of towers wider at the tops than at their bases. Just to the other side of the cairn rose a high ridge, and beyond that we'd find the *Compass Rose*, nestled in a low valley.

::...ptain! Can you hear me?:: crackled a voice in my ear.

My pace not slacking, I answered, glancing to Jida to see if she was getting the signal, too, and her nod indicated that she was. ::Maruti?::

::Oh, glorious!:: the chimpanzee answered. ::Xerxes, whose vision is considerably better than mine, for all that ey has no eyes, just caught sight of you.::

Jida and I raced on. I realized a considerable advantage of communicating by subvocalization was that one need never try to talk when out of breath. It was a good thing, because with my aching lungs and the stitch in my side, I doubted I'd be able to string together more than a few words, if spoken.

::Where are you?:: I asked.

::Just inside the edge of the cairn forest, Captain,:: Xerxes answered.

::Can you get to the ship? We need to get out of here.::

::Not quite yet, Captain,:: Maruti said.

::*What*?:: Jida snapped.

::We've made a surprising but profoundly disappointing discovery,:: Maruti said.

::I told you so,:: Xerxes put in.

::Never mind the cross talk, just tell me what it is,:: I said.

::Well, in the cave system, we found the remains of a downed ship. It's millennia old, almost entirely cannibalized, with only fragments remaining.:: Maruti's tone was strange, an odd mix of disappointment and excitement.

::A terrestrial ship?:: Jida asked.

::Sadly, yes,:: Xerxes answered, with a nonvocal sigh. ::Just another bit of flotsam from the Diaspora, it appears, and no sign of extraterrestrial intelligence.::

::So why can't you get to the ship?:: I asked. ::What's the delay?::

::Do you recall the unicellular organisms responsible for the cairns?:: Xerxes asked.

::No, I've forgotten all about them,:: I answered hotly. ::Yes, of *course* I remember them. What about it?::

::They're terrestrial in origin, too,:: Maruti said. ::We've worked out their genetic sequencing, and it's clear they were derived from terrestrial strains of radiation-resistant anaerobic bacteria. They were engineered to survive in this environment by the survivors of the crashed ship.::

::Whyever for?:: Jida asked.

::Xerxes was right about the autoinducers. The bacteria has been designed as a kind of biological distributed computing system, with the individual organisms acting in tandem, using signal molecules to pass information back and forth.::

::What information?:: I asked.

::We're currently taking readings, so a picture is still emerging,:: Xerxes said, ::but the forest appears to contain almost ten zettabytes of information. Even though the processing speeds involved in organic molecular signaling would mean extremely low clock speeds, that amount of data is sufficient to store a number of uploaded human consciousnesses.::

"*What?*" I sputtered, talking out loud, echoed and transmitted out via interlink.

::It's our supposition that the minds of the surviving crew exist in the bacteria network as a kind of gestalt, an organic equivalent of a digital incarnation emulation like your friend Amelia.::

Just the mention of her name stung, but I didn't let it slow me down.

::And you can't leave yet because you think you'll be able to... what?::

::We think we can save them, Captain.:: Maruti's tone was energetic, hopeful.

::I was afraid you were going to say that.:: I continued on, my feet pounding on the gray surface. I chanced a glance back over my shoulder and saw the Iron Mass following just at the edge of vision, with only the undulating surface of the planet preventing them from firing off another round with their light cannon.

Jida and I reached the edge of the cairn forest, but I rounded it to one side and continued ahead to the ridge beyond.

::OK, here's the plan,:: I said. ::The guys behind us don't know that you two are on the planet, much less where you are. So you've got exactly as long as it takes for me and Jida to get to the *Compass Rose* and get off the ground to get this bacteria farm uploaded. Whether you can or not, I expect you to be ready to roll when we fly over, and then we're getting off this rock. Agreed?::

::Captain, I think that—:: Maruti began.

::Good,:: I said, cutting him off. ::We'll see you momentarily.::

SEVENTY-SIX

Jida and I crested the ridge and saw the *Compass Rose* lying directly below us, escape just within our grasp. Then my faceplate went completely opaque as a gout of white light blazed between us, a shot fired from the Iron Mass far behind us. Jida's wordless howl rang over the interlink channel, rattling around in my head.

Blinded, I reached in Jida's direction, grabbed hold of the first thing that met my hand, and leaped down the far side of the ridge, sliding headfirst down the rocky slope.

::Jida?:: I instructed my mantle to go transparent and turned to see that Jida's left arm was completely gone below the elbow, ending in a charred stump.

Jida's faceplate went transparent, and I saw her tortured expression beneath. She was still conscious but didn't seem able to concentrate enough to form words.

::Come on,:: I said, helping her to her feet with an arm around her back. ::They won't be far behind us now.::

In the end, I had to more or less drag Jida bodily across the floor of the canyon, taking an eternity to cover a distance of only a few steps. Finally, we reached the *Compass Rose*, and I keyed the airlock to cycle open.

::Hang on, Jida,:: I told her. ::We're getting out of here.::

As the airlock cycled shut, I heard a familiar voice in my head.

::Captain Stone?::

::First Zel i'Cirea,:: I answered, in mock formality. ::Please tell me you're calling with good news.::

::That depends entirely on your definition of 'good,' Captain, but I doubt your standards are low enough for it to make a difference.::

The airlock cycled, filling with air and pressurizing, and finally, Jida and I stumbled into the shuttle's interior.

"*Compass Rose*, prepare for takeoff," I said out loud as my mantle retreated below my neck, addressing the shuttle's subsentient governing intelligence. Then I helped Jida into a chair and fit her with restraints to keep her immobilized. Fortunately, she'd at last lost consciousness, and I only hoped that by the time she woke again—assuming we lived long enough for her to do so— her medichines would have gone to work damping down the pain her severed arm must be causing her.

::Go ahead, Zel,:: I said, sliding into the ship's command chair and bringing up a control display on the wall before me. ::What's happening up there?::

::I take it from your apparent position that your plan worked and that you and the others have escaped?::

::Yes, but only Jida and I made it back to the ship. Bin-Ney didn't make it, I'm afraid.::

::I'd instruct the *Further* to begin fabricating a new body for him to be restored into, but I'm afraid we have other, more pressing uses for the power at the moment. Evidently, as a consequence of your escape, a short time ago the Iron Mass ship initiated an attack on the *Further*.::

::*Further*, what's your condition?::

::The damage is nontrivial,:: answered the voice of the ship's avatar, ::but so far, I've been able to maintain hull integrity, and there's been no loss of vital systems.::

::You've returned fire, I take it?::

::I've employed both launchers and emitters, to varying effect.::

::They've taken damage,:: Zel said, ::but so far, they're in much better shape than us.::

The *Compass Rose* was almost ready to take off, its drives nearly ready to create the tiny bubble of distorted space that would break the bonds of gravity holding it to the surface.

::How much longer until the metric engineering drives are charged enough to leave?::

::More than half a standard day, I'm afraid, Captain,:: answered the *Further*.

::If we last that long,:: Zel said.

::OK, keep at it, guys,:: I said. ::I'm rounding up the rest of the party and we'll be with you shortly.::

"*Compass Rose*," I said, "let's go."

SEVENTY-SEVEN

As the *Compass Rose* lifted off, an even more familiar voice rang from the ship's speakers.

"RJ? Are you reading me?"

It was a radio-frequency signal, picked up by the shuttle's transceiver. I tapped on the smart matter of the display and drew up a communication interface.

"Amelia?"

Her face appeared on the display, as big as life. She appeared to be floating in a featureless white void, positioned right in front of the "camera."

"I've just managed to take control of the platform's communication array."

"Are you OK?" I asked, even as I realized that I had no notion what an appropriate answer might be for a digital incarnation infecting a strange computer network.

The image of Amelia smiled slyly and gave a slight shrug. "Ah, you know me, RJ. Always looking for a bit of excitement." She averted her eyes momentarily, as though looking at something off-screen. "I'm monitoring the Iron Mass communications, and it looks like they're almost on top of you. Did you and Jida make it there OK?"

I glanced over at Jida, strapped to the chair beside me, short an arm. "We made it, at least. Bin-Ney got shot just—"

"I know," she said, nodding. "I've been reviewing their communications logs. That's too bad, he seemed like a nice guy."

"No, he didn't," I said. "He seemed like kind of a pillock, if you ask me. But he was under my command, and I let him die."

"Maruti can bring him back, I'm sure."

I nodded slightly as the *Compass Rose* angled over the valley and rose over the crest of the ridge. "Maybe. But if Maruti doesn't make it either, who's going to bring *him* back?"

"Look," she said, her tone growing more serious. "Take this."

The display threw up a symbol, indicating that it had just received a considerable amount of data.

"What's this?" I asked.

"That's me," Amelia said simply. "My memories, at any rate. Assuming you get back to the ship and the ship makes it out of here in one piece, you should be able to restore my consciousness from backup. Then it'll be like nothing ever happened."

I looked at her image on the screen, my eyes narrowed. "Except it *will* have happened, won't it? You'll have died. Again."

Amelia looked away, refusing to meet my eyes. "Look, RJ, don't make this harder than it has to be. I'm sure it's just our parochial, primitive mindsets that make it difficult for us to accept the idea of death and resurrection, right? Even when we've experienced it ourselves."

I glanced over at Jida, who had clutched at her throat whenever she remembered what the Iron Mass had done to her in the past and who fought tooth and nail to make sure they wouldn't be able to do it again.

"I don't know, Amelia. These future folks seem pretty concerned about the idea, too."

"Look…" she said, but then her words were cut off with a loud, penetrating squeal.

A new face filled the screen. Jet black, a wicked scar down the left side of the face, the right ear missing the lobe, long horns sticking out from the dome of the hairless skull.

It was Commander-of-the-Faithful Nine Precession Radon.

"Ah, unbeliever," Radon said, with snarling satisfaction. "Our network defenses have finally detected your little intrusion and are in the process of isolating the perversion of consciousness you've set loose in our system."

"You leave her alone!" I shouted, rising up out of my chair.

"Calm yourself," Radon said, eyes glinting. "You'll soon have more to worry about than one digital ghost. Your ship in orbit, for instance?"

"My ship's been taking everything you people have been throwing at it and returning fire in kind. I wouldn't be so quick to claim victory, Radon."

The Iron Mass nodded, miming an expression of thoughtfulness.

"Perhaps," he said serenely. "But that will all change. Even now, my men are preparing to blow your ship out of the sky."

SEVENTY-EIGHT

I maneuvered the *Compass Rose* over the ridge and out over the cairn forest.

Radon kept ranting over the radio frequency, but I killed the audio and concentrated on the task at hand.

::Maruti. Xerxes. You guys ready to go?:: I subvocalized.

::Oh, Captain Stone,:: Maruti effused, ::we've actually been able to record the data contained within the organic network, storing the gestalt consciousness in a repurposed part of Xerxes's own body. It's left him not entirely communicative, but—::

::I take it that's a yes?:: I cut in.

From a short distance away, our Iron Mass pursuers began firing energy bursts from their spears, which deflected harmlessly off the *Compass Rose*'s bubble of distorted space. Even the larger white-light cannon, which had ripped through Zaslow and

Bin-Ney, and tore Jida's arm off at the elbow, rebounded without effect off the bubble. But the failure of their weapons to make an impression didn't seem to deter them from continuing the effort.

The *Compass Rose* glided out over the forest of cairns, homing in on Maruti's interlink signal.

::Oh, we see you, Captain!:: called Maruti's voice.

::Great,:: I said, with little enthusiasm.

I brought the shuttle to a halt just over their position and configured a display to give me a view straight down. I could see the chimp looking up, the robot beside him standing impassively.

::Erm, how are we to…That is, how do we get from here to…?::

::Just hang on, Maruti.::

I wasn't sure this was going to work. But Arluq had mentioned that it was a feature of the metric engineering drives that hadn't been much explored.

::*Compass Rose*,:: I said, addressing the shuttle's intelligence, ::distend the gravity field downward to the surface of the planet below us.::

The shuttle indicated that it would comply, and I felt a shifting in my stomach, as though I were in an elevator that suddenly began to descend at great speed.

::Hold onto yourselves, guys,:: I said, calling down to the surface. ::This might be a little rough.::

::What do you mean? Oh no!::

On the display, I watched as the pair of them suddenly fell *up* toward the underside of the shuttle, accelerating at full standard gravity. With the ship's gravitational field extended to include them, their relative "down" had suddenly shifted from the ground beneath them to the center plane of the shuttle high overhead.

Xerxes hit the hull with a resounding clang, Maruti with a sickening thud.

::Oh dear…:: Maruti said.

::Look,:: I called out, ::there isn't time to cycle the airlock, so you guys will have to ride back outside. Just key your mantles for full protection and instruct them to adhere to the hull, and you should be fine.::

::But—: Maruti began.

::No time,:: I said, regretting my snappish tone but having no choice.

The *Compass Rose* began to rise up, lifting higher above the surface.

::Zel, do you read me?::

::Yes,:: came the voice of the first.

::You're about to get hit—and hard—by the Iron Mass, so it's time to hit them first. *Further*, what was the name of that big gun of yours, the one that has a devastating impact but that you can use only once?::

::The field inverter?:: the ship's avatar asked.

::That's the one. It redirects the ship's bubble of altered space outward, correct? And can change the characteristics of space in a targeted region? Like near-infinite gravity, or slower time, or such like?::

::Yes, but it's a tremendous drain on the ship's stores of energy.::

::I know, I know. And you've only got a half charge in the drives. But is there any chance you can pull power from other systems and give us one big shot?::

::If I cut life support on all but a few areas of the ship, I suppose it would be possible. But I don't know how long I can maintain—::

::Good. Evacuate those parts of the ship.::

::Already done,:: Zel put in. ::We moved everyone into the center of the ship, into the Atrium and adjoining sections, when we came under attack.::

::Great. The ship'll be a sitting duck after you take this shot, but if you don't, it sounds like you'll just be roasted instead.::

::Sir?:: the ship's avatar asked, confused.

::Never mind. Radon might be bluffing, but I don't want to risk it. Charge up the big gun and fire on the ship.::

A long moment passed in anxious silence as the *Compass Rose* drifted higher and higher above the surface of the planet below.

::We're ready, Captain,:: the *Further* said. ::I can pipe you a visual feed from my hull, if you like.::

::Do it,:: I barked, and then thought to add, ::please.::

::My pleasure.::

Suddenly, another panel of the wall before me reconfigured into a new display, and I could see the wicked shape of the Iron Mass houseship hulking against the sea of stars, the curve of the pulsar planet just visible at the edge of the image.

::OK, *Further*,:: I said, taking a deep breath. ::Fire!::

Space rippled and rucked, and while I watched, the Iron Mass houseship seemed to shimmer and flex. One end of the ship suddenly collapsed in on itself, like an aluminum can crushed underfoot, and from the other side of the hull, a stream of debris jetted out. It was working!

But then, without warning, space smoothed back out, and aside from the visible damage done to the houseship, everything seemed normal again.

::I'm sorry, Captain Stone,:: the *Further* said. ::I was able to produce the field and invert it, but as I indicated, the drives lacked power to sustain it. We clearly inflicted some damage on the Iron Mass vessel, but I'm not sure if it was sufficient to disable it.::

::Well, they haven't fired their big shot yet,:: I said, cautiously hopeful. ::Maybe we can—::

"RJ!" shouted the voice of Amelia from the display, her eyes wide and frightened. "I've been listening in on Radon while trying to keep ahead of his network defenses. It isn't the *ship* that's going to fire on the *Further*. It's the *platform*!"

"What?"

"They're loading the mass launcher with enough fissionable material to blow up a planet!"

SEVENTY-NINE

::*Further*?:: I called out.

::We are completely immobilized, Captain,:: the ship answered. ::Firing the inverter used up virtually all our stores of power. We'll be able to maintain limited life support within the Atrium and the bridge, but it will be the better part of a day before we can move again, much less mount any kind of defense.::

"Damn!" I slammed my fist against the arm of the command chair, my teeth gritted.

::If it comes as any consolation,:: Zel said, ::we appear to have incapacitated the Iron Mass ship. If that had been the sole danger presented to us, your plan would have apparently worked.::

::You'll forgive me if I find that pretty cold comfort, First,:: I said.

"RJ," called Amelia, "I may be able to help."

I spun around in the chair, turning to face her image on the display.

"What is it, Amelia?" I said eagerly, desperately. "Anything at all?"

"Well, I'm still working out the specifics of the platform's mining operations, but it appears that the mass launcher is controlled by two separate command systems. It's essentially just a big electromagnetic catapult, like a giant gauss gun. One system controls the electromagnets that accelerate the payload to escape velocity."

She paused meaningfully.

"And?" I said.

"And the other controls the gimbals that are used to aim the launcher."

She fell silent for another moment, her mouth drawn into a tight line, and I recognized her expression. This wasn't the Amelia who stayed up late nights with me, telling stories about her brothers or her favorite graphic albums from childhood or the names of the characters in the fantasy novels she loved. This was Amelia the soldier. This was the Amelia who'd been trained to kill with her bare hands and who'd piloted warships and exchanged fire in border wars all across the solar system. This was the Amelia you didn't want to meet.

"I can control the one, not the other," she went on grimly. "I can't stop it firing, but I can control what it's aimed at."

"Bless you," I said, and blew her a kiss.

Radon was still on the other display, though his attention was elsewhere, shouting orders at someone off-screen. I toggled the audio channel back on and interrupted.

"Atari," I said, a force of habit. I had him boxed in now, though he didn't know it. "It's time to stand down, Radon. You've hurt us and we've hurt you, but it's time for this to stop now."

"Do you mock me, unbeliever? When I have the advantage in my hands?"

"You don't, though, Radon," I said, no trace of warmth or humor in my voice. "This doesn't end well for any of us if you don't stop right now. Leave us be, and we'll go on our way, and you can keep mining to fuel your crazy crusade across the stars. But if you fire that mass launcher, it'll end in tears."

"Your tears," he shouted, sounding unreasonable, manic. "You'll bathe in your tears as you watch your ship blow to atoms above you, and then you'll beg for release before I end your meaningless existence."

"No," I said simply, shaking my head. "You won't, and I won't. Stand down, let me and my ship go, or you won't like what happens next."

"I tire of your misbelief and madness," Radon raged. "This ends—now."

He turned to someone out of view, and raised a spurred fist.

"Fire!"

I opened my mouth to shout for him to wait, but by then it was too late.

EIGHTY

The projectile from the mass launcher shot up with a tremendous amount of force, enough to reach escape velocity and still be moving fast enough after shedding speed-overcoming gravity that it impacted with considerable inertia. It wasn't the impact that did the damage, but the fissionable material inside the ferric shell, arranged into an incredibly powerful nuclear bomb. When it exploded, it far outshone the dim light of the dead star overhead, blinding bright.

The Iron Mass vessel never stood a chance.

On the display screen, Radon sputtered, looking with disbelief as he watched his spacefaring home go up in a ball of nuclear fire.

"Divine Ideal!" Radon cursed.

The *Compass Rose* had slipped the bonds of the planet's gravity and was well away as the Iron Mass ship began to plunge downward toward the planet's surface.

"Amelia?" I said as I watched the houseship drift ever lower, until finally it exploded in a fiery conflagration that reached for kilometers in every direction.

The mining platform was far away from the blast, and had the leading edge of the shock wave not hit the refinery, they'd likely have been able to weather the storm. But it did, and they didn't.

The refinery, triggered by the impact of the exploding ship, quickly approached a runaway meltdown.

"Good-bye, RJ," said the image of Amelia on the display, and then was gone.

A second new sun raged from the planet's surface as the refinery went up in an atomic holocaust that consumed Radon and Amelia, the mining platform and the cairn forest, the bodies of Bin-Ney and Zaslow, and everything else for a range of dozens of kilometers.

EIGHTY-ONE

Maruti and Xerxes weren't happy about having to ride back to the *Further* affixed to the bottom of the *Compass Rose*, and less so that they had to wait even longer while the ship's generators built up enough power to open the hangar bay doors. But once we were back on board, with the solid deck beneath us, all was forgiven.

Xerxes was unable to properly communicate, having devoted a large part of eir intellect to storing and sustaining the uploaded gestalt of crash survivors from the planet below.

Maruti, as much as he wanted to talk, was kept busy helping Jida to grow a new arm, fabricating new bodies for Zaslow and Bin-Ney and decanting their consciousness backups into their new homes, and integrating the backup of Amelia's mind with the compressed memories that her previous incarnation had sent me from the mining platform.

Amelia remembered nothing of the final moments on the mining platform, her final memories being those of contacting me on board the *Compass Rose* as Jida and I were making good our escape. She knew that her previous iteration had sacrificed herself for us, but until I told her about changing the mass launcher's aim, she'd had no idea that she'd been responsible for saving the entire crew of the *Further* as well. As I described the events to her, though, with her projected in holographic miniature on the palm of my hand, I could tell that she was grateful not to have any memory of those final deeds. For all that Amelia the soldier was necessary from time to time, Amelia the good-hearted friend was no more comfortable around her than I was.

Jida was happy to be rejoined with the rest of her mind, as small as it was, and I could see the looks of shock, fear, and pride as they flickered across her other two faces as the memories spread throughout the legion fragment. Jida, speaking in three voices in unison, thanked me for my part in sparing her another death at the hands of the Iron Mass, and then waited patiently for me to thank her for her part in sparing me the same. After sufficient thanks had been passed around, the three Jida bodies crushed me between them in a massive hug, and then she wandered off, talking to herself about the possibilities of fabricating a new body for herself, perhaps one a bit better adapted for adventure.

And that was that. Everyone was restored, wounds were licked, and we had nothing to do but wait until the ship's drives accumulated enough power for us to move on. Fortunately, by the time we'd all gotten squared away, the *Further* had generated at least enough power to turn on life support in the rest of the ship, so I could at least go back to my quarters for some much-needed rest.

EIGHTY-TWO

After taking a well-deserved nap, I showered and dressed, and wandered down to Maruti's quarters. I felt bad about having been so short with him through much of our recent misadventure and wanted to apologize for being so curt.

I needn't have bothered, I suppose. Maruti was so caught up in his most recent discovery that I doubt he even noticed the slight in the first place, much less my apology after the fact.

"Oh, Captain!" he said as I entered his rooms. I noted that he'd taken the opportunity to clean and groom himself, and was now wearing a purple velvet tuxedo, a yellow flower in his lapel, with a huge cigar smoldering at the corner of his wide mouth and a martini glass in his hand. "I was hoping you'd stop by!"

He waved me over to a large, flat, table-like object he'd erected at the center of the room. As I approached, I could see that its surface was configured as a display and that a strange, low-resolution kind of virtual environment could be seen within.

"What is it?" I asked.

"These are our new friends, of course," Maruti said, beaming. "The gestalt—I've taken to calling it the 'Hive,' and Xerxes had advanced no serious objection, so I suppose we should simply call it the Hive, yes? Well, the Hive from the bacteria network has been transferred from Xerxes's memory into the *Further*'s computational array."

I gazed down into the virtual environment and saw indistinct gray shapes moving deep within.

"So that's them?"

"Exactly. A fairly limited existence, to be sure, but they've survived, which is a remarkable achievement. They must have uploaded their minds into the bacteria network as a final resort, turning themselves into little more than messages in a bottle, hoping against hope that they might be rescued. And though it's taken thousands upon thousands of years, at last they have."

"What do they think about all of this?"

"Oh, so far as they're aware, no change at all has occurred. We're still working out the best way to establish contact with the Hive consciousness, but for the time being, we've managed to duplicate the limited environment they've existed in all of these years."

"But we *will* be making contact with them?"

"Absolutely! And in time, we'll be able to slowly integrate them back into the real world." He paused and took a sip of his martini. "Assuming, of course, that they haven't grown to prefer it in there. After all," he said, flashing me a chimpanzee smile, "I imagine things out here could be a mite too exciting for those not quite as adventurous as you and me, eh, Captain?"

I smiled right back. "You might just be right, Maruti. The world is pretty exciting at times, isn't it?"

"That it is," the chimp said with a smile. "And in light of same, can I offer you a drink?"

I shrugged. "Why not? And how about one of those bidis while you're at it?"

EIGHTY-THREE

Later, properly lubricated after a few rounds with the chimpanzee, the strong smell of bidi smoke clinging to my hair and clothes, I left Maruti's quarters and made for the bridge.

Aside from Zel, sitting in the command chair, and the *Further* avatar perched high overhead, the bridge was empty.

"Captain," Zel said, inclining her head slightly. "I'm glad to see that you're well."

"Thanks, First," I said, stepping down the tiered layers of the bridge to the control center. "I could easily say the same about you."

Zel shrugged and, reaching up, tapped the sapphire patch over her eye. "I've been in worse spots, believe me."

"You'll have to tell me about them sometime." Smiling, I stopped just short of the command chair.

"Perhaps," Zel said through a slight smile, unmoving. She glanced down at the chair's arms, at the control center before her, and then sighed deeply before looking up at me.

"I believe you're in my seat," I said good-naturedly.

"Oh, I know," Zel said, waving her hand absently. "I just find, when you vacate it, that it suits me so well."

I grinned. "Well, you kept the ship in one piece while I was away. I couldn't ask for more from a second-in-command. Good job."

"Yes." Zel nodded languidly. "It was a good job, wasn't it? And while I wouldn't have risked using the field inverter, I must admit that it seems to have been the right decision, after all." She paused, then narrowed her eye and added, "Though it was a stroke of incredible good fortune that your digital friend was in position to save us from the mass launcher strike."

I shrugged. "We all got lucky. I just hope that our luck doesn't run out when we need it most."

"You and me both," Zel said. Then, reluctantly, she rose to her feet.

Stepping away from the command chair, she motioned toward it.

"I believe this is yours?"

"Thanks, First," I said, and sat down unceremoniously.

Zel turned and started for the exit.

"Hey, Zel?" I called after her, thoughtfully.

"Yes, Captain Stone?"

"This isn't the kind of relationship where we start off hating each other and end up romantically involved is it? Are we that clichéd?"

Zel looked surprised and crossed her arms over her chest.

"You…" she began, and then trailed off. "You don't…?" She shook her head. "I'm sorry, this is just…unexpected. Captain, has no one told you about Pethesileans, then?"

"Um, no?"

"It would appear not," Zel said, an unfamiliar tone of kindness in her voice. "Captain, we Pethesileans decoupled reproduction from sexual intercourse millennia ago. We're genetically adapted to be parthenogenic and can reproduce at will. The genetic material can come entirely from the mother or can be taken into the mother's body from any number of donors and incorporated into the embryo. But we have no fathers, no males—only females."

"You mean…?"

"You met my mother above Aglibol. Cirea is my isomorphic parent, my sole genetic donor."

"So, wait, I'm confused. You're a clone?"

Zel sighed and shook her head. "I'll try not to be offended by that. I'm a clone in precisely the way that you are the corrupted diploidic copy of the spliced genes of two donors."

"I…I didn't…"

Zel smiled, a thin smile that didn't reach her eye. "Pethesileans are seldom romantically involved, but never for long. And never with males. I'm sorry to disappoint, Captain Stone."

With that, she turned on her heel and walked out the door.

"But…" I said, trying to object that I'd not actually been propositioning her, but only making a halfhearted joke, but the door closed behind her and the moment was gone.

I sat in silence for a long moment, shaking my head ruefully. Then, sighing, I turned and looked up at the silver eagle perched high on the wall.

"Well, *Further*, I think it's high time we had a talk, don't you?"

EIGHTY-FOUR

"What do you mean, Captain Stone?"

"I mean, *Further*, that I'd like an answer."

I swiveled around in the command chair, propping my feet up on the surface of the control center.

"An answer?"

I crossed my arms over my chest, but kept silent.

"An answer to what?"

"Well," I said, "to the question that hasn't been asked but that shouldn't *need* to be asked."

The silver eagle cocked its head to one side and regarded me for a moment.

"You want to know why, then?"

"Yes," I said. "Now, I don't believe that the Plenum created me out of whole cloth, like Zel suspects. I believe that I'm

Ramachandra Jason Stone. I *have* to believe that, I think, or I'd go a little crazy. But what I can't figure out is why I'm not just a museum piece or a relic in someone's personal menagerie of oddities. I'm a pretty capable and clever guy, sure, but I don't kid myself that I'm the best qualified to command the most expensive ship ever made, with the fortunes of untold numbers of Entelechy citizens in his hands."

"No," the *Further* said simply. "You're not." It paused, and after a moment, added, "At least, not if the only consideration were the cost of the ship or the fortunes of Entelechy citizens—not fortunes in terms of profit and loss, at any rate. When discussing the fortunes of the Entelechy as a whole, though, in perhaps a less tangible but much more meaningful sense, then I would argue that you are, in fact, the *perfect* being for the job."

I narrowed my eyes and slid my feet down to the floor. Leaning forward over the control center, my palms flat on its surface, I stared up at the avatar. "And why is that?"

"Because, Captain Stone, you bring a unique perspective. You are the product of an era of exploration and discovery to rival any in human history. The century of your birth, while plagued with ills and corruption, was at the same moment one of the high watermarks of human achievement. In the span of a few dozen decades before your birth, humanity learned more about the world around them than in all of human history to that point combined, expanding the bounds of knowledge and understanding from the quantum to the cosmic. You threw off the shackles of irrationality and mysticism, and brought to bear the penetrating light of human reason. Everything that is best and brightest about the Human Entelechy, every technology and science and art and craft, has its origins in your era. But the humans of the current era, the inheritors of this wealth of greatness, have become too complacent, too comfortable in their utopian splendor. They motivate themselves to explore the heavens only in search of profit, or proof of their pet theories and beliefs, or for a thousand other selfish motives. Of them all, only *you*, Captain Stone, have come out here into the uncharted blackness of space simply because you *can*."

I took a deep breath, soaking in all it had said.

"And that's why the Plenum chose me to represent its interests on the ship? I don't get it. Why the cost? Why the expense? What does the Plenum have to gain?"

"The future, Captain. You are our insurance against stagnation and decay. The Entelechy, for all its size and variation, has become increasingly insular, an endogamic superculture. Though it may take millions of years, in time that isolation will lead to the same ills found in primitive cultures when a genetic pool was too small to sustain itself. Defect, decay, and death. In the time of the Diaspora, countless offshoots of humanity spread throughout the stars. The future health of humanity in all of its guises—biological and synthetic, corporeal and digital—depends on the intermarriage, if you will, of these disparate human branches. The Plenum projects that for every new culture that is brought back into contact, the Entelechy gains another few millennia of health and vibrancy, if not more. But without an infusion of new concepts and new ideas, it is only a matter of time before the Entelechy collapses in on itself, decaying from within."

"And you threw in with the *Further* fund and manipulated me into becoming the ship's captain…"

"Because you had nothing to lose, and we had everything to gain."

EPILOGUE

I found Xerxes in the Atrium, the domed ceiling overhead displaying a true-color image of the hull's exterior view.

"May I join you?"

Xerxes waved absently to the bench beside em, eir eyeless face lifted, watching birds wheel high overhead.

"Sorry you didn't find your extraterrestrials, Xerxes," I said, sitting.

"It was an unlikely outcome." Ey made a noise almost like a sigh, though for my benefit or eir own, I wasn't sure. "It always is, I suppose. But there's still the hope that our next destination may prove more fruitful." Ey paused, and then said, "What is our next destination, for that matter?"

"A nebula a hundred or so light-years away," I answered. "The brothers Grimnismal think there's a chance we might find their exotic matter in the vicinity."

The robot shrugged, an almost imperceptible gesture. "It seems as good a destination to me as any."

I smiled. "You know, that was pretty much my feeling exactly."

The birds overhead swooped and darted, and the robot and I sat quietly for a long moment.

"Tell me, Xerxes. Do you regret not moving into your final stage yet, breaking your body down and beaming your signal out into space?"

Ey turned eir eyeless face toward mine and smiled. "If I had, Captain Stone, I wouldn't be sitting here, talking to you, watching these birds. We don't know what will happen tomorrow or the day after or the day after that. The future lies before us with all its endless promise of possibility, discovery, and surprise. How could I *possibly* want to give all that up?"

I laughed. "Xerxes, I couldn't agree more!"

The stars beyond the curve of the Atrium ceiling began to shift, growing gradually redder, moving slowly but steadily toward our sky's north pole.

We were on our way into the future.

–End–

ABOUT THE AUTHOR

Photograph © Kevin Church, 2011

New York Times bestselling writer Chris Roberson is best known for his Eisner-nominated ongoing comic book series *iZombie*, co-created with artist Mike Allred, and for multiple *Cinderella* mini-series set in the world of Bill Willingham's *Fables*. He has written more than a dozen novels and numerous short stories, as well as numerous comic projects including *Superman*, *Elric: The Balance Lost*, *Star Trek/Legion of Super-Heroes*, and *Memorial*. Roberson lives with his wife and daughter in Austin, Texas.